# AN AMISH QUILT

# Other Books by the Authors

## Beth Wiseman

### The Amish Secrets Novels
*Her Brother's Keeper*
*Love Bears All Things*
*Home All Along*

### The Daughters of the Promise Novels
*Plain Perfect*
*Plain Pursuit*
*Plain Promise*
*Plain Paradise*
*Plain Proposal*
*Plain Peace*

### The Land of Canaan Novels
*Seek Me with All Your Heart*
*The Wonder of Your Love*
*His Love Endures Forever*

### Other Novels
*Need You Now*
*The House that Love Built*
*The Promise*
*An Amish Year*
*Amish Celebrations*

## STORIES

*A Choice to Forgive* included in *An Amish Christmas*

*A Change of Heart* included in *An Amish Gathering*

*Healing Hearts* included in *An Amish Love*

*A Perfect Plan* included in *An Amish Wedding*

*A Recipe for Hope* included in *An Amish Kitchen*

*Always Beautiful* included in *An Amish Miracle*

*Rooted in Love* included in *An Amish Garden*

*When Christmas Comes* included in
*An Amish Second Christmas*

*In His Father's Arms* included in *An Amish Cradle*

*A Love for Irma Rose* included in *An Amish Year*

*Patchwork Perfect* included in *An Amish Year*

*A Cup Half Full* included in *An Amish Home*

*Winter Kisses* included in *An Amish Christmas Love*

*The Cedar Chest* included in *An Amish Heirloom*

## KATHLEEN FULLER

### THE AMISH LETTERS NOVELS

*Written in Love*

*The Promise of a Letter*

*Words from the Heart*

### THE AMISH OF BIRCH CREEK NOVELS

*A Reluctant Bride*

*An Unbroken Heart*

*A Love Made New*

THE MIDDLEFIELD AMISH NOVEL

*A Faith of Her Own*

THE MIDDLEFIELD FAMILY NOVELS

*Treasuring Emma*

*Faithful to Laura*

*Letters to Katie*

THE HEARTS OF MIDDLEFIELD NOVELS

*A Man of His Word*

*An Honest Love*

*A Hand to Hold*

STORIES

*A Miracle for Miriam* included in *An Amish Christmas*

*A Place of His Own* included in *An Amish Gathering*

*What the Heart Sees* included in *An Amish Love*

*A Perfect Match* included in *An Amish Wedding*

*Flowers for Rachael* included in *An Amish Garden*

*A Gift for Anne Marie* included in
*An Amish Second Christmas*

*A Heart Full of Love* included in *An Amish Cradle*

*A Bid for Love* included in *An Amish Market*

*A Quiet Love* included in *An Amish Harvest*

*Building Faith* included in *An Amish Home*

*Lakeside Love* included in *An Amish Summer*

*The Treasured Book* included in *An Amish Heirloom*

## KELLY IRVIN

### EVERY AMISH SEASONS NOVELS

*Upon A Spring Breeze*

*Beneath the Summer Sun*

*Through the Autumn Air*

*With Winter's First Frost* (Available February 2019)

### THE AMISH OF BEE COUNTY NOVELS

*The Beekeeper's Son*

*The Bishop's Son*

*The Saddle Maker's Son*

### STORIES

*A Christmas Visitor* included in
*An Amish Christmas Gift*

*Sweeter than Honey* included in *An Amish Market*

*One Sweet Kiss* included in *An Amish Summer*

*Snow Angels* included in *An Amish Christmas Love*

*The Midwife's Dream* included in *An Amish Heirloom*

# AN AMISH QUILT

## THREE STORIES

Beth Wiseman

Kathleen Fuller

Kelly Irvin

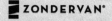

ZONDERVAN

*Amish Quilt*

Copyright © 2018, 2016, 2015 by Beth Wiseman, Kathleen Fuller, and Kelly Irvin

This title is also available as a Zondervan e-book.

Requests for information should be addressed to:
Zondervan, *3900 Sparks Dr. SE, Grand Rapids, Michigan 49546*

**Library of Congress Cataloging-in-Publication**
Names: Wiseman, Beth, 1962-author. | Fuller,
Kathleen, author. | Irvin, Kelly, author.
Title: An Amish Quilt: patchwork perfect, a bid for love, a midwife's dream /
    Beth Wiseman, Kathleen Fuller, and
Kelly Irvin.
Description: Nashville: Zondervan, 2018.
Mass Market ISBN: 978-0-7852-1759-6
Subjects: LCSH: Amish—Fiction. | GSAFD: Love stories. | Christian fiction.

All Scripture quotations, unless otherwise indicated, are taken from The
Holy Bible, *New International Version*®, NIV®. Copyright © 1973, 1978, 1984,
2011 by Biblica, Inc™ Used by permission. All rights reserved worldwide.
www.zondervan.com. The "NIV" and "New International Version" are
trademarks registered in the United States Patent and Trademark Office by
Biblica, Inc.®

Any Internet addresses (websites, blogs, etc.) and telephone numbers in
this book are offered as a resource. They are not intended in any way to be
or imply an endorsement by Zondervan, nor does Zondervan vouch for the
content of these sites and numbers for the life of this book.

All rights reserved. No part of this publication may be reproduced, stored in
a retrieval system, or transmitted in any form or by any means—electronic,
mechanical, photocopy, recording, or any other—except for brief quotations
in printed reviews, without the prior permission of the publisher.

Publisher's Note: This novel is a work of fiction. Names, characters, places,
and incidents are either products of the author's imagination or used
fictitiously. All characters are fictional, and any similarity to people living or
dead is purely coincidental.

*Printed in the United States of America*

18 19 20 21 22 / QG / 5 4 3 2

# CONTENTS

*Patchwork Perfect* by Beth Wiseman............................1

*A Bid for Love* by Kathleen Fuller............................109

*The Midwife's Dream* by Kelly Irvin........................201

# PATCHWORK PERFECT

BETH WISEMAN

# PENNSYLVANIA
# DUTCH GLOSSARY

*ab im kopp*—off in the head; crazy
*ach*—oh
*bruder*—brother
*daed*—dad
*danki*—thank you
*Englisch*—non-Amish person
*fraa*—wife
*gut*—good
*haus*—house
*kapp*—prayer covering or cap
*kinner*—children
*maedel*—girl
*mamm*—mom
*mei*—my
*mudder*—mother
*nee*—no
*rumschpringe*—running-around period when a teen-ager turns sixteen years old
*sohn*—son
*Wie bischt*—How are you?; Howdy
*wunderbaar*—wonderful
*ya*—yes

*To Kiki and Katie*

# CHAPTER 1

Eli walked toward a group of men gathered in the front yard. He'd met several of them over the past couple of weeks, but he was having a hard time remembering names. Back home, there weren't nearly as many people to keep track of. Then he reminded himself, *This is home now.*

Amos Glick extended his hand when Eli joined the men. Amos was an easy name to remember since it was his father's.

"It was a fine worship service today," Eli said as he greeted the other men with a handshake. Amos introduced everyone to Eli. Some were repeat introductions, but Eli was grateful to hear their names again.

"For those of you who haven't met Eli before now, he comes to us from a small church district near Bucks County." Amos stroked his beard, a mixture of brown and gray streaks, though Eli suspected the gray was premature. Amos looked about Eli's age, early thirties, and couldn't be over five foot five. He'd also met Amos's wife, Sarah, who towered over her husband. One thing Eli liked right away about Amos was that he smiled a lot. Eli remembered a time when he smiled often, and he wondered if he'd ever be that man again.

"What brings you to Lancaster County?" one of the other men asked, an older fellow with a big black mole above his left eye. Eli had already forgotten his name.

Eli had practiced how he would respond to this question. "More opportunities for work here." He forced a smile, content that he'd told the truth, even if it wasn't the entire truth.

"Do you farm?" The same man squinted one eye, still stroking his beard.

"*Ya*, mostly farming." Eli tipped the brim of his hat to block the sun that had reached its midday peak. This was his favorite time of year, when the foliage shifted into soft hues of amber and crimson. His former home was only an hour and a half from here, and they'd enjoyed the same type of Octobers in the past. Not only was the shift in seasons a feast for the eyes, but cool breezes drifted beneath the brilliant blue skies. Soon they could expect low clouds that floated like billowy cotton overhead. Best of all, it signified that the fall harvest would soon be upon them. It was always a lot of work, but following the harvest there would be time for rest. And weddings. Almost everyone waited until the fall to get married.

"Eli bought the old Dienner place," Amos said as he looped his thumbs beneath his suspenders. "And Gideon had already done all the planting, so it'll be ready for harvesting in a few weeks."

Eli was grateful to the prior owners of his new farm, though Gideon had planted alfalfa before he knew he'd be moving away. The kindly older man had met with unfortunate circumstances of the financial type. That was all Eli knew. It was the only reason Eli had been able to buy the Dienners' farm. It was worth more than he'd offered Gideon, but it was all he could afford. Eli had been surprised when Gideon had accepted his bid, but somehow it seemed like a win-win situation for both men. A chance for Gideon to relocate with his wife to a smaller house now that their *kinner* were grown and living in a different district, and a fresh start for Eli, Ben, and Grace.

The men began to disassemble when the ladies starting bringing out trays of food, placing them on tables set up in a shaded area. But Amos lingered behind with Eli until they were alone.

Amos's smile grew as he nudged Eli. "*Ach*, let's get down to business." He pointed toward the group of women and lifted up on his toes, closer to Eli's ear, so Eli leaned down a bit. "See that woman in the maroon dress, the one carrying the tea pitcher? She's a widow."

Eli nodded, grinning. He'd told Amos that he lost his wife two years ago in an accident. Eli would always miss Leah. But he was ready to find a wife and a mother for his children. He'd been ready for the past year, but with no more than twenty Amish families in his area, his choices had been limited.

"Her name is Elizabeth," Amos whispered as two men walked past them. "She's twenty-five, no *kinner*, and her husband passed a few months ago."

Eli stretched his neck to have a better look at her. She was a petite woman with dark hair, but he couldn't make out her features.

Amos tapped him on the arm. "Let's walk that way."

Eli fell in step beside Amos, who slowed down as they approached the crowd. Most of the men were finding seats at the tables as the women delivered pitchers of tea and glasses filled with ice. "She's pretty," Eli said as he studied her. He could tell by the way she moved around the table carrying glasses of ice that she was graceful and feminine, flowerlike. Her eyes were dark brown, set against an olive complexion, and when she smiled, Eli instinctively smiled too.

"*Ach*, and not only is she pretty, but she might be the best cook we have around here." Amos raised his chin as he also looked at Elizabeth. "I'll introduce you to her after the meal."

Eli wondered if Elizabeth was too young for him. Probably no one would think so, but eight years was stretching it. He had been married at seventeen, widowed at thirty-one, and now was raising a fifteen-year-old and an eleven-year-old. He felt older than his thirty-three years. And would someone Elizabeth's age want to step into a family with older children? He scratched his chin as he watched her.

Amos cleared his throat, then whispered again. "Sarah told me that Elizabeth is in a hurry to get remarried. She wants *kinner*. Her husband died of cancer." Amos shook his head. "A real shame. He took sick not long after their wedding. He had lots of treatments in the hospital. I don't think they ever had a chance to think about starting a family. Elizabeth took care of him for their entire marriage, right up to the end. I think everyone was surprised at how strong she was, and what a *gut* caregiver she was to John." Amos turned to Eli and sighed. "We're all praying Elizabeth will find a nice fellow. There are several vying for her affection, but if the truth be told, I don't think a one of them is right for her."

Eli was seeing Elizabeth in a new light. Taking care of someone like that lent her a maturity that was uncommon for her age. *Pretty, can cook, graceful, and wants more children.* Eli wanted more children too. "I'd like to meet her." He took a step forward, but Amos tugged on his shirt.

"Hold on there, fellow." Amos nodded to his left. Almost everyone was seated now, and Eli could feel several sets of eyes on them. Amos must have, too, because he was whispering so softly that Eli had to ask him to speak up a little.

"We have one other widow in our church district that I'll point out to you as soon as I find her. Her name is Ruth." Amos turned to Eli. "There are plenty of younger women who are available, but . . ." He grinned. "They got their eyes set on the young bucks. You'd be an old man in their eyes."

Eli took a deep breath and blew it out slowly. He knew Amos was right. But at least there were two widows in his new church district. It would be nice if he was properly suited to one of them and didn't have to travel outside of the community to find a *fraa*.

Amos scanned the tables looking for Ruth. Eli's stomach rumbled, and his need to eat was becoming more important than being introduced to anyone. But when he heard a screen door slam in the distance, he turned his attention to the tall woman floating down

the front porch steps as if she had angel wings on her
back. Even from a distance, Eli was mesmerized as she
strode across the yard. The closer she got to him, the
more her beauty shone, and he had to force himself to
breathe. From beneath her *kapp* wisps of red hair blew
against her rosy cheeks. But it was her green eyes twin-
kling in the sunlight that kept Eli from being able to
look away. He'd been taught that pride and vanity were
sin, and most of the time he did his best not to let them
dominate his choices.

"She's a beauty, isn't she?" Amos said as they
finally started making their way to two empty seats.
"That's Ruth."

Eli nodded, finally pulling his gaze from Ruth.
After he was seated, he bowed his head in prayer, then
reached for a slice of bread. He was glad to see Ben two
tables over talking with two boys who looked to be
around his age, maybe ten or twelve. But as his eyes
traveled from table to table, he didn't see Gracie. He
took a bite of bread, assuming his daughter must be
inside. Maybe the bathroom. Or maybe just sitting in
the living room avoiding everyone. His fifteen-year-
old hadn't been happy about the move and leaving her
friends behind. But Eli was certain a fresh start was
just what they all needed.

. . .

Grace loved kissing as much as chocolate pie, a warm
bath on a cold winter's night, and reading *Englisch*
magazines on the sly, the ones she kept hidden between

her mattresses. But Wayne Huyard was interested in a lot more than just kissing, and she was having a hard time guiding his hands away from places they needn't be. They'd barely been in Lancaster County a week when she'd met Wayne at a Sunday singing. He was sixteen, a year older than Grace, and with his dreamy blue eyes and blond hair, he was cuter than cute.

"*Mei daed*'s going to come looking for me," she said, latching onto one of Wayne's roaming hands. Actually, she doubted that was the case. The only thing her father was looking for was a wife. She'd met Wayne behind the far barn on the property. As everyone was getting ready for the meal, they'd slipped away as planned.

"I love kissing you," he said as his mouth covered hers again. She loved the way he cupped her cheeks in his hands, thankful to know exactly where those hands were for the moment. But within seconds, they wandered again.

"I can't," she said as she eased her lips away from his, stepping back until his hands finally fell to his sides.

Wayne gently touched her cheek with the back of his hand. "You're so pretty. I *really* like you."

Grace felt herself blush as he slowly inched forward, kissing her again. She tried to relax. Wayne had kissed her one other time, after the singing the night they'd met. Maybe he thought she was easy, as the *Englisch* girls would say, since she'd allowed him to kiss her that first night. But his roaming hands could get them both into trouble. She'd seen it happen with other girls.

Grace put her hand on top of his, hoping she wasn't going to make him mad. She was grateful to have met someone so cute not long after moving here, and she'd only kissed one other boy; that was about a year ago. He'd been shorter than her and didn't seem to know what he was doing. Wayne was a take-charge man. Handsome. And he knew what he was doing. Grace had never had anyone like him take an interest in her.

"I want to spend time with you," he said between kisses. He pushed away a strand of hair that had fallen from her *kapp*, a gesture that caused her to shiver. "Some of us guys play baseball in a big field at the Lantzes' *haus* on Saturdays." He kissed her tenderly on the lips. "I want you to come watch." He pulled her closer and whispered, "As my date."

Grace felt herself relaxing a tiny bit and she wasn't as quick to latch onto his hand. She'd never had a boyfriend, and for the first time in two years, she wondered if maybe she could be happy again. But no matter how good looking and sweet Wayne might be, some things were just off-limits. She grabbed his hand again, but he didn't leave the area. She eased him away.

"I'm sorry, Wayne. I just can't." She took a deep breath and held it, knowing that some boys—even *gut* Amish boys—wanted a girl who was willing to go further than just kissing.

"It's okay," he whispered in her ear. "I like you so much, I don't mind waiting. I think you're someone I could really fall for."

Grace was sure the clouds were opening up and raining down blessings on her, and for a brief second, she considered giving him some freedoms that went against what she believed was right, but at the last minute, she took his hand and repeated, "I can't."

Wayne trailed his kisses down her neck, and Grace wasn't sure what was happening to her. She was a bit weak in the knees, but a rustling in the leaves to their right caused both of them to stop and turn. Grace's heart was beating hard, but she quickly thanked God that it wasn't her father.

"Wayne Huyard, what are you doing back here?" A woman a few years older than she and Wayne walked toward them, stopping a couple of feet away. Grace remembered meeting her earlier that morning before the worship service. Her name was Miriam, and Grace was pretty sure her last name was Fisher. The woman didn't look as old as Grace's father, but she had those feathery lines women get when they start to age. Miriam had a smudge of dirt on her chin.

Scowling, Miriam put her hands on her hips. Grace was pretty sure this woman was going to haul them back to the group, and her father would know she'd been alone with a boy. And so would everyone else. She swallowed hard, wondering exactly how much Miriam had seen.

# CHAPTER 2

M iriam felt like punching Wayne, even though it
wasn't their way, and she'd never hit anyone in
her life. But why was it that some boys felt the need to
welcome the new girls in a way that wasn't appropriate?
Especially on a Sunday.

"Miriam, this ain't none of your business." Wayne
shrugged. "We weren't doing nothing anyway."

Miriam rolled her eyes as she folded her arms across
her chest. "If that's what *nothing* looks like, I don't
need to see *something*." She'd known Wayne since he
was born. She'd been about twelve when she used to
babysit him. And at sixteen, he'd already grown into
the type of young man that mothers feared.

She glanced at the girl, who appeared to be quaking
in her loafers, her big brown eyes as round as saucers.
Miriam wasn't sure Wayne's prey was even breathing.

"Have we met?" Miriam squinted one eye as she
tried to remember. She knew a new family had moved
to their church district, but she didn't recall formally
meeting any of them.

The girl let out a breath. She was a cute little thing,
but she was no match for Wayne.

"*Ya*. We met this morning. I'm Grace Byler. My family moved here a couple of weeks ago."

Miriam recalled being introduced to the girl early this morning. "You have a *bruder*, too, right?"

Grace nodded. "*Ya*. Ben."

That morning, Miriam had left the house before having a cup of coffee, something she tried never to do. But she'd overslept, tripped over the threshold between the kitchen and den, and landed on her right knee. By the time she'd cleaned up her wound, she was late for worship and ran to her buggy, bypassing her cup of coffee. She glared at Wayne, wanting to give him a good talking-to, but Miriam didn't want to embarrass Grace even further. And it wouldn't do any good.

"Are you going to tell *mei* father?" Grace blinked her eyes a few times and her lip was trembling.

"Did I meet your father too?" Miriam frowned, vowing never to start her day without coffee again. She should have just been late. Relief washed over her when Grace shook her head.

"*Nee*. I don't think you met him yet. He wasn't with us when Ben and I were introduced to you."

"*Nee*, I'm not going to tell your *daed*," Miriam finally said. She was wise enough to know that Grace and Wayne were going to do whatever they wanted, but she wasn't sure she could live with herself if she didn't try to warn Grace. She turned to Wayne. "You go join the others. If Grace goes back with you now, it will be obvious you two snuck off together."

Wayne nodded, picked his straw hat up off the

ground next to him, and quickly disappeared around the corner.

Miriam thought for a few moments. She wanted to warn Grace about Wayne without making him sound like the resident bad boy. Even though he was.

Miriam sighed, thinking *bad boy* was probably too strong a description. Wayne was a teenager finding his way into adulthood, like a lot of other young men here. But he seemed to have an overabundance of cuteness, hormones, and confidence. A dangerous combination when it came to the teenage girls. Miriam knew of two girls who hadn't been able to resist Wayne's charms, and they'd both been left brokenhearted after he'd won their affections and then tossed them aside later for reasons Miriam could only speculate about. Miriam didn't want to see that happen to the new girl.

"Grace, I know you're new here, so I'm going to tell you about Wayne." She paused, wondering how to structure her words in a way that Grace would understand, without Miriam having to spell it out. "Wayne is . . . well . . ." She blew out a breath, then scratched her chin. "Wayne is probably not the best person for you to spend time with right now. Maybe get to know the other young people before settling on the first boy who shows interest."

Miriam hoped the other girls would talk to Grace about Wayne soon, but just in case they didn't, Miriam wanted to walk away with a clear conscience. Some of these boys seemed to swoop in on the new girls like vultures, even before they had time to make close girlfriends. Not many new families came into their community, but those with teenage daughters needed to be warned about this particular teen boy.

Grace raised her chin as she lifted one shoulder, then let it drop slowly. "We really weren't doing anything, and I can handle boys like Wayne."

Miriam stifled a grin. It was a very *Englisch* thing to say, and Miriam doubted it was true, but she just shrugged. "If you say so. I tried to warn you."

"Well, I don't need a warning, but *danki* anyway." Grace folded her hands in front of her and stiffened.

Miriam stared at the girl for a few moments, but her eyes hadn't deceived her. Grace could have used two extra hands to ward off Wayne during their little kissing extravaganza. If Grace allowed Wayne to kiss her like that, how long before she allowed him to go further? Maybe things were different in the district Grace came from.

"*Ya*, okay," Miriam finally said. "I guess we can go join the others now."

. . .

Eli was relieved to see Gracie coming across the front yard. He would ask her later where she'd been, but for now, he was just glad she was okay. After breathing a sigh of relief, he noticed the woman walking next to his daughter.

"Don't get any notions," Amos said, then snickered. "That's Miriam Fisher, and she ain't the woman for you."

"I just assumed she was married." Eli had noticed

Miriam earlier in the day, mostly because she had blood seeping down her leg. He'd been about to ask her if she needed help when another woman handed her a paper towel. "You said there were only two widows in this district."

"There are." Amos grinned. "Miriam has never been married."

Eli opened his mouth as Gracie and Miriam took seats at different tables. "But she looks like she could be close to thirty."

Amos whispered, "*Ya*. She's our resident old maid. She's twenty-eight."

Eli watched Miriam reach for a slice of bread, thinking she was pretty. Not beautiful, like Ruth, but pretty. "What's wrong with her?" he finally asked.

Amos chuckled. "The list is too long to recite, *mei* friend. Just take my word for it and keep your eyes focused on Elizabeth and Ruth. Either of those two ladies would make a fine *fraa* and *mudder* to your *kinner*."

Eli nodded, but he couldn't stop wondering about her. "Is she . . . sick? Or maybe *ab im kopp*?"

"*Nee*, she's not sick that I know of or off in the head. Miriam grew up here, and for as long as I can remember, she's been . . ." Amos grinned. "Strong willed."

"That is *gut*, a strong woman." Eli pulled his eyes from Miriam and put another slice of bread on his plate, then lathered it with church spread and took a bite, savoring the flavor. Nothing in God's perfect world was better than marshmallow and peanut butter mixed together and swiped across a piece of homemade bread. It had been Leah's favorite too.

"Miriam isn't just strong willed," Amos went on. "She's different. I ain't been in her house in years, but rumor has it that she can't host worship service because the *haus* is barely fit for living in. Sarah says Miriam don't cook, have a garden, or know how to sew." Amos raised his eyebrows. "Does that sound like a woman you'd want to be married to?"

Eli stole another look at Miriam. "Doesn't she want to be married? You would think she might work on some of those skills to marry a *gut* man."

"She's a mystery." Amos tapped a finger to his chin. "Although . . . I recall her dating someone a long time ago. She was barely of age. But the courtship seemed to end before it really got going." He pointed a finger at Eli. "And another thing. She plays baseball with the young people when they gather on Saturdays, and most think she's a mite too old to be doing that. And she's got cats . . . lots and lots of cats."

Eli had loved playing baseball as a boy, but Amos was right—there comes a time when a person must put the joys of their youth behind them in order to work, marry, and raise a family. But for a few moments, Eli imagined hearing the crack of the bat when it collided with the ball and the adrenaline of running with all he had. And he loved cats, although he hadn't been around many since finding out he was allergic to them.

Amos was still talking when Eli said, "Who is that?" Eli pointed to where Gracie was standing with an Amish boy who looked to be around her age. His daughter was grinning as the boy whispered in her ear. It was still hard for him to believe that his daughter was old enough to be interested in boys. But he reminded himself that he and Leah had gotten married at seventeen. Most Plain people married young, but Eli hoped Gracie would wait awhile.

"That's Wayne Huyard," Amos said as he glanced up before grabbing the last pickle on a nearby platter. "He's a *gut* boy, a hard worker. I ain't heard nothing bad about him. His parents are fine people. They've raised the boy well."

Eli was glad to hear that, but he remembered being Wayne's age, and he planned to keep a close eye on his daughter, no matter what. He stood up and eased his chair back. "I think I'll go introduce myself to Wayne." He pushed his chair in and began making his way toward his daughter and her new friend. While walking, he took the opportunity to catch a better look at Elizabeth and Ruth, both of whom were busy cleaning tables with the other women. He wasn't sure which one of them he might like to ask out, or if they'd even accept his invitation, but he couldn't help but feel hopeful that he might find love again.

He was several yards from reaching Gracie and Wayne when Miriam crossed in front of him carrying at least six empty plates, three glasses piled on top, and a half full pitcher of tea. Some of the tea was sloshing over the side as she struggled to keep everything balanced. Eli reached for the pitcher. "Here, let me help you." It was customary for the women to serve the men and children, then they'd eat, and after the meal, the women cleaned up. But Eli couldn't help but think it was a bit unfair. Over the past two years, he'd been forced to learn to cook, and he realized he enjoyed cooking almost as much as eating.

*"Danki,"* she said as she got a better grip on the plates and glasses. "If you'll put that pitcher on the table, someone will get it, or I'll come back for it." She smiled at Eli, and when she did, tiny dimples indented her cheeks, which deepened even more when Eli smiled. Eli couldn't tell if her rosy cheeks were sun kissed or windburned, but either way, it made her dark eyes stand out even more. And when her long eyelashes swept down over her high cheekbones, Eli thought she might be flirting with him. He recalled everything Amos had told him about her, but Eli believed in forming his own opinions.

"I'm Eli Byler," he said. "We just moved here a couple of weeks ago."

*"Wie bischt."* She set the stack of plates and glasses on the table and brushed back a strand of dark hair. "I think I met your *kinner*. But, um . . . oops. I can't remember their names."

Eli grinned. "I'm not *gut* with names either. Grace is my daughter. She's fifteen. And Ben, my son, is eleven."

She nodded. "Welcome to Paradise; it's *gut* to meet you."

Shrugging, Eli said, "I don't have a *fraa*." He felt his face turning red. *Why in the world did I say that?* He felt silly when she grinned at him.

"I hope you find one." She picked up the plates and glasses again. "I'd better get these inside and help with the cleanup. Again, nice to meet you."

"Nice to meet you too." Eli told his feet to stay where

they were, that Amos had made it perfectly clear that Miriam was not someone he should pursue, but within seconds, he'd sauntered up beside her.

"Would you like to go to supper with me sometime?"

Miriam didn't even slow down or look at him. "*Nee*, but *danki* anyway. It's kind of you to ask."

"Wait." She was almost to the porch steps when Eli gently touched her arm.

She turned to face him. "*Ya?*"

She wasn't smiling anymore, and maybe that should have been his clue to walk away, but something outside of his own thoughts seemed to be controlling his movements. "I could, uh . . . cook for you. I like to cook." He grinned. "And I heard you don't cook. I like to," he repeated. Eli held his breath as he waited, wondering who had taken over his brain. *What a dumb thing to say.*

Miriam's expression softened. "So, you are asking me to come to your *haus,* and you will cook for me?"

Eli looped his thumbs beneath his suspenders, feeling a little bit taller all of a sudden. He nodded, smiling. "*Ya*, I am."

"Aw," she said softly as she took a step closer to him, so close he could have kissed her. "I guess it's pretty well known that I'm not very handy in the kitchen. And I've never had a man offer to cook for me. Are you any *gut* at it?"

"*Ya*. I am. After *mei fraa* died—Leah—I had to learn how. Grace was thirteen, but she was still in school, and she tended to cook things that weren't all that healthy, so I started spending some time in the kitchen and realized . . . I enjoy it." He chuckled. "And I'd be happy to cook for you."

Miriam looked down at her feet for a few seconds, then back up at him. She flashed him a thin-lipped smile. It was an expression he recognized. Leah used to give him the same look when she was irritated, before she scolded him for something. *Uh-oh.*

"Eli . . ."

He waited, feeling hopeful by the gentle tone of her voice. Maybe he'd read her expression wrong. *"Ya?"*

"I can't come to your *haus* for you to cook for me. And I will never go on a date with you. But I wish you God's blessings and a happy life here for you and your family." She turned and headed up the porch steps, and this time, Eli's feet remained rooted to the ground beneath him.

# CHAPTER 3

Grace sat on the makeshift bleachers that faced the baseball field at the Lantzes' place the following Saturday. The bleachers were six logs lined up in a row behind home plate. Bases were marked with large bags of rice. There were eight boys and . . . *Miriam*?

Grace was sitting next to three girls she didn't know very well. She'd tried to talk to them the couple of times she'd been around them—once at the singing when she'd met Wayne, and then again after worship service. They were friendly enough both times, but when they saw Grace and Wayne walk up together today, the girls met her with a stony expression and hadn't said much. Jealousy was a sin, but that was clearly the girls' problem. Grace had never wanted to move here. Their former community was small, but at least she'd had a couple of close girlfriends she'd grown up with, even if the shortage of available boys was disappointing.

Grace turned to the girl sitting to her right, Rachel. "Why is Miriam playing with the boys?" She waited until Rachel finished whispering to Naomi and Linda. Hopefully they weren't talking about Grace.

Rachel pulled her sweater snug as she turned to face Grace. The first cold front had blown in, and it was starting to feel like fall. Grace was wishing she'd brought a sweater too. "The boys all think she plays to show them up." Rachel grinned. "We don't think that's it." She pointed to Naomi and Linda, who had leaned forward to hear. "Miriam babysat all of us when we were young, and since she's not married, she seems to make it her job to look after us."

"More like spying," Naomi added. "I think she reports back to our parents if she sees us with a boy, doesn't approve of something we're doing, or finds us somewhere we aren't supposed to be."

If that was the case, why didn't Miriam tell Grace's father that she'd been kissing Wayne? Or maybe Miriam cared about these girls since she'd known them so long.

"We're in our *rumschpringe*," Linda said. "So it's really none of her business what we do."

Grace nodded, recalling that Wayne had said the same thing to Miriam: *none of your business*. Grace couldn't wait until she turned sixteen in a few months. Then she'd be able to enjoy her running-around period too. In a way, she already was—with Wayne. Her father hadn't even missed her on Sunday when she'd snuck off. He was too busy identifying the widows in the community. *Daed* could say whatever he wanted, that they'd moved for more work opportunities, but Grace knew the truth. *Daed* was on the hunt for a *fraa*, and there hadn't been much to choose from back home.

"She looks old not to be married," Grace said as

Miriam pitched the ball to the other team. Her arm was as good as or better than the boys'.

"That's what she is, an old maid." Rachel chuckled. "It probably has something to do with the fact that she can't cook, her house is always a mess, she doesn't garden, and she's a tomboy."

Linda leaned forward until she met eyes with Grace. "Don't listen to Rachel. Miriam is a *gut* person." She shrugged. "She's just different than most of the grownups here. But she'd do anything for any of us." Linda glared at Rachel. "Shame on you, Rachel."

Linda leaned back, and they all went back to watching the game. Naomi and Linda cheered the loudest each time a boy named Jessie made a good play. Grace couldn't help but smile when Wayne hit a double and slid into second base, but when she glanced to her right, Rachel was glowering in her direction.

Grace knew it would take time to make friends. But at least she had Wayne. She smiled again when he winked at her from second base. And she didn't bother looking over at Rachel.

. . .

Eli sat down in the rocking chair in his bedroom and thumbed through the cookbook he'd bought last week. It was his guilty pleasure, and after the day he'd had, he deserved some downtime. He and Ben had repaired a long stretch of fence along the back of the property, and then they'd cut enough firewood to last most of the winter. Ben was as exhausted as he was, and last he saw his son, he was napping on the couch. Eli glanced down at his paint-splattered clothes at about the same time he got a whiff of himself. Next stop, bathtub. But he'd allow himself a few more minutes to skim the cookbook. He ran a hand through his beard, a gesture that made him think of Leah and the way she'd playfully yank on his whiskers to get his attention.

Eli lifted the bottom of his beard. Tiny threads of gray had emerged over the past year, and he found himself checking it often. Sighing, he refocused on his book. A moment later, someone knocked on his bedroom door.

"*Daed*, there's a lady here to see you," Ben said as he rolled his eyes.

Eli wondered if Ben made the gesture because he'd been disturbed while napping, or if he was just irritated because a woman was visiting. Neither of his children had made a big secret about not wanting Eli to date and therefore stayed suspicious about all females close to Eli's age. Eli got another whiff of himself and grimaced. "Who is it?" he whispered as he lifted his stinky self from the rocker.

"She said her name is Elizabeth." Ben yawned. "And she's carrying a pie."

Eli put a finger to his mouth, narrowing his eyebrows at his son. "Whisper," he said. "And where is she?"

"On the porch." Ben closed the door, and Eli made a mental note to speak with his son about manners.

He couldn't just leave her on the porch while he got cleaned up. Shaking his head, he hurried into the living room, and when he didn't see Ben, he assumed his son must have gone upstairs to finish his nap. Eli had briefly been introduced to Elizabeth and Ruth last Sunday after worship service, but he still hadn't decided whom he might be interested in courting. He'd ruled out Miriam right away, since she'd ruled him out before he'd even put his best foot forward. He opened the wooden door and saw Elizabeth through the screen.

"*Wie bischt*, Elizabeth." He eased the screen door open and motioned for her to come in, noticing Ben's almost-empty plate on the coffee table; just one half-eaten cookie remained. "I apologize for my son leaving you on the porch." He nodded to the coffee table. "And please forgive the mess." Although the biggest mess was himself.

"*Nee, nee,*" Elizabeth quickly said. "Not to worry." She handed Eli a pie, and the aroma of freshly baked apples swirled in the air. "I wanted to bring your family a welcome present, so I made this apple crumb pie." She smiled as she lifted up on her toes for a second. "My own recipe."

Amos had told him that Elizabeth might be the best cook in the community. She seemed mighty young to have earned that title at twenty-five, but Eli loved apple pie. "*Danki*. It's so nice of you to do this." He looked down at himself. "Please don't take notice of the way I'm dressed. Ben and I repaired the fence and chopped wood today."

"I feel awful for just dropping in like this, but I felt a proper welcome was in order, and I didn't have a shanty number . . . or cell phone number, if you happen to have one."

Eli was pretty sure that was a hint for his phone number, and as a warm and flattering feeling wrapped around him, he pondered what to say.

"I-I think I'm going to go now. I caught you at a bad time." She gave him a quick wave, then turned to leave.

"Wait."

She turned to face him, her hand on the doorknob.

"I *never* eat pie alone. It's a rule I have. So you have to stay and have a slice with me. I'll get some coffee percolating too."

A full smile swept across her face as she folded her hands in front of her. "I would love to."

"This way." Eli motioned for her to follow him into the kitchen, and once he had the percolator on the stove top, he pulled a knife from the drawer, along with two plates.

"Allow me," Elizabeth said as she gently took the knife from him. "You sit down and let me serve you." She pulled out a chair, and when Eli didn't move, she added, "I never let a man serve me. It's a rule I have."

Eli grinned but shook his head. "*Nee*, you are in my home. Please let me—"

"I insist. It is obvious you have done a hard day's labor, so you rest."

After hesitating a few more seconds, Eli sat down. His own exhaustion had won that argument.

"This is the best apple pie I've ever had," Eli said a few minutes later. And he meant it. "Where did you learn to bake like this?" He shoveled another piece in his mouth, fully aware that his manners weren't any better than his son's at the moment. "You said it's your recipe?"

She nodded, taking tiny bites of the small slice she'd cut for herself. "I like to play around with recipes. If I see one that looks *gut*, I'll usually make it as written, but then I make a list of things I'd like to try to make it better. Sometimes it takes two or three times before I get it exactly the way I want it."

Eli swallowed and sat taller, tempted to tell her that he loved to cook, but he wasn't sure if that would sound unmanly, so he chose another version of the truth. "I've done a lot of cooking since *mei fraa* died two years ago."

Elizabeth gazed at him from across the table. "I bet you miss someone cooking for you. I met both your *kinner* last Sunday; they are lovely. Does Grace do most of the cooking?"

Eli swallowed the last of his pie, then chose another safe version of the truth, since he did most of the cooking. "She does some of the cooking, but she stays busy keeping the *haus* clean, doing laundry, and mending Ben's clothes. I think my *sohn* is growing so fast that he's popping buttons. It seems like Gracie is always letting out hems or sewing on buttons."

"That is a lot for a young girl to do." Elizabeth shook her head. "My husband passed recently. I miss him very much, but I also miss having someone to take care of. I bet you miss being taken care of?"

"I did in the beginning. Leah—that was *mei fraa's* name—did all the cooking, and there wasn't a day that I didn't come home to a hot supper." He paused when he saw that Elizabeth had a faraway look in her eyes. "I know it hasn't been long since you lost your husband.

I'm sure you've heard this a hundred times, but it does get easier."

She seemed to force a smile. "It's lonely sometimes."

Eli nodded as he recalled the months following Leah's death. Even in a roomful of people, he'd never been lonelier in his life. "I heard that your husband had a long battle with cancer. I also heard that you took very *gut* care of him."

"*Danki* for saying so." Her cheeks took on a rosy hue as she tipped her chin down.

"Leah died instantly." Eli took a deep breath, remembering the heavy steps he took to the morgue to identify his beloved wife. "She was in her buggy when a car hit her." As much as Eli missed Leah, he'd thanked God every day that Ben and Grace hadn't been with her. Elizabeth's eyes locked with his, and Eli had to wonder which was worse—losing someone unexpectedly or watching them suffer month after month.

Elizabeth shook her head, still watching him. "I'm very sorry for your loss."

Eli nodded. "*Danki*. And I'm sorry for yours. What kind of cancer did your husband have?"

"A brain tumor. When we found out about John's cancer, he was already in a bad way, and . . ."

Eli listened to Elizabeth for the next hour, detailing every phase of John's battle. He commented when the conversation called for it, but it was clear that Elizabeth was in a different place than he was in the grieving process. The first year is the hardest. Amos had obviously thought Elizabeth was ready to move on, but Eli wasn't sure. But they did have two things in common.

They both liked to cook, and they'd both endured a terrible loss. Elizabeth was also easy on the eyes. Just the thought made him think of Ruth and her incredible beauty. But pretty on the outside didn't always mean pretty on the inside, and he was going to keep an open mind about his possibilities.

When the room grew silent, Eli snapped back to the present.

"I am so sorry," Elizabeth said as she covered her face with her hands. "I have spent the past hour boring you with details about a man you didn't even know."

Eli reached over and lightly touched her arm until she uncovered her face. "Elizabeth, if anyone understands, I do." He offered her a tender smile and held it until she smiled back.

"*Danki*, Eli." She eased the chair back and stood up. "I have overstayed my welcome, but please let me know if there is anything I can do for your family. If your daughter Grace needs help with anything, I'm a stone's throw away. I live alone, and I'd welcome the company." She winked at Eli. "Tell her I'll even cook, if she'd like."

"That sounds *gut*." Eli said a quick prayer asking God to forgive the lie. Grace was worse than Ben when it came to Eli finding a wife, and he doubted his daughter would enjoy spending time with anyone who might be vying for her father's attention. Eli had never approved of courting more than one person at a time, so if he asked out Elizabeth, he would be passing on Ruth. At least for now.

Elizabeth moved around the table and stopped in

front of Eli, then touched him on the arm. "Please call on me for anything you or your family might need," she said again. She exhibited such sincerity, mingled with a loneliness Eli remembered well.

"Would you like to go to supper with me next Saturday night?" Eli filled with warmth when Elizabeth's face lit up, but when she frowned after that and shook her head, Eli felt his heart drop.

"*Nee*, I am not going to let you take me to supper. You are going to come to my *haus* where I can make you a proper home-cooked meal." She gave her head a taut nod. "You deserve that."

Eli smiled. "It's a date then."

# CHAPTER 4

Miriam ran her hand across sweat beaded on her forehead. The crisp October air was refreshing.

"You played *gut* today, Miriam." Wayne brushed by her, smirking, as he made his way to where Grace was sitting. The other girls had already left, but when Wayne leaned down and kissed Grace, Miriam's stomach churned. A tasteless show of public affection. Once again, she found herself wanting to smack that boy. But instead, she glared at him as she walked by, then nodded at Grace, whose face immediately flushed.

As Miriam untethered her horse, she glanced at Grace again. Even though she didn't know the girl, it was hard not to worry about her. She kept hearing a tiny voice in her head, asking if she'd really done enough to warn Grace about Wayne Huyard. But Wayne had been right about one thing. She'd played *gut* today—even hit a home run. They'd been taught not to keep score, but Miriam knew that every person on that field was tallying points, and today Miriam's team had won.

When she pulled up to her small *haus*, Kiki was waiting on the porch.

"*Wie bischt*, sweet girl." She scooped up the orange-and-white tabby, scratched behind her ears, and opened the door with her other hand. A pungent odor met her, and she carried Kiki with her until she found the source. The trash can in the kitchen.

Pinching her nose, she bundled the trash and headed for the door. She was almost down the steps when she heard horse hooves. She spun around, still holding her nose, and peered down the road. It wasn't until the buggy got much closer that she recognized the driver. The new guy. She couldn't remember his name.

Miriam hurried down the remaining steps, dropped the bag next to the house, and met him before he even got out of his buggy. *"Wie bischt,"* she said as he stepped down. *What could this man want? Is he going to ask me out again?* She was pretty sure she'd made her answer clear. Miriam didn't date. She couldn't. What was the point? She'd accepted God's plan for her years ago.

*"Wie bischt,"* the man said. "We met briefly after worship service. Eli Byler."

Miriam folded her arms across her chest. *"Ya,* I remember. You asked me out. You're not here to do that again, are you?"

He held up both palms, grinned slightly, and shook his head. *"Nee.* I think you made it perfectly clear that taking you out was never going to happen."

Miriam stifled a smile as she took in Eli's appearance, wishing things were different. Eli had a gentle smile that crooked up on one side, and his dark hair and beard were specked with gray, even though his features suggested he was in his thirties. "Then why are you here?" she finally asked.

"I'm looking for *mei* daughter, Grace." Worry lines

creased his forehead. "She said she was going to the Lantz *haus* to watch her friend Wayne play baseball, but she didn't come home when she said she would." He paused, shrugged. "Anyway, Amos told me that you play baseball sometimes, and I wondered if you saw her there. I drove by the Lantz *haus*, but all the players had left."

"She was there. And I saw her and Wayne leave together." Miriam took a quick breath. "How old is Grace?"

"She's fifteen. And very responsible. It's not like her not to come home when she says."

Miriam squinted as she stared at Eli. "She's not even in her *rumschpringe*, but you let her date?"

Eli frowned. "She's not dating. She just went to watch a friend play baseball." He looped his thumbs under his suspenders and stood taller. "Besides, she'll be sixteen in a couple of months. She's had such a hard time with this move, I guess I've given her some liberties a little early. And Amos said Wayne is a *gut* boy, a hard worker."

Miriam rolled her eyes. "*Ya*, he's a hard worker all right."

"What does that mean?" Eli folded his arms across his chest like Miriam's.

She wasn't sure whether or not to spill the beans about Wayne. All the girls already thought she was a snitch, but she loved those girls and felt a certain responsibility. She didn't even know Grace.

"I'd just keep a close eye on your daughter," she said. "Boys that age . . ." Biting her bottom lip, she watched the furrows of Eli's brow deepen. "I'm sure she's fine," she added, trying to backtrack, but it was too late. She'd already set the stage, and she could tell by the way Eli was scowling that she'd said too much. But Eli was a man. Surely he remembered what it was like to be a teenage boy.

"I'm sure I'll find her, or she'll show up at home. I'm sorry to have bothered you." He got back into his buggy.

"Eli, wait." Miriam took a few steps until she was right next to the buggy. She was pretty sure she knew where Wayne and Grace had gone, but when she opened her mouth to tell Eli, the words didn't come out. Grace would be horrified if her father caught her in an inappropriate situation with Wayne. But maybe that's exactly what needed to happen so Eli could keep his daughter safe. She thought about it for a few more seconds, then said, "I'm sure she's fine, and if I should happen to hear anything, I'll make sure she knows you are looking for her."

"*Danki.*"

Miriam stood in the yard until she saw Eli turn the corner, then she let out a heavy sigh and huffed back to the side of the house to grab the trash. It would have been nice to curl up on the couch with Kiki and bury her head in a good book. But now she was going to have to go tell Grace that her father was looking for her.

. . .

Grace wiggled free of Wayne's tight hold as he kissed her in a way that was making her uncomfortable, and his hands were traveling again. "I can't, Wayne."

He eased away, breathing hard and frowning.
Cupping her cheek gently in his hand, he said, "I know
it might seem wrong, but when two people really like
each other, it's just natural to want to be closer."

Grace's breathing was ragged, and alarms were going
off in her mind, but Wayne spoke with such tenderness. And he was so cute. If he really cared about her,
maybe there was no harm in letting him take things a
little further. But she quickly tossed the thought aside
as her mother's face flashed in front of her, and the
thought of disappointing her was too much to bear,
even if *Mamm's* view was from heaven. She shook her
head, and Wayne dropped his hand.

"I think you'd better take me home. I'm already
late." Grace doubted her father had even noticed, but
if she was gone much longer, he might. Or maybe not.
From her seat next to Wayne in the buggy, it was easy
to see why he had chosen this spot. From the highway,
they'd turned onto a dirt road, followed wagon-wheel
ruts across a pasture, and arrived at this cluster of
trees with barely enough room for a buggy. There was
an overlook about fifty feet away and a creek below.
Secluded and pretty. The perfect make-out spot.

"Fine." Wayne twisted in his seat, and Grace was
startled by his gruff tone.

"Are you mad?" She reached for his hand at the same
time he grabbed the reins, so she slowly returned her
hand to her lap.

"*Nee*. I'm not mad." He dropped the reins and sighed.
"It's just . . ." He turned to look at her and pressed his
lips together, and for a moment, she thought she saw

his lip tremble. "I've never felt this way about anyone before. I know we haven't known each other long, but I'm feeling something I've never felt before. And it wonders me if you are feeling the same way. I'm worried that you're not." He hung his head, and this time Grace reached for his hand and latched on.

"*Ach*, Wayne." Her words sounded dreamy, but she felt like she might burst with emotion. "I *am* feeling something. I really am." As he turned to face her, she leaned over and kissed him on the mouth, and as he returned the kiss, Grace knew that it was going to take more than just a few kisses to hold on to someone like him. But they both jumped when they heard a buggy come up the path.

"You have got to be kidding me," Wayne said as he abruptly pulled away from Grace and stepped out of the buggy. "This is *ab im kopp*, you following us around."

"I'm not off in the head, Wayne. I don't want to be here any more than you want me here." Miriam spat the words as she approached them. "But Grace's *daed* showed up at *mei haus* looking for her."

Grace brought a hand to her chest, then stepped out of the buggy. Following a brief thrust of adrenaline that shot through her veins, she realized that even if she got in trouble, her father did care about her. Deep down, she knew he did, but he'd been so preoccupied that it was good to know she'd been missed.

Miriam scowled at Grace before she looked back at Wayne. "And I knew you'd bring her to make-out mountain, or whatever you boys are calling it these days." She pointed a finger at him. "You'd best get Grace home. Now!"

Grace couldn't get back in the buggy fast enough. She wasn't sure who she was more scared of, Miriam or her father.

Surprisingly, Wayne didn't respond to her. He just hurried back to the buggy and stayed quiet on the ride home.

. . .

Grace sat on the couch, staring at the floor as Eli paced the living room. He wasn't sure how strict he should be with Gracie. He wanted her to make friends and to be happy here, but too much freedom could also lead to trouble at her age. And how much had Leah talked to Grace about boys?

"I was worried about you. When you didn't come home, all I could think about was . . ." He stopped pacing and locked eyes with Gracie when she looked up. "You know, your *mamm*. What if there had been an accident?"

She pulled her eyes away, leaned back on the couch, and folded her arms across her chest. "Sorry."

*You don't sound very sorry.* Eli stroked his beard, thinking and praying he was saying the right things. Grace had already told him that Miriam had gotten word to her that Eli was looking for her. He was grateful to Miriam for that.

"Can I go upstairs now?"

Eli stared at his beautiful daughter, and in his mind's

eye, he could still see her as a little girl, running into his arms. Now he couldn't recall the last time Gracie had initiated a hug, and it was hard for him to acknowledge that his little girl was growing up.

"There's someone here anyway," she said, standing up.

Eli looked out the window, and sure enough, a buggy was heading up the driveway. "All right. We can talk more about this later."

Grace padded across the living room in her socks, then scurried up the stairs.

"See what Ben's doing up there," Eli hollered before he walked onto the porch. When he saw who his visitor was, he couldn't keep the smile from his face. Two female visitors in one day.

Ruth floated her way to him in total perfection, like the angel he'd made her out to be the moment he'd laid eyes on her.

"Please forgive my unannounced visit, but I wanted to welcome you and your family to Paradise." She handed him a pie. "I've brought you an apple crumb pie."

When Ruth smiled, Eli went weak in the knees. *"Danki,"* he managed to say, even though he felt tongue-tied. "How nice of dooo . . . I mean, you." He nervously chuckled. "Um . . . would . . . would you like maybe to come have a chunk?" He blinked his eyes a few times. *What is wrong with me?* "I mean a *slice*. Not a chunk."

Ruth laughed, and Eli felt like his body was lifting off the ground when she said she'd love a slice. So together they floated into the house, and Eli had never been more grateful to be freshly bathed and dressed in his Sunday blue shirt. He hadn't realized until this moment that he'd grabbed his newest shirt reserved for worship service. He invited Ruth to sit in the living room, and he fetched two slices of pie, then two cups of coffee. The pie wasn't nearly as good as Elizabeth's, but it was merely a passing thought.

"I met your precious *kinner* last Sunday, Grace and Ben. I'm guessing Grace is fourteen or fifteen, and Ben . . . maybe ten?"

Eli nodded from his spot on the couch next to Ruth. "Close. Gracie is fifteen, almost sixteen, and Ben is eleven."

"How wonderful," Ruth said, setting her plate on the coffee table after only a couple of bites. "I have four *kinner*. Stephen is six, Carolyn is seven, Eve just turned eleven—same age as your Ben—and Mary is thirteen."

"Aren't big families *wunderbaar*? Together we have six *kinner*." Eli felt his face turning fire-engine red, since he apparently already had them married off and raising their six children together, but when Ruth smiled, Eli smiled too. Then he hung on Ruth's every word for the next thirty minutes.

. . .

"What is wrong with *Daed*?" Ben whispered to Grace from the top of the stairs. "He don't sound right."

Grace rolled her eyes. "He's trying to impress that lady."

"What's that mean, imperess?"

"Not imperess, impress. It means he's trying to put on a *gut* show for her so that she'll like him."

Ben grinned. "I don't think he's doin' too *gut* a job. Sounds like he can't say his words right."

Grace had to put a hand over her mouth to keep from laughing. She'd never heard her father stutter before, or sound so nervous with a woman. She held a finger to her lips before whispering to Ben. "Listen, that lady just asked *Daed* if he wanted to come over for lunch next Saturday. Guess she wants to be our new *mamm*," Grace said as she rolled her eyes again. Maybe it wouldn't be so bad. With six kids, Grace could just stay lost in the crowd; lost with Wayne. She smiled.

"I don't know. Maybe the other woman will be *Daed*'s *fraa*."

Grace scowled. "What other woman?"

"A lady named Elizabeth was here earlier. She brought *Daed* a pie, too, and before she left, I heard *Daed* say he'd see her for Saturday supper."

Grace heard the door shut and the house go silent. "What is he doing? Someone needs to explain to him how dating works." She tromped down the stairs, Ben on her heels.

Ben laughed. "Uh, you gonna explain it to him? Like you'd know anything about it."

When they hit the landing, Grace spun around. "As a matter of fact, I do. I have a boyfriend."

"You're as bad as *Daed*. You didn't waste any time either. But you ain't old enough to date."

"Well, *Daed* is letting me go out with Wayne."

They were quiet when the front door opened and

their father came in. Grace walked to the middle of the living room and slammed her hands to her hips. *Daed* was grinning in such a way that he looked like a little boy. Grace lifted her chin.

"*Daed*, please tell me that it isn't true . . . that you have a date for lunch next Saturday and a date for supper? Don't you think that's a bit much? I've heard you say that you never date two women at the same time, that it isn't right."

"I . . . I did say that." *Daed* scratched his forehead. "But these aren't really dates." He smiled as he shrugged. "Just friends having a meal."

"It's still dates." Grace shook her head. "You need to go to dating school or something. I know you didn't go out much back home, but you need to use some discretion." Grace had recently learned that word from Rachel, who liked to throw big words around. She nodded to Ben. "You have a young child at home."

"Hey!" Ben said, scowling. "You ain't much older than me."

"Dating school?" *Daed* stroked his beard, grinning. "Is there such a thing?"

"Be serious, *Daed*. You made two dates that could overlap. Dinner at noon and supper at four. Do you know what they call that in the *Englisch* world?" She waited, lifting her chin higher. "It's called double-booking, *Daed*. That's what they call it. You've double-booked."

Grace clicked her tongue, then turned and went upstairs, certain that her father was going to embarrass her by acting like a silly schoolboy.

# CHAPTER 5

Eli tucked his shirt in and pulled his suspenders over his shoulders. He'd spent all week looking forward to his lunch with Ruth and supper with Elizabeth, even though he was guilty of breaking his own rule. Double-booked, Gracie had called it.

Thirty minutes later, he was knocking on Ruth's door, praying that he wouldn't stutter or act stupid. But when she opened the door and gazed into his eyes, his knees got that weird feeling again, and he wished he'd brought her flowers. As it were, she might as well have been holding his heart on a platter. Eli knew Leah would want him to be happy, but he couldn't help but wonder if she was frowning from heaven and saying, "*Ach*, Eli. Pick up your jaw before you slobber on yourself." Eli was well aware that looks shouldn't play a part in his decisions, but Ruth was an exception that he'd never been faced with before.

"Come in, Eli. Welcome to our home." Ruth stepped aside, and Eli walked into the living room, surprised at how fancy it was. She had green shades covering the windows, which he'd learned was customary in

Lancaster County, but she had ivory lace valances as well. Above the fireplace were several decorative figurines and even two pictures hanging on the wall. The rug atop the wood floor was colorful and looked expensive. As he took a deep breath, he could vaguely smell something cooking, but mingling with a meaty aroma was a lemony scent, like the kind of cleaning solution Leah used to make. Eli couldn't recall a time when his home was ever this clean, even when Leah was alive, especially after Gracie and Ben were born. And Ruth had twice as many *kinner* as he did.

"Your home is very nice," he said, proud of himself for speaking clearly this time.

"*Danki.* So nice of you to say so." She motioned for him to sit down on the couch, and he noticed how quiet it was. "I'm anxious to meet your *kinner*."

Ruth sat down in a rocking chair across from Eli. She crossed her legs and cupped one knee with her hands. "I was looking forward to them meeting you, but they aren't here today. *Mei* sister has them for the day, and they love going to their aunt's *haus* since she has young *kinner* too." Ruth smiled. "I just couldn't tell them no."

Eli swallowed hard and nodded as he shifted his weight on the couch, wishing he wasn't so nervous. And when Ruth got up and walked to the couch, the knot in his throat grew to the size of a walnut. She sat down beside him. So close that her black apron brushed against his blue slacks.

"I don't date much, Eli, so this is a little awkward for me." She tucked her chin, then looked up and batted her eyelashes at him. "But when I saw you after worship service for the first time, I felt like you were someone I wanted to get to know."

"It is a little awkward for me too." Eli swallowed twice, then coughed. "I dated a little back home, but never anyone—anyone . . . as pretty as you."

Ruth's lashes swept down over her high cheekbones as she bit her bottom lip, then she looked up at him and smiled. "What a nice thing to say."

"And . . . and I would like to get to know you too."

"Are you ready for dinner?"

Eli nodded, then followed Ruth into her kitchen where two white china plates were laid out at opposite ends of a table for six. In addition to the green blinds, green-and-white-checked valances hung on the windows, and cool air blew through the screened windows. The lemony smell had faded, replaced with the aroma of roast. There was another colorful rug on the floor underneath the table, and several kitchen gadgets on the counter, along with a set of green canisters. It was a large room that was painted light beige. Eli had sought information about the bishop before he chose to move here, and he'd learned that the man was lenient. *Very lenient, apparently.*

After they ate, Ruth insisted Eli wait in the living room while she cleaned things up and started some coffee. A few minutes later, she joined Eli on the couch with two cups of coffee. Eli thanked her for the meal. She twisted to face him, tucking one foot underneath her, and even though her cooking skills weren't the best, he could overlook that.

"Tell me everything about you, Eli," she said as she leaned her shoulder against the back of the couch.

Eli gave her a condensed version of his life thus far, anxious to hear about her. She listened intently when he got to the part about Leah dying.

"That must have been so hard." She touched his arm and hung her head for a few moments.

Ruth's life story was similar to Eli's. She'd married young and started having children right away, and her husband had died a year and a half ago, six months short of how long Leah had been gone. Cancer had taken him, too, like Elizabeth's husband. Ruth was in a much better place emotionally than Elizabeth, but time made loss more bearable. Eli knew he would never forget his first love, and the pain was still present, but he was learning to live again. And for the first time in a long time, he was excited about his future. As Ruth started talking to him about the kind of books she liked to read, her favorite foods, and how important it was to her that her children stay in the community, they fell into a comfortable conversation. He shed his nervousness, and eventually he surprised himself by sharing his love for cooking with her.

· · ·

Miriam wasn't surprised to see Grace watching the baseball game again since Wayne was playing. But she was surprised to see the girl still sitting there after everyone had left the Lantzes' house, including Wayne. Miriam got in her buggy and started to back up when she noticed there weren't any other buggies left, except those belonging to the Lantzes. She glanced at Grace, whose head hung low, her shoulders moving up and down.

As she backed the horse up, she recalled how she'd felt called to go find Grace last Saturday, a girl she didn't even know. It hadn't been her responsibility, but Eli had been so worried. Today, she was going to do what she'd planned to do last Saturday, curl up with Kiki and read a book. But she hadn't even made it off the Lantzes' property when she turned the buggy around, grumbling to herself. She tethered the horse and walked to Grace.

"Do you need a ride?" Miriam silently prayed that Grace hadn't already done something she regretted. "Your *haus* isn't that much out of the way, and I'd be happy to take you home."

Grace sniffled as she stood up, then pulled her sweater around her. "*Nee*, I can walk."

"That's a far piece to your place from here." Miriam studied Grace's tearstained face, and for the third time in the past two weeks, she felt like smacking Wayne. But where were the girls she'd been sitting with? "Did your girlfriends just leave you here?"

"They aren't my girlfriends," she snapped back. "And I didn't ride here with them anyway. I came with Wayne." Glaring a little, she added, "But you probably know that."

Miriam had been late today, but she had assumed Grace had come with Wayne. She cringed a bit when Grace continued to shoot daggers at her. Nothing worse than a hormonal teenager who had been wronged by a boy. *Walk away, Miriam.*

"*Mei maedel*, I tried to warn you about Wayne. There are lots of nice boys here, and—"

"I don't want to talk about this with you." Grace took long strides toward the driveway, continuing to swipe at her eyes.

Miriam glanced up at the dark clouds overhead, the reason they'd cut the baseball game short. "Did Wayne just leave you here?" she asked as she scurried to catch up with Grace.

"Just leave me alone. I hate it here. I wish we'd never moved here." Grace stopped and faced Miriam, her eyes red and swollen. "The only reason we're here is so *mei daed* can find a *fraa*."

"I gathered that." Miriam bit her lip, trying not to grin, but when a smile broke through anyway, Grace grunted and started walking away. "Grace, wait!"

When Grace didn't slow down, Miriam ran to catch up to her. She grabbed her by the arm. "Please wait."

"What do you want, Miriam? You were right. I wouldn't give Wayne what he wanted, and he left me here. When I said I needed to go straight home today, he said he was going to town to visit two girls he knew, *Englisch* girls."

Relief washed over Miriam, but she knew Wayne wouldn't give up that easily, and Grace didn't have a mother to confide in, or apparently anyone else. Miriam wouldn't have gone to her mother about something like this when she was Grace's age anyway.

"Just let me take you home. A storm is coming, and I can't let you walk all the way to your place."

"*Ach*, well, you're not my boss, so you can't stop me." Grace folded her arms across her chest.

Miriam smiled broadly. "Really, Grace? You sound like a five-year-old. *You're not the boss of me*," Miriam mimicked as she waved her hands playfully in the air, although it was apparent by Grace's blazing eyes that she wasn't amused. "I'm taking you home. Come on." Miriam looked up at the sky as thunder rumbled in the distance. "Please. We don't even have to talk."

"Fine," Grace huffed as she headed toward Miriam's buggy. It was everything Miriam could do not to say something about her smart mouth and lack of appreciation, but the important thing was to get her home safely, so she bit her lip again. It started drizzling not five minutes after they got on the road. She didn't dare tell Grace that Mr. Ed got spooked by thunder, but when he whinnied and tried to pick up the pace, Miriam had to pull back on the reins.

"Whoa, Mr. Ed." She eased him back into a steady trot, hoping to beat the storm that was fast approaching.

"What kind of a name is Mr. Ed?" Grace spat the words at Miriam.

"It was the name he had when I got him. He was put out to pasture after he was no *gut* on the racetrack anymore. Things like trains, thunder, and the fire alarms in town tend to spook him, but I've learned how to handle him."

"I hope so," Grace said under her breath as she leaned out the window and looked up at the sky.

Miriam only had one buggy, and she was glad it was covered. "He wasn't treated very well where he was, and someone got word to me, and I took him in." She glanced at Grace and smiled. "He's a lovable fellow."

"The *Englisch* don't always treat their animals very *gut*," Grace said as she kept her eyes on the road. Big drops of rain had started to slam against the windshield.

"I got him from an Amish farmer, not *Englisch*." Miriam had to pay twice as much as the horse was worth, but after seeing the whip marks across his flanks, she wasn't leaving without him.

They were quiet until the horse reared up in response to a loud clap of thunder, and it took a little longer for Miriam to get him settled down.

"I think I would have been safer to just walk," Grace said as she clutched the dashboard.

"That's my *haus*. I think we'd better wait out the storm there. It's still a ways to your place."

"*Ya*, okay."

Miriam was a little surprised that Grace was so agreeable. Miriam would have kept going if it was just herself in the buggy, but she had Grace to think about.

"Do you have a cell phone?" Miriam asked as she pulled into her driveway. Grace nodded. "Call your *daed* and tell him that I'll bring you home after the weather gets better."

"I doubt he'll be too worried." Grace finally let go of the dash when Miriam pulled back on the reins and Mr. Ed was stopped in front of the barn.

"Of course he will be worried. I could tell he was concerned when he was looking for you last weekend."

"Well, he's on a date, so I'm sure he's preoccupied interviewing a new *mamm* for me and Ben." She paused, turned to Miriam, and held up two fingers. "Actually, he has *two* dates today."

"Busy man," Miriam mumbled as she wondered whether or not Eli had asked her out first, second, or maybe even third. "Who is he out with?" *Not that I care.*

"His dinner date at noon was with someone named Ruth."

"Ruth Zook?"

"I think so. And the other one is someone named Elizabeth Petersheim."

Miriam was quiet for a few moments. She knew Elizabeth wanted to get remarried and start a family, but it seemed that she might not be ready. Elizabeth still cried a lot. Ruth, on the other hand, easily lured men in. She was beautiful. But the few she'd dated hadn't worked out. "I wonder who the lucky lady will be. He asked me out too." Miriam said the last part under her breath, although Grace must have heard.

*"Ach, nee."* Grace had her hand on the door handle, but she threw her head back and let out an exaggerated sigh. "Please tell me that you are not trying to be our new *mamm* too."

Miriam glared at Grace. "I assure you, I want nothing to do with your father in that way, so you'll never have to worry about me being your new mommy." She thought this news would make Grace happy, but the girl just sat there staring blankly at her.

*"Mei daed* is a wonderful man." Grace's tone was defensive.

*Touching.* "I'm sure he is. Now let's get Mr. Ed settled in the barn and make a dash for the *haus* before this weather gets worse. Then you can call Mr. Wonderful and let him know you're safe." She grinned, and surprisingly, Grace did too.

# CHAPTER 6

Eli pushed his horse harder than ever through the downpour, wondering if he could blame the rain as his excuse for being so late to Elizabeth's house. "*Ya, ya!*" he yelled. When he'd realized what time it was, he'd made a mad dash out of Ruth's house, promising to call her later. He'd already made his decision about whom he wanted to date. Ruth was everything he wanted in a woman, aside from just being beautiful. But he owed it to Elizabeth to be polite, and he was angry with himself for being so late.

When Elizabeth opened her front door, she handed Eli a towel to dry off. Eli took the towel, but he'd never felt like such a heel in his life. Elizabeth's eyes were red and swollen. "I'm so sorry." It had to be nearly five thirty by now, and he was due at Elizabeth's house at four.

"It's no problem." Elizabeth waited on the other side of the threshold, and for a few moments, Eli wasn't sure he was going to be invited in, but once he'd finished drying off, she eased the screen door open and stepped aside. "Supper is cold, but I can reheat everything if you'd like."

"*Nee, nee,*" he quickly said. "I'm sure it will be wonderful like it is." Shivering, he followed her into the living room, a much plainer room than at Ruth's house, more like what Eli was used to. "It sure smells *gut* in here."

Elizabeth didn't say anything but motioned for him to follow her.

When Eli walked into the kitchen, he'd never seen such a spread laid out, especially for just two people. There must have been ten different offerings, including two pies. Elizabeth's table wasn't as big as Ruth's, to be expected since she lived alone. There was seating for four and two place settings, which barely fit amidst all the food. Eli pulled out a chair and sat down. He wasn't all that hungry since he'd eaten a heavy meal a few hours ago, but he planned to force himself to eat generous portions since Elizabeth had gone to so much trouble. "*Ach*, Elizabeth . . . this looks *gut* beyond words."

She smiled, but there was something not quite right about the way she pressed her lips together. Eli knew that look. "I hope you like it. I worked on it all day."

*Ouch.* He deserved that. Worst of all was that she looked like she'd been crying, and Eli felt like a louse. "I can't apologize enough for being so late. There's no excuse. I was busy and lost track of the time."

"It is fine." She took a seat across from him, then they both bowed their heads in prayer. After Eli filled his plate, he took a bite of chicken casserole. And that was all it took for his appetite to return. He'd wondered if the pie was a fluke, just her best recipe. But after trying a little bit of everything, he had to admit—she was a better cook than Leah. And certainly better in the kitchen than Ruth. Eli had jokingly thought, *If I marry Ruth, I'll have to do the cooking,* and it was an idea he liked. But first he was going to get through this meal.

As they ate, the silence grew awkward. "How was your day?" Eli scooped up a forkful of mashed potatoes. Even the potatoes were better than most, with just the right amount of butter slightly browned on top.

"I cooked all day," she said again, barely picking at her food and not looking at him.

Eli needed to do something to redeem himself, even if he had no plans to pursue Elizabeth in a romantic way. He was sorry for being late, but he couldn't help but think maybe she was overreacting a little. This situation didn't seem to warrant tears, but just the same, he wanted to cheer her up. But visions of his time with Ruth were distracting him. He couldn't wait to see her again.

"You have a very pretty home." Eli was getting full, but he accepted a slice of coconut pie when Elizabeth inched the pie closer to him. "Coconut pie is a favorite of mine." He took a bite. "And this is surely the best I've ever had." The truth. But Elizabeth stayed quiet.

When they were done eating, they moved into the living room. There was no mention of coffee, and the brittle silence was even worse now that they weren't busy eating. Eli decided to break the ice.

"I can tell you're upset about me being late, Elizabeth. It wonders me what I can do to make you feel better.

I'm usually punctual, so I apologize to you again." They were each sitting in a rocking chair, a small table between them with a lantern on top, a box of tissues, and several books.

"It's fine, really," Elizabeth said with a stone-faced expression that Eli knew meant trouble. *Fine* never meant fine when a woman said it like that, accompanied by that look. Eli used to be able to talk his way out of trouble with Leah.

Eli picked up the book on top of the pile, a Christian devotional guide for women. "I love to read when I have the time," he said, casually thumbing through the pages. He put it down, smiled, then picked up the next book, a novel with a woman on the front cover, a prairie in the background.

"I have plenty of time to read," she said as her voice cracked a little bit. Eli had a strong urge to hug her, to comfort her, but in a fatherly sort of way. But he just nodded as he put the book back.

"*Danki* for supper. It was the best meal I've had in a very long time. But I reckon it's best to get home. Gracie went to watch the baseball game at the Lantzes' *haus*, and I'm anxious to make sure she got home safely." Eli stood up, but Elizabeth remained seated, kicking her rocker into motion as she folded her hands in her lap. Eli should have already called his daughter, but Grace was the worst about leaving her cell phone lying around or not answering it. He was glad the use of cell phones was acceptable in Lancaster County.

"*Danki* again," Eli said when it appeared that Elizabeth wasn't going to walk him to the door. "See you soon." He forced a smile and moved toward the door, but when he heard a whimper, he turned around. Elizabeth had covered her face with her hands. Eli suspected this was going to be a long evening. He needed to call Gracie. Ben was spending the night at his new friend's house, so he just needed to make sure his daughter was okay before he tried to make amends with Elizabeth, whose whimpering had turned into full-blown sobs.

· · ·

Grace lagged behind Miriam and stayed on the porch to talk on her cell to her father, then walked into Miriam's living room and closed the door behind her.

"*Daed* is with date number two, and he'll pick me up in a little while," she said as she looked around Miriam's house. "No wonder you're not married," Grace mumbled as Miriam started a fire in the fireplace. It wasn't very cold, but the fall afternoons and evenings were cool enough to enjoy a fire, and within a few minutes, orange sparks shimmied up the chimney. Grace tossed her sweater on the couch, which was filled with . . . stuff. There wasn't even room to sit down.

"Okay, now we have warmth." Miriam brushed her hands against her dress. "Now, what did you say?"

"I said . . ." Grace twisted her mouth back and forth but didn't have the heart to come out and tell Miriam that this place was a wreck. Newspapers, books, and empty plates were piled high on the coffee table, and a further inspection of the couch revealed laundry that needed folding, more books, and . . . a cat. "Aw, who's this?" Grace picked up the orange-and-white tabby. "I love, love, love cats. But *Daed* is allergic, so we've never had one." She held the kitty close and stroked her ears, and within seconds she purred.

"That's Kiki."

Grace recalled hearing someone say that Miriam had lots of cats, like a crazy cat lady. "Where are the others? Don't you have more cats?"

Miriam shook her head. "*Nee*, it's just me and Kiki." She gave the fire another poke, then turned to Grace. "Are you hungry?"

Grace had figured she and Wayne would eat after the baseball game, but his only suggestion had been to go back to the same place as last Saturday to make out. When Grace had said no, that she better get home, there was no mention of food or even a ride home. *Jerk*. "*Ya*, I'm a little hungry."

"Come on." Miriam motioned for Grace to follow her into the kitchen, so she set Kiki back on the couch. They both had to step around three big boxes on the way.

"Did you just move here?" Grace walked into the kitchen behind Miriam. Dishes were piled in the sink, but otherwise, it wasn't too bad. Kind of pretty. Plain and simple, but with just a little color here and there.

"*Nee*, I've been here about four years. My parents moved to Colorado after both of my grandparents died. Some of the Amish folks here have been moving out there. Land is cheaper, and there's more of it. My two younger *bruders* went with them, but I chose to stay here." She shriveled up her face. "It's cold there." Then she shrugged. "Besides, I couldn't imagine leaving here. But they are all happy and that's what counts. Both my *bruders* got married in the past year, and one of my sister-in-laws is expecting. But I miss them all." She opened the pantry and pulled out a box of macaroni and cheese. "This okay?"

Grace was speechless. She'd never had boxed macaroni and cheese. "Okay," she said hesitantly as she pulled out a chair at the small kitchen table and sat down, briefly wondering how her father's two dates had gone. She wanted him to be happy, but it was unsettling to think about anyone besides their mother living with them. "Why aren't you married?"

"I'm not planning to get married," Miriam said as she turned the gas up on the burner before placing a pot of water on top.

"Why?" That was unheard of to Grace. Everyone wanted to get married and have children. "Um . . . are you sick or something?" Maybe Miriam didn't want to burden a man if she wasn't well.

"*Nee*, not that I know of." Miriam turned to face Grace and leaned against the kitchen counter. "I know those girls you hang out with call me an old maid." She smiled. "They can be a bit rude sometimes, but I think once you get to know them, you'll find that they really are *gut* girls. I know it's hard to make friends at your age, but give it some time. All of those girls have grown up together. It will just take awhile for them to warm up to you."

"But why aren't you married? I don't understand."

Grace propped her elbows on the table, then cupped her cheeks as she and Miriam locked eyes. "I mean, you're . . . um . . . pretty."

"For an old maid, huh?" Miriam chuckled. "I just choose not to get married. I spend my time trying to do for others, trying to live a *gut* life, and worshipping my heavenly Father as often as I can."

"But lots of people do all those things and still get married and have *kinner*. I don't understand," she said again.

. . .

Folks in their community had stopped asking these questions a long time ago. It was just accepted that Miriam planned to live her life alone. But every time a new single man came along, the questions started again. Miriam was tempted to tell Grace the truth, that she wished more than ever that she could share her life with a wonderful man, and why that wasn't possible anymore. But this was a teenage girl she barely knew.

"You don't have to understand," she finally said. "It's just the way I choose to live my life."

"It's weird."

That wasn't the first time Miriam had heard the popular *Englisch* word used to describe her. "*Ya*, you are correct. I am a weird old maid." Miriam had grown used to laughing at herself. She wished things were different, but this was the path God had chosen for her, and she made do, trying to stay focused on the positives.

But sometimes, late at night, in the darkness when no one was around, she'd allow herself a good cry.

"Do you date?"

Miriam sighed, hoping Grace would move on to something else soon. "*Nee*, I stay busy doing other things."

"Like what?" Grace nodded toward the sink full of dishes, then strained her neck to look into the living room. "You don't stay busy cleaning *haus*."

Miriam folded her arms across her chest and raised an eyebrow. "Anything I want to do. How many people can say that?"

"Do you work? I noticed you don't have a garden. What do you do?"

"You are a curious creature, are you not?" Miriam grinned, tempted to make up a fun story to tell Grace, but instead, she dumped the noodles in the boiling water before motioning for Grace to follow her. They walked down the hall to Miriam's extra bedroom that she'd turned into a sewing room after her parents left for Colorado. She pushed the door wide and kept her eyes on Grace, not wanting to miss her expression.

Grace's jaw dropped as she walked into the spacious room toward the quilting table, then took in the dozens of quilts on racks around the room.

"Did you do all of these on your own?" Grace took another look around, then gingerly touched the project on the table, a quilt filled with bold colors, a special order that Miriam was almost done with. "Or do you have quilting parties in here?"

"*Nee*. I've done all of these myself." She picked up

an old red suitcase and set it on a nearby chair. "This suitcase is filled with scraps from Widow Hostetler's life. I've been piecing them together for weeks, until the patchwork is just perfect." She eased closer to where Grace was standing and pointed to the square in the middle. "This piece represents Widow Hostetler. It's a scrap from her swaddling cloth when she was born." Miriam touched each of the six squares surrounding the center. "Each of these scraps represents what Widow Hostetler believes to be the most important events in her life. Her baptism into the faith, marrying her husband, and the birth of her four children."

She pointed to the next eight larger squares. "These squares represent things to do with her baptism, husband, and children, things relevant to them. Then it branches out from there, until the quilt becomes her entire life story." Miriam smiled. "I love doing these story quilts. I know more about Widow Hostetler than I ever would have known otherwise." She walked around the table and pointed to a maroon square. "This was the dress she was wearing when she packed up and left the community. She was shunned for doing so." She glanced at Grace. "She was sixteen when she left."

"But she came back?" Grace was still running her hand along the tightly sewn patches.

"*Ya*. But not for six years." Miriam touched the square with the white cross etched in the middle. "This represents her return to Christ."

"What's this one?" Grace touched a square with a cross-stitched pie in the middle.

Miriam smiled. "Against the bishop's wishes—it was a different bishop back then—Widow . . . Annie Hostetler . . . entered her key lime pie at the county fair. And she won."

Grace smiled. "This is the neatest thing." She looked up at Miriam. "Are all your quilts like this? Do they all tell a life story?"

"*Nee*, some people just order a regular old quilt. But these are my favorites to make. Annie plans to write up a list of what each scrap means, then she'll give it to her *kinner*. She has arthritis, so it's hard for her to do any type of quilting these days. But most of my orders are from the *Englisch*."

"So . . . I guess someone wouldn't do this until they were old, right?"

Miriam shook her head. "*Nee*. I do them for all different reasons." She walked to a rack on the far wall and pulled down a small quilt. "I just need to finish the edges on this, but each scrap represents a child's life— when she was born, when she took her first step—see the picture of baby shoes sewn in? And it goes all the way until she starts her first day of school, represented by the book in this square."

"These are the most beautiful quilts I've ever seen." Grace lifted her eyes to Miriam's again. "Beauty goes so much deeper than what our eyes can see, and the beauty in these quilts isn't just on the outside."

Miriam smiled, warmed by Grace's mature comment. "*Danki*, Grace."

Her eyes lit up. "Where's yours? Surely you've started one for yourself?"

This was the bad part about showing newcomers her quilting room. It was the question that ultimately came up. She didn't want to lie to Grace, but she'd never shown anyone her quilt, and she doubted she'd ever have anyone to hand it down to. "It's not very far along, a work in progress," she finally said.

Grace opened her mouth to say something, but they both looked toward the hallway when they heard a buggy coming.

"Probably *mei daed*," Grace said softly. "*Danki* for showing me this, Miriam."

"You're welcome. Ready for mac and cheese?"

Grace smiled and nodded, so they headed back to the kitchen. Miriam supposed she would have to ask Eli to stay for supper. She smiled to herself. *Unless he's too full from all his dates.*

But when Eli walked into the house, Miriam had to ward off the sadness that threatened her sometimes in the presence of someone she might have been interested in. *Oh, how I wish things were different.*

# CHAPTER 7

Eli was sure he'd never eaten so much in one day, and he'd surely never had noodles and cheese that came from a box. Gracie had tapped him on the arm and nodded to the empty box when Miriam wasn't looking. Eli forced himself to take a few bites. It was awful, but Grace ate most of her serving.

"I'm sorry it's not a better meal, but I didn't know I'd have company for supper," Miriam said, smiling. Eli wondered if her house was tidier when she was expecting visitors.

"*Danki* for asking me to stay." Eli would have preferred to go home, but Gracie wanted to stay. And now that he was here, he was having a hard time keeping his eyes off of Miriam. He'd never had a woman shoot him down so fast. Eli knew he was no expert when it came to dating, but her rejection had left him wondering if there was something outwardly wrong with him. He tried to clear his thoughts. It had gone from a wonderful afternoon with Ruth to a terrible time with Elizabeth. But when Eli had finally left Elizabeth, she'd stopped crying. They'd both decided she wasn't ready for any type of courtship yet, a decision that would make it easy for Eli to move forward with Ruth, especially since they'd set another date before saying good-bye earlier. Ruth wanted Eli to come for lunch again next Saturday. And he would meet her four children.

Grace laughed out loud, which caught Eli's attention. She and Miriam had been chatting about quilts, and Eli hadn't heard most of what was said. But as he eyed his daughter, such merriment shining in her eyes, he tuned in to their conversation.

"So the *Englisch* lady wanted the entire quilt to have shoes on it? All different ones?"

"*Ya*. She loved shoes and she had many, many pairs." Miriam shook her head. "Can you imagine? So wasteful, but she paid a *gut* sum of money for me to make her the quilt."

Grace chuckled again. "*Nee*, I can't imagine. I wish I could have seen that."

Miriam tapped her finger to her chin for a few seconds, then she glanced at Eli before excusing herself. "Be right back."

After Miriam was out of earshot, Grace raised an eyebrow and said, "How were your dates?"

Eli shrugged. "One was *gut*. The other . . . not so *gut*."

"So, who was the winner? Elizabeth or Ruth?"

"*Ach*, it's not really about being a winner because neither one of them is a loser."

"You picked Ruth, didn't you?" Grace slouched into her chair.

"It's not about picking, but *ya*, I think Ruth and I are

better suited to each other. And Elizabeth isn't really ready to date. She wants to be ready, to get on with her life, but she is still grieving."

"If you're going to insist on dating, it's too bad you can't date Miriam." Grace stretched her neck and looked around the corner, apparently to see if Miriam was coming. "I like her," she added.

"You'll like Ruth too." Eli set his fork on the plate still half filled with the cheesy noodles from a box. "And besides, I *did* ask Miriam if she would like to go out, and she said no." He kept his eyes on Gracie's, curious how she'd react. She slouched even deeper into her chair.

"Don't take it personally. She doesn't date anyone because she says she is never getting married."

"Maybe it's because she has a dozen cats, a messy *haus*, and eats noodles from a box." Eli realized he hadn't sneezed once since he got here.

"She only has one cat, and her name is Kiki." Gracie narrowed her eyebrows at Eli. "Why aren't you sneezing?"

Eli shrugged. "I don't know."

Gracie sat up tall in her chair and smiled. "Maybe you're not allergic anymore." She pressed her palms together. "Maybe we can get a cat?"

"We'll see. I imagine if I was around a cat all the time, I would take to sneezing again." Eli wanted to follow up on Gracie's earlier comment. "Why is Miriam never getting married?"

"I'm not sure." Gracie paused, then opened her mouth like she had more to say, but quickly closed it when Miriam came back into the room holding a photograph.

"This is our secret," Miriam said as she handed the picture to Gracie. "It took me awhile to find it. The *Englisch* woman took pictures of the quilt, and she gave me one. I've never shown it to anyone. We have a very *gut* and lenient bishop, but the one thing he frowns on is photographs of any kind. The younger folks are using their mobile phones to take pictures, and the bishop *really* dislikes that."

Eli had heard of phones taking pictures, even though his and Gracie's phones flipped open and didn't do such things. Eli was all for embracing certain technology that was necessary, and cell phones had become a necessity. He could recall several emergencies back home when folks could have died if they hadn't had a phone with them. Even though it didn't help Leah. But phones that took pictures were just too much luxury for Eli.

"I wish my phone took photographs," Gracie said as she glanced at Eli.

*"Nee."* Miriam spoke up before Eli had a chance to tell his daughter no. "It's not *gut*. We're all forced to move forward, to be more like the *Englisch* in many ways. But I think we need to remember the second commandment: 'Thou shalt not make unto thee any graven image, or any likeness of any thing that is in heaven above, or that is in the earth beneath, or that is in the water under the earth.'" She frowned. "I probably should not have even kept this photo, but . . ."

"I'm glad you showed me the picture. It's odd, but

pretty." Gracie giggled, which was music to Eli's ears. "What a strange *Englisch* woman."

"Her shoes were like her *kinner*," Miriam said softly as she eased the picture from Gracie's hand. "She loved them all. She didn't have a husband or any *kinner*."

Eli kept his eyes on Miriam's. Such sadness in her voice, like regret. Possibly at her own situation? He waited until they'd left before he asked Gracie about it again.

"Um . . . so Miriam is never getting married—why?"

"I told you. I don't know." Gracie shrugged, then turned to him and grinned. "*Daed*, I can't believe you asked her out *too*."

Eli maneuvered the buggy around a pothole in the road filled with water, thankful it had stopped raining. "*Ya*, well, I did." They were both quiet for a while, then Eli said, "Next Saturday, I'm going to Ruth's again to meet her *kinner*, and I would like it if you and Ben would come too."

Gracie didn't respond.

"Will you do that for me?" Eli glanced at his daughter, and in the darkness, he saw her nod.

They were quiet again, until Gracie cleared her throat. "*Daed?*"

"*Ya?*"

"Who did you ask out first? Elizabeth, Ruth, or Miriam?"

Eli turned into their driveway. "I didn't ask Elizabeth or Ruth out. They both asked me to their homes for dinner and supper." He paused, thinking. "The only one I asked out was Miriam."

"Why?"

Eli slowed the horse to a stop in front of their barn.
It had been a spontaneous gesture asking Miriam to
dinner, but he knew what prompted him to do so.

"She's pretty," Gracie said before Eli answered.

"*Ya*, she is. But she's different, and that interests
me." He met Gracie in front of the buggy and they
walked toward the house.

"I really like her," Gracie said as the glow from the
propane light lit Gracie's features. Eli smiled, knowing
Miriam had won Gracie over. Not an easy thing to do.

. . .

Monday morning, Grace shivered as she pinned a towel
on the line, not realizing until today that she'd left her
sweater at Miriam's. Maybe Miriam had found it and
taken it to worship service, but Grace had no way to
know since her family hadn't attended the service yesterday. *Daed* was sick with a stomach bug, and it was
raining, so he didn't want Grace and Ben going alone.
Her father had tried to blame his stomach troubles on
the boxed noodles and cheese, but finally admitted
that it could have been any dozen of things he'd eaten
on Saturday. Ben woke up this morning complaining
of an upset stomach, so *Daed* let him stay home from
school, but Grace wasn't sure that Ben didn't just want
the day off.

Grace was picturing her mother next to her, showing her the best way to hang clothes on the line while
they sang songs. *I miss you, Mamm.*

She looked over her shoulder when she heard footsteps. "You could help me, you know."

Ben sidled up beside her. "That's girls' work. But I'll do it if you'll go clean the barn."

Grace shook her head, clipping another towel to the line. "*Nee*. I don't think so."

Ben pulled a wet towel from the basket anyway and pulled two clothespins from the bag. Grace smiled. "You seem to be feeling better."

"Um . . . *ya*. When's *Daed* going to be back?" Ben dropped one of the clothespins, leaned down to pick it up, then the other pin came loose and the towel landed in the grass. "See, girls' work." He grimaced but set to hanging the towel again.

"He's opening an account at the bank and said he had some other business to take care of in town. He shouldn't be much longer." Grace's teeth chattered as she hurried to finish. "Did he tell you about wanting us to meet his new *friend* next Saturday, and her family?"

"*Ya*. I hope whoever he picks to replace *Mamm* is nice."

"No one can replace *Mamm*. And I don't want anyone living with us."

Ben was quiet. "Maybe . . . maybe . . ." He shrugged. "Maybe it wouldn't be so bad to have a replacement *mudder*."

Grace dropped the towel she was holding into the basket and put her hands on her hips. Ben had always said he didn't want their father to remarry. "What are you saying? And no one can replace *Mamm*."

"I'm just saying . . ." Ben threw his hands up. "You

have a lot to do. Cleaning, sewing, laundry, and other things. Don't you want some help?"

"*Nee.* I don't need help. I thought we both agreed that we like things the way they are."

Ben stared at Grace until his eyes filled with water. "*You* like things the way they are." Then he ran to the barn. Grace called out to him and started toward the barn, wondering how long her brother had felt like this. She reminded herself that Ben was only eleven. Grace had done her best to nurture him when he seemed to need it, but she could also recall trying to bandage his knee before they'd moved here, and how he kept telling her she was doing it wrong. He'd also mentioned how their mother used to read to him. And now that Grace thought about it, she wondered how much her own opinions had rubbed off on Ben. Did he need a mother figure in his life?

She'd slowed her pace and was trying to organize her thoughts before she went into the barn. A buggy turned in, so she waited. Maybe it would be best to let her father handle this, father to son. But as the buggy got closer and the driver came into view, she realized it wasn't her father returning from town. She draped an arm across her stomach, took a deep breath, and walked across the yard toward the approaching buggy.

# CHAPTER 8

W hat are you doing here?" Grace asked Wayne as he stepped out of the buggy.

"You weren't at worship service yesterday, and it wondered me if you were okay."

"We're fine." Gracie glanced toward the barn, then looked back at Wayne. "I've got to finish getting the clothes on the line." She nodded over her shoulder. "*Danki* for checking on us."

Wayne stared at her. "I can tell you're mad at me."

Shivering, Grace looked down at the moist, dewy grass, then back at him. "You left me at the Lantzes'. Just because I didn't want to . . ." She swallowed back the lump in her throat.

"Your teeth are chattering." Wayne took off his jacket and put it around her shoulders. "Please don't be mad. It's just . . . you scare me."

Grace's jaw dropped. "Scare you? What are you talking about?"

Wayne sighed, shifted his weight, and stuffed his hands in his pockets. "I've never liked anyone as much as you, so when you don't want to be closer to me, it makes me feel like you don't like me as much as I like you."

Grace locked eyes with him. "I do like you, Wayne. I'm just . . . not ready for . . ." She could feel her cheeks flushing, and she forced herself to recall how she'd felt Saturday. "If you like me so much, I don't understand why you'd leave me to go be with *Englisch* girls."

"I had to go," he said, sighing again. "My feelings for you are so strong, and when I'm around you, I just want to show you."

Grace glanced at the barn again, then met Wayne's gaze, wanting to believe him. "I like you, too, Wayne . . . but . . ."

"Why do you keep looking at the barn?" Wayne looked over Grace's shoulder.

"*Mei bruder* is in there. I'm a little worried about him."

"What's wrong?"

Grace scratched her forehead as she wondered how much to tell Wayne. "It's just . . . well, it's hard for me to think about our father possibly marrying someone. And I always thought Ben felt the same way. But we just had a conversation that makes me think otherwise, like he might actually want and still need a mother. But no one can replace our *mamm*."

Wayne touched Grace lightly on the arm, then pulled the coat snug over her shoulders. "Poor guy. At his age, he probably does need a *mamm*, but I bet he feels guilty for even thinking that way." He paused, looking toward the barn again. "Do you want me to talk to him?"

"Um, I don't know."

"Come on. Let's go together." Wayne put an arm around her, and Grace got in step beside him. He opened the barn door for Grace to go first. Ben had hoisted himself up on *Daed's* workbench and was kicking his legs back and forth.

"This is my friend Wayne," Grace said to Ben as they walked toward him. "I think you met him at worship service."

Ben nodded, but didn't say anything.

"*Wie bischt*, buddy." Wayne sat on the stool near the workbench. "Whatcha doin'?"

Ben shrugged as he kept his eyes on the floor. "Nothing."

"Grace, I'm a little thirsty. Could you maybe get me a glass of water or tea?" Wayne winked at Grace. She glanced at Ben, then back at Wayne, who gave a nod.

"Um, sure. *Ya.* Ben, do you want something to drink?"

Her brother still didn't look up as he shook his head. Grace hesitantly left, got a glass of tea for her and Wayne, and hurried back to the barn, but when she heard voices, she stopped outside and listened.

"I know how you feel," Wayne said. "When *mei mamm* died, it was real weird for a long time."

Grace froze. She'd seen Wayne with his parents, and she'd just assumed that the woman he called *Mamm* was his mother. She leaned her ear closer.

"And when *mei daed* married someone else, I was confused. I wanted *Daed* to be happy, and he married a real nice woman, but I felt a little bad, like *mei mamm* was being replaced and forgotten about. But I wanted a mom, someone to look after me."

"Grace doesn't want *Daed* to marry anyone else," Ben said softly. "But I miss things. You know, those things a mother does. But it ain't like I want to replace *Mamm*."

"I know what you're saying. And I think that your *mamm* would want your *daed* to be happy. She'd want you and Grace to be happy too."

"I know all that," Ben said a little louder. "It's Grace that doesn't want anyone living with us. And she gets mad about *Daed* dating anyone."

Grace's eyes filled with tears. Why hadn't she given more consideration to Ben's needs? And her father's.

"Do you want me to talk to her?" Wayne's voice was filled with tenderness, and this was a beautiful side to him that she didn't know about. She sniffled, then leaned her face to Wayne's jacket still around her shoulders and blotted her eyes on it.

"Here's tea," she said as she walked into the barn. "Everything okay?"

Wayne stood up and accepted the glass. Grace set hers on the bench near Ben. Her teeth were still chattering, and a cold drink didn't sound all that good. But Wayne chugged his down, then put his glass on the workbench. "Everything is *gut*," he said to Grace, winking again.

"I gotta clean the barn." Ben jumped down from the workbench, the hint of a smile on his face.

"Someone's coming." Grace nodded toward the driveway. "Probably *Daed*."

Wayne walked out of the barn. Grace lagged behind, but when Ben started putting away tools that had been left out, Grace followed Wayne.

As her father stepped out of the buggy, he shook hands with Wayne, and after pleasantries about the weather turning cooler, Wayne said, "I know Grace isn't quite sixteen yet, but I would like to ask your permission to take her to eat pizza next Saturday for dinner. We're not having a baseball game at the Lantzes' because the womenfolk are having a baby shower that day."

Grace held her breath. She'd just assumed that Wayne wouldn't want anything to do with her anymore. And that had started to be okay. But maybe he'd realized that there were other ways for a couple to be close, besides what he had in mind. And after hearing him with Ben, and now so politely asking Grace's father to take her out . . . Grace would go crazy if her father didn't say yes.

"Wayne, I'm told you're a fine fellow," Grace's father said as she continued to hold her breath. "But we have plans next Saturday. Maybe another time, though."

"*Daed.*" Grace locked eyes with her father, willing him to change his mind. "Please, *Daed.* I'd rather go eat pizza."

Her father frowned as he stroked his beard. Grace shouldn't face off with her father in front of Wayne. "Please," she added, glancing at Wayne and hoping she didn't sound too desperate.

"I was hoping you'd be able to go Saturday." Grace's father scratched his cheek, glanced at Wayne, then back at Grace. "I guess it will be okay."

Grace let go of the breath she was holding and smiled.

"Pick you up at noon?" Wayne smiled, and Grace took off his coat and handed it back to him.

"See you then," she said.

*Thank You, God. And thank you, Daed.*

. . .

Eli felt all warm and fuzzy, as Leah used to say, watching Gracie clean the kitchen later that evening. She was humming and had been chattier than usual during supper, which she'd also prepared. A beef and potato casserole, her mother's recipe. Eli rarely made the casserole, but it was Ben's favorite, and the boy had enjoyed two generous helpings. Eli was well aware of the source of his daughter's joyful mood, and his name was Wayne Huyard.

"*Daed*, I have something to tell you." Gracie tossed the kitchen towel over her shoulder, then pulled out a chair at the table, across from Eli. Ben had already excused himself to go feed the pigs and get the other animals secure for the night.

"You're welcome," Eli said, grinning.

Grace sat down, smiling herself. "I am grateful that you are letting me go with Wayne next Saturday, but I want to tell you something else."

Eli leaned back in his chair, then picked up his cup of coffee, a little concerned about the serious tone of his daughter's voice. "What is it?"

"I haven't really wanted you to remarry." She crinkled her nose as she pressed her lips together.

This wasn't news to Eli, but he just nodded.

"I've been worried about replacing *Mamm*. It just didn't feel right."

Eli swallowed his sip of coffee and put the cup on the table. "No one can ever replace your mother."

Grace put her palm up for a couple of seconds, then laid both hands on the table as she sat taller. "I know that now. And I want to let you know that it's okay with me for you to find someone to spend your life with." She smiled. "I won't always be living here anyway. And I think Ben really needs a mother figure. He's still at a tender age."

Eli was watching his daughter grow up before his eyes, and it was lovely and terrifying at the same time.

"I'm sorry I won't be going with you to Ruth's on Saturday. I briefly met her *kinner* at worship service, but it would have been nice to get to know them better."

Eli had been praying that Gracie would feel this way, but hearing her talk in such a mature manner about a subject so close to their hearts was giving him a lump in his throat. He knew good and well that he didn't need his daughter's permission to remarry, but he'd always wanted hers and Ben's blessing. He nodded. "I'm sure there will be other opportunities to spend time with Ruth and her family."

Gracie got up, walked around the table, and kissed Eli on the cheek. "I'm sure there will be." Then she left Eli sitting at the table, knowing that God was giving his family a second chance at happiness.

He couldn't wait to spend some time with Ruth. Saturday wasn't going to get here soon enough.

# CHAPTER 9

"You look very nice," Grace told her father the following Saturday, before turning to Ben. "And you clean up pretty *gut* too."

Her father slipped on his jacket and his Sunday black hat. "I hope you and Wayne enjoy the pizza." Frowning, he said, "Don't be late."

Grace wasn't sure who'd been looking forward to Saturday more—her or her father. "I won't."

Once they were gone, Grace ran upstairs and found her lip balm. Since seeing a different side of Wayne, she felt sure he'd be better about respecting her boundaries. But kissing was on her "okay" list. She ran downstairs, pleased to see Wayne out the window, right on time.

Wayne was all worked up about some chores his father wanted him to do later in the afternoon, so he talked about that most of the way to the restaurant. Grace felt warm inside despite the cool temperature.

At the pizzeria, Wayne chose the booth in the far corner, and they shared a pepperoni pizza and each had a soda.

"*Danki* again for talking to Ben. I had no idea that your *mudder* had passed. How long ago?"

"When I was little, about four. I don't even think about it anymore." Wayne took a drink, then reached for the last slice of pizza.

"I still miss *mei mamm* all the time." Grace pictured her mother looking down from heaven and seeing her with the cutest boy in their community, out on a real date.

"You ready?" Wayne wiped his mouth. "I've gotta get going so I have time to do all that stupid extra work for my *daed*."

"*Ya*, sure." Grace stood up when Wayne did and glanced at the clock on the wall. She was going to get home way before she'd expected. Maybe she would surprise her father and walk to Ruth's house since it wasn't too far.

They were about halfway home when Wayne turned off the main highway. It took Grace a few seconds before she recognized where he was heading. "I-I thought you needed to get home?"

Wayne looked her way. "I do. But now that we're back together, I thought we could spend some time by ourselves."

Grace swallowed hard. She didn't want to make Wayne mad, but she didn't want to lead him on either. "Wayne . . ."

He glanced her way again. "*Ya?*"

"I-I just need you to respect my boundaries."

Wayne chuckled. "That sounds very *Englisch*, the way you said that."

Grace felt her cheeks turning red as she grinned. "*Ya*, I guess it does." But at least she'd said it before any kissing started. That way, Wayne wouldn't have expectations.

• • •

Eli glanced at the empty chair at Ruth's table for eight, wishing Gracie were here, but hoping she was having a good time with Wayne. Ben was quiet. Ruth's only boy, Stephen, was only six, and the girls—Carolyn, Eve, and Mary—chatted among themselves at one end of the table. Eli cleaned his plate and laid his fork across it. It hadn't been a bad meal, although he had thought about Elizabeth's mashed potatoes. And he would have seasoned the roast more than Ruth had. But all in all, things were going well. Ruth's *kinner* were polite and well behaved.

"Eli, are you ready for dessert?" Ruth pointed to the stove. "Shoofly pie."

"*I* am," Stephen said. "And I ate all my roast," he added, sitting up taller.

"Let's serve our guests first." Ruth stood up to get the pie, then brought it to the table, along with a stack of small plates.

"*Danki* for a wonderful meal, Ruth." Eli allowed himself to envision the seven of them—eight with Gracie—as a family. He knew it was way too soon to be having such thoughts, but he loved the idea of having a large family. He and Leah had wanted more children, but it just never happened after Ben came. Eli and Ruth hadn't discussed whether or not either of them wanted more children.

When Ruth's three daughters finished their pie, they asked to be excused, leaving Ben and Stephen. Eli's son was starting to fidget, and he was glad when Ruth's oldest daughter, Mary, asked if he'd like to go with them to the barn to see a calf that had been born two days ago.

"Don't you want to go with the other *kinner*, Stephen?" Ruth began to clear the table, and when Eli stood up and picked up a plate, she said, "*Nee, nee.* You sit. Let me do this."

Eli sat back down across from Stephen, who was shaking his head. "I would like another piece of pie, please."

Ruth walked to the pie plate. "Just a small piece, Stephen." She looked over her shoulder. "What about you, Eli? Another slice of pie?"

Eli put a hand across his stomach. "I don't think I can eat one more bite. It was all very *gut*."

"So, Stephen," Eli said to the boy, "is this your first or second year of school?"

"He's six, so this is his second year," Ruth said as Stephen took another bite of pie.

Grace had been out of school for almost two years, but he could still remember her first day at the one-room schoolhouse back home like it was yesterday. Ben's first day was just as memorable.

"What is your favorite thing to study?" Eli said to Stephen as Ruth scurried around the kitchen.

"Anything but my numbers," Stephen said with a mouthful. "*Mamm* says I'm stupid when it comes to my numbers."

"Stephen!" Ruth spun around and walked toward him, her face as red as the beets still in a bowl on the table. "I didn't say *stupid*." She looked at Eli and smiled. "He has a hard time with math; it's not his favorite subject."

"I hate math, so that makes me stupid." Stephen shrugged, and for a few tense moments, everyone was quiet. Eli could tell that Stephen's behavior was embarrassing Ruth as her face turned even redder.

"I disliked math as a young scholar too," Eli finally said. "But it's important to know. You'll use your numbers in many ways for the rest of your life."

Ruth cleared her throat. "Stephen, don't you want to go join the other *kinner* and check on the new calf?"

"*Nee.*" The boy eyed his empty plate. "I would like another piece of pie, please."

"No more pie, sweetheart." Ruth turned to Eli. "Coffee, Eli?"

"I would like one more piece of pie, please," Stephen repeated as he slammed his fork down on the plate. Eli stifled a grin. He remembered this age with both of his children, a time for testing the boundaries.

"If you eat another piece of pie, you might turn into a pie," Eli said, winking at Stephen. He glanced at Ruth, but she wasn't smiling.

"No pie, Stephen. Now, do not ask me again." Ruth cleared the beets and a bowl of chowchow from the table as Stephen slouched down in his chair until he was barely still in it.

"But I ate all my dinner, and my second piece of pie was small. I want another one." He eased his way back up the chair. "You're mean," he grumbled under his breath, but after a quick glance toward Ruth, Eli knew she'd heard.

"Eli, can you excuse Stephen and me for a minute?" Eli nodded, and Ruth walked to Stephen's side, then pointed to the doorway in between the living room and kitchen. "March," she said to her son.

Stephen slowly stood up, and before he even hit the threshold, Ruth grabbed his shirt and pulled him along at her side. He'd tell her when she got back not to be embarrassed. *Kinner*, especially at that age, could make a parent want to pull their hair out at times. And they always seemed to put on the best show in front of visitors.

After a few moments, Eli decided to find the bathroom, then maybe he'd go have a look at the new calf. He'd seen plenty, but he mostly wanted to see how Ben was interacting with the girls.

He turned down a long hallway, thinking maybe the bathroom was at the end, like at his house. But when he heard muffled voices, then what sounded like a slap followed by crying, he stopped in his tracks.

"Stop crying."

It was Ruth talking to Stephen, but she spoke to the boy in a deep whisper, almost like it wasn't even her. Eli knew better than to eavesdrop, but his feet were rooted to the floor as Stephen's sobs got quieter.

"I told you that you would be in trouble if you didn't act right in front of *Mamm*'s friend, didn't I? You stay in this room and don't come out. If I hear one peep out of you, I will give you much more to cry about."

The door flew open, and Ruth ran right into Eli. She brought a hand to her chest as her jaw dropped. "Eli?"

"I-I was looking for the bathroom."

. . .

Miriam eased the pile of clean clothes over to make room for Kiki, who had joined her on the couch. She opened her book and settled back into the love story she was reading, hoping Landon would ask Mary Beth to marry him in this chapter. Ever since she was a teenager, she'd chosen to read Christian fiction because those books always had happy endings.

She jumped when she heard a ruckus on the front porch, then hurried to the front door when someone started knocking.

"I forgot my sweater," Grace said, breathless, gulping in air.

Miriam pushed the screen door open. "*Ya*, you left it here." She closed the door behind Grace and took note of her red, swollen eyes. "Did you run here?"

"*Ya*." Grace pushed back several strands of hair that had fallen from her *kapp*.

Miriam walked to the couch and dug around the clean clothes until she found Grace's black sweater and handed it to her.

"*Danki*." Grace slipped it on and didn't seem to notice the orange cat hair that clung to it. She waited for Grace to do or say something, but the girl just stood in the middle of the room.

"Um, do you want to stay for a while? Need a glass of water?"

Grace was still catching her breath when she nodded, so Miriam left her in the middle of the living room and brought her back a glass of water, deciding that she wasn't going to find out if Landon proposed to Mary Beth today.

Grace chugged the water and handed the glass back to Miriam, but the girl still didn't move.

Miriam put the glass on the table. "Grace, what's wrong?"

Grace didn't say anything for a few seconds, then she tearfully recounted the time she'd spent with Wayne.

Miriam's blood was boiling. "He did *what*?"

"I can't say, I can't say." Grace ran into Miriam's arms, and Miriam held her tightly as she also started to get teary eyed. This was so similar to her own experience when she was Grace's age, the day that changed everything for Miriam. She eased Grace away and cupped her cheeks with her hands. "First, are you okay physically? Did Wayne force himself on you?"

"I'm okay, and *nee*, he didn't force me to do anything. But when I wouldn't do what he wanted, he got really mad and said ugly things to me."

Relief washed over Miriam as flashbacks of her and Luke filled her mind. Luke hadn't forced Miriam to do anything either. Miriam had made that decision on her own, and now she lived with the consequences. She was thankful that Grace had the courage to walk away—or run, as it appeared.

"He told me he could have any girl he wanted, girls

that were prettier than me. Like Rachel. He said he'd been pursuing Rachel before I came to town, but had put her on hold for me." She sniffled. "And that if I didn't grow up, I was never going to have a boyfriend here."

"That's all rubbish. Boys can be jerks." Miriam guided Grace to the couch, hoping Rachel wouldn't fall for Wayne's charm. Rachel wasn't the sweetest girl in the community, but Miriam didn't want to see any of them get hurt. "And if Wayne was trying to get you to do something you're not comfortable with, then you did the right thing, no matter how much he says he cares about you, and no matter what kind of ugly things he might have said."

"If he liked me so much, he shouldn't even ask me to go further than kissing," Grace said between sobs. "And then he was so mean about it and didn't talk to me all the way home. *Mei daed* is at Ruth's *haus*, and I couldn't have talked to him about this anyway. I don't have any girlfriends here, and I'm just so mad at myself for believing that he really liked me when all he really wanted was . . ." She covered her face with her hands.

Miriam sat down, put an arm around her, and let Grace bury her face in her shoulder. "I'm glad you came here, Grace." She kissed the top of Grace's head, knowing she was going to have a little chat with Wayne.

# CHAPTER 10

Eli sat alone on his couch. He could hear Ben upstairs tinkering, probably digging in his closet looking for a book his mother had given him. The subject had come up on the way home, and Ben was frustrated that he didn't know where the book was.

Sighing, Eli was wondering if this move was a good idea. Miriam had left a message on Eli's phone saying she would bring Grace home in a little while. When Eli had asked if his daughter was okay, Miriam told him that she was fine. But Miriam said she needed to talk to Eli, which caused Eli's stomach to sour.

He recalled the abrupt way he and Ben had left Ruth's house. Children needed discipline, and Eli was all for that, but his and Ruth's way to reprimand their *kinner* wasn't the same. On the ride home, he'd asked Ben if he had a good time, but his son had only shrugged and said it was okay. Eli wasn't sure he could afford to move again, and a month really wasn't long enough to give Lancaster County a chance.

Gracie walked into the house, and Eli stood and went to her. "Gracie?" Her cheeks were red, eyes swollen. "What happened?"

"*Daed*, I don't want to talk. Can I please be excused?"

Miriam walked in behind Gracie and nodded to Eli. Eli told Gracie that was fine. Once she was upstairs, he motioned for Miriam to sit down. Eli sat down beside her on the couch. "What happened?"

Miriam's cheeks were flushed, and her eyes were a bit swollen as well, which caused Eli's stomach to roil even more.

"Eli, I don't have any *kinner*," she said softly. "And I would never try to tell you how to raise your children. But I would strongly suggest that you not allow Grace to spend any more time with Wayne."

Eli's hair prickled against the back of his neck. "Did that boy hurt Gracie?"

"Not physically." Miriam kept her eyes down as she spoke. "But he's . . . pressuring her to do things that aren't right, things that would cause her regret later on, things that aren't right in God's eyes."

Eli started to tremble as anger boiled to the surface. Amos had told him Wayne was a good lad from a good family. He wanted to grab that boy by the shirt collar and throw him to the ground, an unfamiliar emotion that went against everything Eli believed.

"Wayne isn't a terrible person," Miriam said. "But he isn't respectful of the boundaries that girls set for him. I've seen this with other girls. And I know about boys that age." She lifted her eyes to Eli's. "I care about Grace, and I just thought you should know. I'm planning to have a talk with Wayne. It probably won't do any *gut*, but I'm tired of watching him pursue these young girls like an animal on the hunt."

"*Nee*, you don't need to do that. I will take care of him."

A hint of a smile crossed Miriam's face. "I thought you might say that, and maybe Wayne would heed a man more than me."

Eli stared at Miriam for a few moments. Too long, apparently, since her face took on a pinkish glow as she pulled her eyes from his. "*Danki* for bringing Grace home," he said.

Miriam looked up at him again. "Sometimes young girls are so smitten with a cute boy that they eventually give in, believing that the boy loves them and they will be together forever. But that isn't always the case. And sometimes the girl isn't strong enough to walk away and she does something that leaves her feeling unworthy for the rest of her life, undeserving of a husband." Miriam paused as she looked away from Eli, blinking her eyes a few times. "And it's those choices that we make as young girls that we have to live with."

Eli was quiet, knowing they were no longer talking about Grace. "But God forgives our sins the moment we ask Him to," he said softly, moving his head to search her eyes, but she wouldn't look at him. "Many times, the challenge is to forgive ourselves."

Miriam finally lifted her eyes to his and took a deep breath. "I must go." She stood up abruptly and smoothed the wrinkles from her black apron. "Do you mind if I go upstairs and say good-bye to Grace?"

Eli stood up, too, and as he looked at Miriam, he had a strong urge to hug her, so he did. It took her several seconds before she embraced him as well, and when she tried to pull away, Eli gave her a final squeeze and whispered, "*Danki* again."

Miriam hurried up the stairs after Eli told her which room was Gracie's. And once she was up there, Eli tiptoed up the stairs. He wanted to believe that Miriam's intentions were all good, but he'd been so wrong lately—about Ruth . . . and Wayne. He listened outside Grace's door, feeling guilty, but not enough to walk away. This was his daughter, one of the two greatest gifts the Lord had blessed him with, and he'd do whatever it took to keep her safe.

Miriam and Gracie spoke softly to each other, but Eli could hear every word.

· · ·

Miriam tried to choose her words carefully. She and Grace had talked for a while before Miriam had carted her home, but she wanted to make sure Grace was going to be okay. Miriam understood teenage heartbreak, and at Grace's age, it could seem like the end of the world.

"You are strong and did the right thing, Grace," Miriam said. "And don't be mad, but I talked to your father about this."

Grace hung her head. "How mad is he?"

Miriam cupped her chin and smiled. "He isn't mad at you, but I do think he might have a little talk with Wayne."

Grace swiped at her eyes. "I really liked him. And I've never had anyone that cute want to be my boyfriend."

"You are a beautiful *maedel*, Grace. The right boy, one who truly loves you, won't pressure you to do things you aren't comfortable with, things that should be saved until marriage. You are special, and you must always remember that."

Grace stared at her long and hard. "You are special, too, and you deserve to be happy."

Now it was Miriam who feared she might cry again. Maybe she'd said too much to Grace while they were still at Miriam's house. She knew she'd said too much to Eli just now, and she was wondering why that was. Something about Eli made her feel safe, and she was growing fond of Grace. But now she was embarrassed to even face Eli, fearful he'd read between the lines.

"*Danki* for saying that," Miriam said as she reached for Grace's hand and held it for a few moments before she stood up. "I should go. I just wanted to make sure you would be okay." She turned to leave, feeling the need to go home, curl up with Kiki, and have a good cry. Landon and Mary Beth weren't of much interest to her at the moment.

"Miriam?"

With her hand on the doorknob, she turned to face Grace. "*Ya?*"

"Everything is going to be okay."

Miriam forced a smile. "*Ya, mei maedel*. You will be just fine."

Grace stood up and walked to her. "*Nee*, that's not what I meant. What I meant was . . ." She smiled. "*You* will be just fine." Grace wrapped her arms around Miriam and hugged her as genuinely as Eli had downstairs.

*This is a gut family*, she thought as she went back downstairs. Eli was standing in the middle of the room, and Miriam needed to leave before she burst into tears, the events of the day catching up with her. But she couldn't stand the question dancing around in her mind.

"How did things go with Ruth? Grace told me she was cooking for you and Ben. I hope things went well." Miriam cringed, knowing that wasn't entirely true. She'd never deny Eli and his family happiness, but she wasn't sure Ruth was the right person for them.

Eli walked up to her, standing entirely too close, and softly said, "It's not going to work out for me and Ruth."

Miriam avoided his eyes. "*Ach*, I'm sorry to hear that. Maybe Elizabeth?"

"*Nee*," Eli said softly. "Not her either."

Miriam rushed around him, mumbling about how she had to get home. She didn't stop when he called her name.

. . .

A week later, Grace walked into Ben's room. "Are you ready?"

Ben rolled his eyes, but the smile on his face let Grace know he was happy. "*Ya, ya.* You've asked me that three times. I'm coming."

"Okay. Be downstairs in five minutes." Grace ran down the stairs, excited and nervous about what she was about to do. She'd prayed hard about her decision, and she was glad Ben was excited too.

Grace scribbled out a note to her father, turned the oven off, and picked up Ben's gloves from the kitchen counter, as he was sure to forget them . . . again.

"Ready?" she yelled upstairs.

"*Ya.* But it's cold outside," he said as he hit the landing. Grace handed him his gloves.

"It's not that cold outside yet, and next week is the harvest, so you'd best get used to the cold."

They both bundled up, then moved to the porch when the blue van pulled up. Grace knew her father would be upset if she and Ben ventured out on foot this time of day, with darkness almost upon them.

"Come on," she said, almost pulling Ben along. "We've got to go before *Daed* gets home."

• • •

Eli had spent the first part of his day readying up the plows for the fall harvest, greasing the parts and going through a safety checklist since his two most prized possessions would be helping him next week. Then he'd given the mules an extra helping of feed and reminded them that hard work and nurture of the land was a God-given blessing, and he prayed over the horses. Talking to his animals wasn't something Eli would want a living soul to see, but it was a common practice for him.

Earlier in the afternoon, he'd visited the bishop, a courtesy he'd been meaning to get around to in an attempt to get to know the man better. And now it was time to visit Wayne. As he pulled up to the boy's house, he quickly asked God to give him the right words and help him control the urge to sling the lad onto the ground. Wayne swaggered toward Eli's buggy as if he didn't have a care in the world.

"*Wie bischt*, Eli." Wayne looped his hands beneath his suspenders. "What brings you this way?"

Eli took in a deep breath as he stepped out of his buggy and reached for the reins, not planning to tether his horse or stay longer than he had to.

"I need to speak to you about my daughter."

Wayne stood taller as he pulled his hands from his suspenders and folded his arms across his chest, but he didn't say anything.

Eli stared at him for a few moments, then forced himself to shake the images from his mind that were probably far worse than what had actually happened. Just the same, he moved closer to Wayne. Close enough to be able to take a swing at the boy and knock him to the ground. He inhaled another deep breath but kept his gaze fixed on Wayne's eyes. Eli wanted to see fear in the boy's eyes when he was done speaking.

"My Gracie, and every *maedel* is this community, deserves to be treated with respect." Eli spoke in a whisper, but he could feel himself trembling. "We can have a long conversation about what this means, or you can take me at my word when I say that I will be watching you. And if I hear of you behaving inappropriately with any of these girls, I won't be coming back here to talk."

The knot in Eli's throat pulsed. He'd never hit any-one, but if Wayne didn't heed his warning, he might be tempted to do something he didn't believe in. He clenched his teeth and watched Wayne's eyes for any sign of fear, but the boy didn't flinch, still remaining quiet.

Eli took a small step closer to the boy, close enough to poke Wayne's chest. "Do you understand what I'm saying?"

Wayne stumbled backward, blinking his eyes a few times. "*Ya, ya,*" he said, his eyes widening.

Eli stared at him, wondering if what he'd said would make a bit of difference, and not feeling proud of himself for resorting to physical intimidation, even if it was just his finger. He'd ask God for forgiveness later, but for now, he wanted Wayne to understand that Eli meant business. When he saw a hint of fear in Wayne's eyes, Eli left.

It was almost dark when he pulled into his driveway, and he was surprised to see another buggy parked out front. And Miriam sitting on the porch.

"I'm a little early," Miriam said when Eli walked up the steps. She stood up. "I knocked on the door, but there was no answer. But Grace said it was urgent."

Eli's stomach flipped as he threw open the door and rushed inside. He picked up a note on the kitchen table as Miriam followed him in. "Is everything okay?" she asked.

Eli read the note, eyed the table set for two, and inhaled a heavenly aroma of what smelled like pork roast. Smiling, he handed the note to Miriam and looked over her shoulder, rereading what Grace had written.

Dear Daed,

Me and Ben went to Naomi's haus. She and I went shopping at the market this week, and I think we are becoming friends. She has a younger bruder Ben's age. I knew you wouldn't want us to walk, so we took our money and hired a driver Naomi's mamm said was a nice Englisch lady. Don't be mad. We love you and want you to be happy. Miriam might be mad, but tell her not to be mad either.

Supper is keeping warm in the oven. There is a salad in the refrigerator and a pecan pie on the counter.

Love,

Gracie and Ben

Eli walked to the oven and eased the door open, realizing he'd been wrong about the roast. He slowly closed the oven and took his time turning around, but when he saw Miriam smiling, he said, "How do you feel about meat loaf?"

"I love meat loaf," she said, still grinning.

Eli pulled out a chair for her, and after she sat down, he lit the two candles that his daughter had put in the middle of the table, then he lit the two lanterns on the counter, knowing it would be dark soon. He put the salad on the table, then the meat loaf, potatoes, and carrots that had been keeping warm in the oven. Sitting down, he was having trouble keeping the smile from his face. "I'm not mad at all," he said as he glanced at Miriam, encouraged by the fact that she was still smiling.

"I'm not mad either," she said.

They both bowed their head in silent prayer, and afterward, Eli stared at the woman across from him, the flicker from the candles creating a glow on her face that Eli had always seen. But it seemed to him that maybe for the first time, Miriam was seeing for herself the life she was meant to live.

The life Eli had seen the first time he'd laid eyes on her.

# EPILOGUE

Miriam had settled into her new life almost effort-lessly, and there was no reason to regret that she'd waited until she was twenty-eight years old to do so. If anything had happened differently, she might not be exactly where the Lord had always intended for her to be.

She'd moved into Eli's house after they were mar-ried the following fall. Forgiving herself for past choices hadn't come easily, but over time, she realized that harboring such ill will toward herself was just as much a sin as the inability to forgive others. She had Eli to thank for that. And God. Eli led by example. He was a loving man who forgave easily—most of the time. But when he'd said he was having trouble forgiving Wayne for hurting Grace, Miriam found herself explaining all the reasons God wants us to be forgiving. When she was done, Eli kissed her on the cheek and lovingly told her to follow her own advice. From that moment on, Miriam began to shed the sins of her past and started to let go of burdens that weren't hers to carry, discover-ing that God was ready and willing to take over the job.

Grace hadn't shied away from boys completely. She

still attended the Sunday singings, but Miriam was glad to see her focusing more on new friendships with some of the kinder girls in the community. And Ben had his first crush on a girl. Grace teased him unmercifully at times, but Miriam suspected that when the time came, Grace would be his coach on how to treat the young ladies.

Eli was everything Miriam had always dreamed of. Kind, gentle, forgiving, a wonderful parent, and Miriam's inability to cook a decent meal didn't bother him. He'd tenderly told her not long into their courtship that he didn't think he could eat noodles and cheese from a box. Luckily, Eli loved to cook.

Miriam hadn't heard about any problems with Wayne, and although no one spoke of it, Miriam assumed that had something to do with the visit Eli had paid Wayne not long after the incident with Grace.

Miriam was motivated to keep their home tidy, and with Grace's guidance, she'd become a pretty good housekeeper. But her most important role, aside from being a good wife to Eli, was mothering Ben. He was at a touchy age where he wanted to be grown up but in many ways was still a boy.

Today was a special day. Eli had added a room onto the back of the house not long after they'd married, a sewing room much larger than Miriam had at her home, and she'd asked Grace to meet her here this afternoon to see a quilt that Miriam hadn't shown anyone yet.

"Are you ready?" she asked when Grace came into the room.

"I've been ready." Grace folded her hands in front of her, smiling. "Do I need to close my eyes?"

Miriam watched as Grace closed her eyes, even though Miriam didn't tell her to. She marveled at the beautiful woman Grace was becoming, both inside and out.

"You can open your eyes," she said once the quilt was spread on the table. "What do you think?"

Grace ran her hand gingerly across the colorful squares and tears pooled in the corners of her eyes. She looked at Miriam. "It's you."

Miriam nodded. "And look." She began pointing to all the squares, explaining what each one meant. The day she fell in love with Grace's father was represented by a red heart. There was a piece of her wedding dress, along with many other symbolic squares, some from her life before she found her family, but mostly ones she'd added over the past year. Recently, she'd added a square with an orange cat. Her sweet Kiki had passed not long after she'd married Eli; curiously, no one ever understood why Eli wasn't allergic to the cat, the way he'd always been of other felines. And Miriam had also quilted in a square with a baseball mitt. She'd given up playing on Saturdays, even though Eli had encouraged her to continue. But her happiest times were now at home with her family.

As Grace studied the quilt, Miriam peeked her head out the door and called for Eli and Ben to join them. Eli was grinning ear to ear. Ben was yawning, probably thinking this was girls' stuff. And as Miriam had hoped, Grace found the one square that was going to make her quilt patchwork perfect.

"What's this one?" Grace asked, pointing to a yellow square with a rattle.

Eli put his arm around Miriam. "What do you think it is?"

Grace tapped a finger to her chin as Ben walked to Grace's side, then his face lit up. "A baby!"

"*Ya.*" Miriam couldn't imagine a better moment in life than when Grace and Ben ran into her and Eli's arms. But deep down, she knew there was a lifetime of happiness waiting for all of them. She touched her stomach, acknowledging the tiny life growing inside her, feeling overwhelmed by the love and gratitude she felt for her new family. And for God's love and divine providence.

# ACKNOWLEDGMENTS

This was a fun story to write, and I happily dedicate this novella to Kiki and Katie—my precious kitties who were with me for seventeen years. I miss you girls.

My heartfelt thanks to my family and friends, and also to my amazing team at HarperCollins Christian Publishing. And Natasha Kern, I appreciate you as my agent, but even more so as my friend.

God's blessed me abundantly with stories to tell, and I am grateful for the opportunity to serve Him.

# DISCUSSION QUESTIONS

1. When Eli was introduced to Elizabeth and Ruth in the beginning of the story, whom did you hope he would choose? Did you like one woman better than the other? Were you relieved when Miriam came into Eli's life? Did you root for her?

2. Miriam doesn't cook, clean, or have a garden. She's an untraditional Amish woman who isn't interested in marriage, so she doesn't hone in on those skills to attract a husband. But later in the story, we find out that Miriam can't forgive herself for a choice she made when she was young. Do you think that her inability to get past that is part of the reason Miriam lives the way she does? Do you think she was depressed?

3. From the beginning, Wayne is pushing Grace beyond her comfort zone when it comes to affection. Did you feel like Wayne only wanted Grace for his own reasons, or did you think he really liked her and was just being a boy? As you think about this, remember the kindness that he showed to Ben in the barn.

4. Amos tells Eli that Miriam is their "resident old maid" at the age of twenty-eight. While this might

sound harsh, it is common for Amish folks to get married at a young age. Do you think Eli and Miriam will be happier because they are both older when they got married?

# A Bid for Love

## Kathleen Fuller

*To my husband James. Love you always.*

# CHAPTER 1

*Will he stop by today?*

Hannah Lynne Beiler tried to pull her gaze away from Ezra Yutzy, but it was impossible. Instead of staring at him, she should be focusing on selling the butter and pies at her stand inside the main building at the Middlefield Market. But once she saw him across the room, perusing a table covered with a variety of tools for sale, she couldn't stop looking at him.

Her cheeks heated as they always did when Ezra was around. So what if he was twenty-seven and she was only twenty-two? What difference did it make that he barely spoke to her every time he stopped by her stand to buy butter? Did it matter that the man of her dreams barely knew she existed? Or that everyone knew he was a *very* confirmed bachelor?

"That's a big sigh," Rachael said.

"I didn't notice I was sighing." Hannah Lynne glanced at her sister-in-law, who had joined her a few minutes earlier. Though she married Hannah Lynne's brother Gideon two years ago, and he made a good living running the family dairy farm, Rachael still grew and sold plants. Usually she had a small stand outside, but while today's weather prohibited that, setting up her stand inside the market building hadn't impeded her sales. She'd already sold all she had.

"Is something wrong?" Rachael asked.

Hannah Lynne flicked another glance in Ezra's direction, but he had disappeared. She hid her disappointment. "*Nix* is wrong."

"*Gut.*" Rachael glanced at the dwindling crowd inside the building. The Middlefield Market was held every Monday, rain or shine. Most of the sellers marketed their wares outside, except during the winter months. But Hannah Lynne preferred indoors. She had been selling her own fresh churned butter and her mother's seasonal fruit pies for the past two years, and she rarely had to take any unsold items home. Today might be the exception.

"Not much of a crowd this morning," Rachael commented, smiling at a Yankee woman as she passed by their table.

"I think the rain kept most everyone home." Hannah Lynne tugged her navy blue sweater closer to her body, covering the light blue dress she'd put on that morning. Then she saw Ezra again, and her breath caught. He was coming toward them.

His height made him easy to spot. He wore his straw hat pushed low on his brow, but not far enough to obscure her view of his face. Brownish-black wavy hair curled over his ears, the color matching the thick brows above his blue-gray eyes. What fascinated her most was the small, dark freckle under his left eye, resting right on top of his cheekbone. She could imagine skimming the tip of her finger across it—

"Glad to see you haven't run out of butter yet." He stood in front of her table, his gaze not meeting hers, but focusing on the square packages. "Thought I might have been too late." He finally looked up, his lips curving into a smile.

She gripped the edge of the table, her pulse starting to thrum. She wondered how she could convince him to *un*confirm his confirmed bachelorhood.

Ezra glanced at her price sign. "Five dollars, right?" He dug into the pocket of his dark blue jacket and pulled out a few bills. She watched as he unfolded the money with his work-roughened hands. A carpenter by trade, he was also renovating a Yankee house he'd bought a month ago and converting it to an Amish home for himself. Gideon had commented that it was a strange thing for Ezra to do, considering he wasn't dating a *maedel*. "Why *geh* to the trouble if he's just going to live there by himself?"

Hannah Lynne had no idea, and she wasn't sure she wanted to find out. What if he was secretly seeing someone? If he was, he was doing an excellent job hiding it.

Ezra peeled off a five-dollar bill and held it out to her. "Did you raise *yer* price?"

"Huh?" She looked at him, her face reddening.

"Actually," Rachael said, "we're offering a special deal. Five dollars will get you two packages of butter. Throw in an extra two dollars and you can have three."

He rubbed his chin. "That's a lot of butter for one person."

"It freezes," Hannah Lynne blurted. *Ugh*. Couldn't she have thought of something clever to say? Something *flirty*?

"I don't have a freezer," he said. He glanced at the butter again. "But *mei mudder* has a gas-powered one. I'm sure she'd appreciate the extra butter, and I can't resist a *gut* deal." He counted out the seven dollars and handed it to Rachael, who was already putting the butter in a paper bag.

"Did you find what you were looking for at the market today?" Rachael asked. Thank goodness her sister-in-law's customer-service habits had automatically kicked in. At least Hannah Lynne *hoped* Rachael had no idea she'd become speechless and immobile in this man's presence.

Ezra shook his head. "*Nee.* We need an extra hand planer at the shop. Thought they might have one here, but I didn't see any. Maybe next week." He took the bag from Rachael. "Appreciate it." He turned and left, and Rachael busily rearranged the remaining goods they hadn't sold.

Hannah Lynne finally smiled at him, even though he was already walking away. Carrying her butter . . . and her heart.

Then she frowned, knowing she was fooling herself. Yet a tiny spark of hope remained alive that one day the man she loved would notice her. And maybe one day, if she hoped and prayed hard enough . . . he would love her back.

. . .

Ezra dodged the heavy raindrops as he headed for his buggy, carrying more butter than he knew what to do with. That was the first time he'd seen Rachael Beiler at Hannah Lynne's stand. Rachael didn't know he bought a pound of butter from Hannah Lynne almost every Monday. His purchases were taking up more and more room in his mother's gas freezer, to the point that she had already transferred some of the butter blocks to a portable cooler. Still, he'd been truthful when he said he couldn't resist a good deal.

He also couldn't resist stopping by Hannah Lynne's table.

As he untied his horse, he wondered, not for the first time, why he always went to her table when he visited the market. Sure, he liked butter, especially slathered on a stack of hot pancakes. He also really liked the sayings she wrote inside the paper butter wrapper—a proverb, a joke, a few words of wisdom, a thought-provoking Scripture verse.

But that wasn't enough to keep him going back. There was something else, something he couldn't put his finger on. It wasn't like she talked to him when he bought the butter, which was strange. He knew Hannah Lynne Beiler wasn't afraid to talk. He'd seen her with her friends after church service, often smiling and gesturing with her hands as she spoke. He wouldn't characterize her as quiet, yet each time he visited her stand she became almost mute.

She did have a nice smile. He had to admit that— though unfortunately, he noticed she hadn't smiled today.

He shrugged, tossed the bag of butter on the bench seat next to him, and guided his horse to his parents' home. His new house, which was precisely three doors down from theirs, was barely legal to live in by both Yankee and Amish standards. For some unknown reason he'd been drawn to the house, even though it was too large for just him. Because it needed extensive renovation he'd gotten it for next to nothing. At least the barn was in decent shape. Oddly enough, he also felt a sense of peace once he purchased the property, and he was looking forward to making it his permanent home.

The rain started coming down harder, bringing a stronger breeze. The maples and pin oaks had already started to turn, their green leaves transforming into bright yellows, reds, and oranges. He turned down his street. Their cabinetry shop was behind his parents' house, and he would drop the butter off in his mother's kitchen before he went back to work.

Maybe next week he'd find that hand planer he was looking for. Or maybe not. There was one thing he knew for sure—if Hannah Lynne was there next Monday, he'd stop by her stand. He'd buy her butter. And he hoped he'd get to see her smile.

# CHAPTER 2

"How was the market today?"

Hannah Lynne set down the cardboard box holding two unsold fruit pies on the kitchen table and looked at her mother. "Slow," she said, removing her black bonnet. It had water spots on it from the rain that was still falling. "I brought two pies back."

"Only two?" Her mother smiled as she stood over the cutting board on the counter, her knife slicing through a carrot with quick precision. "You took ten. I'd say that was a *gut* day, despite it being slow." She glanced at Hannah Lynne. "Did you sell all *yer* butter?"

"*Ya.*" She stepped into the mudroom, right off the kitchen, and hung up her bonnet and shawl. Later she would give her mother her share of the money from the sale of the pies, plus a little extra from the butter money. Her mother said she could keep all her money, but Hannah Lynne didn't feel right about that. She wanted to contribute to the household expenses. The rest she was saving for the future . . . whatever it held. "I'll have to make some more butter this week," she said as she stepped back into the kitchen.

"Do you plan on making anything for the auction?"

*Mamm* slid the carrot slices into a pot of boiling water on the gas stove.

Hannah Lynne paused. The annual auction to benefit the DDC Clinic, a special needs care and research facility in Middlefield, was a couple of weeks away. Several years ago the Amish community had organized the auction, and this year it was being held at the Middlefield Market. Over the years it had grown, and Yankees attended as well. Many of the items, from handmade quilts to cords of firewood to simple broom-and-dustpan sets, were auctioned off, and the proceeds given to help support the clinic. Hannah Lynne's family had always made donations.

Last year she put together a basket of butter and cheeses for the pick-a-prize drawings that took place during the auction. A small paper bag was placed in front of each donated item, and participants dropped pre-purchased tickets in the bags for any items they were interested in winning. One ticket was drawn from each bag, announcing the winner of that item.

"Hannah Lynne?" Her mother turned to her, her light-brown eyebrows pushing together. "Did you hear me?"

Hannah Lynne nodded. "*Ya*. I'm not sure what I'm going to do." She didn't want to make the same donation as last year, but she'd have to figure out something soon.

*Mamm* put down the wooden spoon she was using to stir the vegetable soup and went to Hannah Lynne. "Sit for a minute," she said, pulling out a chair from the table and sitting down.

Giving her mother a wary look, Hannah Lynne pushed the box with pies aside and sat down across from her. "Is something wrong?"

"You tell me." *Mamm* folded her hands and rested them on the tabletop. "You haven't been *yer* sunshiny self lately."

"I'm sorry."

"Don't apologize. I just want to know if there is anything you need to talk about." She unfolded her hands and reached for both of Hannah Lynne's. "You know I'm always here for you."

Hannah Lynne nodded and forced a smile. It was ridiculous how her feelings for Ezra were now affecting every aspect of her life. Harboring secret, unrequited love was becoming exhausting.

"Is it Gideon and Rachael?"

Hannah Lynne frowned. "I don't understand."

"There have been a lot of changes in the past two years. Like Gideon getting married, and *yer* older *bruder* moving to Indiana right after that."

"Gideon lives next door, *Mamm*. I see him all the time. Why would I be upset about that? Or about Abraham moving away? We get regular letters from him and his wife."

"I know . . . but it's not the same." Her mother withdrew her hands. "Things aren't the way they used to be."

Hannah Lynne caught a note of sadness in *Mamm*'s voice. This time she grasped her mother's hand. "I'm not going anywhere," she said firmly.

"That's what I'm worried about." She sighed and

looked at Hannah Lynne, who was feeling even more confused. "You should be thinking about a life of *yer* own. A *familye* of *yer* own."

"Oh. But wouldn't that make you even sadder? If I left home too?"

"Sad?" Her mother chuckled. "*Lieb*, I'm not sad. I'm happy for *mei sohns*. They've found the perfect women for them. They're making their way in the world, and doing it while staying true to their faith." She paused. "I'll admit I don't like change very much. But I'll take it if it means *mei kinner* are happy. I want the same happiness for you."

*So do I.* But how could that happen when the one man she thought could make her happy was out of reach? "God's timing," she said softly. "That's what you've always told me."

"*Ya.* God's timing is best." *Mamm* glanced down at their hands, fingers entwined. "I hesitate to ask this, because I know it's not *mei* business." She was looking at Hannah Lynne now. "Is there . . . anyone?"

Hannah Lynne pressed her lips together and looked away.

"Never mind." Her mother gave her hand a squeeze and released it, then stood. "I shouldn't have pried."

"It's all right." Hannah Lynne wished she could give her mother the answer they both wanted. Maybe someday she could.

"Vegetable soup and bread okay for supper?" *Mamm* went back to the stove and stirred the soup. "I guess we'll have pie for dessert."

"Sounds delicious." Hannah Lynne rose, glad her

mother was dropping the subject. And like her mother, she was happy for her brothers. She only wished she had some of that happiness for herself.

She pushed the empty chair to the table, then ran her fingers absently over the smooth pinewood. Her mother was right—being quiet and moody wasn't like her. She missed the sunshiny part of herself too. Maybe if Josiah Miller asked to take her home from the next Sunday evening singing, she wouldn't make an excuse to tell him no this time. In fact, maybe she should start paying more attention to him as soon as possible. He didn't compare to Ezra, but he was a nice guy. Unlike Ezra, he at least seemed a little interested in her.

Hannah Lynne left the kitchen, already feeling more at ease. She'd focus on making more butter to sell at the market and on figuring out a donation for the auction. She had plenty of things to keep her mind off Ezra Yutzy. After a year of pining after him, perhaps it was time to let him go.

. . .

That Sunday, Hannah Lynne put Operation Pay-Attention-to-Josiah-Miller in action. After the service, she lingered outside the barn to wait for him. He was talking to a couple of his friends a few feet away, so she bided her time. She was determined to not try to spot Ezra. That's what she usually did on Sundays, even to only catch a glimpse of him.

*Josiah's the one you're interested in, remember?*

As if he sensed her looking at him, Josiah turned

around and smiled. He gave his friends a short wave good-bye and headed toward her.

"Hi, Hannah Lynne," he said, his hazel eyes shaded by his black hat.

"Hi," she said softly.

He smiled, and she tried to convince herself he was just as striking as Ezra. He definitely wasn't bad looking. Josiah was average height, with nice blond hair and a perpetual tan from working outside as a landscaper most of the year. She returned his smile, waiting for him to say something. But he stared at her, his expression slightly . . . goofy.

Goofy. That was one thing Ezra wasn't.

She steeled her resolve, searched her mind for a topic of conversation, then asked, "Are you going to the auction?"

"Which one?"

"The one for the DDC Clinic," she said, realizing she should have clarified. Auctions were always being held in the area, but this one was special.

"*Nee*. Too crowded." He sniffed, which sounded more like a snort.

"Did you donate something, then?"

Josiah shrugged. "Hadn't really thought about it. It's not something I usually do."

"The clinic is very important to the community."

"I guess. I don't really know what they do there."

She proceeded to tell him, but his eyes started to glaze over. "Anyway," she said, a little irritated that he wasn't interested in the important research the doctors at the clinic conducted, or in how so many children benefited from the special care offered. "If you change *yer* mind, you can come with me." Her eyes widened. Had she really just asked him out?

He shook his head. "I won't be changing *mei* mind. I'll probably be working on rebuilding a lawn mower for Carl Biddle."

She feigned interest as he started explaining to her that by the time he was done with his Yankee friend's mower, he would have improved the power by 20 percent. "That's nice," she said, her gaze straying over his shoulder. She drew in a sharp breath when she saw Ezra walking to his buggy with long, even strides. He was so handsome in his church clothes. He was handsome in anything he wore.

"So would you like to?"

Josiah's question drew her attention. Realizing she was being unfair to him by looking at—and longing for—Ezra, she gave Josiah what she hoped was an innocent smile. "I'm sorry. Could you repeat the question?"

"Would you like me to take you home from the next singing?"

She cut a quick glance at Ezra as he climbed into the buggy, then nodded. "*Ya*," she said, looking at Josiah again. "I would like that."

"*Gut.*" His grin widened, which made his expression a bit more endearing than goofy. Why couldn't she find him as appealing as Ezra? Maybe when they spent more time together she would.

"Then it's a date," he said. "I'll see you then."

As he turned and walked away, Hannah Lynne wondered if she had done the right thing. When she saw

Ezra's buggy leave without him glancing her way, she knew she had.

. . .

Ezra went into his mother's kitchen to grab a sandwich made from some leftover ham. As he continued to work on his own house, the realization that his current living arrangement would be coming to an end became clearer each day. He'd definitely miss his mother's cooking.

His father had left early that morning to go to the local sawmill and haggle about wood prices. The owner of the mill always gave them a fair deal, but *Daed* enjoyed the dickering. Ezra sometimes went with him, especially on a Saturday, but he had a rush, custom-ordered sideboard to finish by the end of next week. It was part of the reason he hadn't gone to the market this past Monday, and he probably wouldn't make it this coming Monday either.

It wasn't like he'd needed more butter, anyway.

He'd seen Hannah Lynne at church, though, talking to Josiah Miller. He frowned as he cut two thick slices of bread from the loaf in the bread box. As he'd walked toward his buggy to go home, he'd been close enough to see both of their faces. They'd paid no attention to him, but it was clear from the wide-eyed way Josiah looked at Hannah Lynne that he was interested in her. It was also clear from the way Hannah Lynne peeked at Josiah from underneath what Ezra knew to be long, brown eyelashes that she was welcoming that interest.

"Ow!" He glanced down at his hand, realizing he'd slid the knife blade across the tip of a finger. The cut wasn't deep, but it stung. He shook his head and turned on the tap, running his finger underneath the cool water. Why was he even thinking about Hannah Lynne and Josiah? Yes, he thought he'd seen Hannah Lynne glance at him for a moment, but he was sure he imagined it. Her focus was all on Josiah.

*Lucky guy.*

Ezra jerked up his head. Where had that thought come from?

A knock sounded on the front door of the house. Ezra turned off the tap, grabbed a dish towel, and dried his finger. The bleeding had already stopped. When he opened the door he saw Sarah Detweiler, one of his mother's closest friends, standing on the front porch.

"Hello, Ezra," Sarah said, smiling.

Ezra had known the Detweilers all his life, and had even been friendly with Sarah's son Aaron, who was a few years older than Ezra. Friendly, until Aaron was arrested for dealing drugs. When Aaron returned from jail he'd straightened up his act, landed a job as a farrier, and married Elisabeth Byler. How long ago was that now? Ezra couldn't remember. All his friends, even his most superficial ones, had either left the community or were married and busy with their own families.

Realizing he was leaving Sarah's greeting unanswered, he opened the door wider. "Hi, Sarah. Come on in."

She nodded her thanks and walked into the living room. He shut the door against the cool outside air.

"*Mamm* isn't here right now. I'm not sure where she went." His mother had left shortly after his father had, and she hadn't told Ezra where she was going.

"Oh." Sarah looked puzzled, her black bonnet shading her wrinkled forehead. "She must have forgotten."

"Forgotten what?"

"I mentioned last Sunday that I would be by today to pick up the quilt for the auction. She said she wanted to donate one." She looked up at Ezra. Sarah wasn't a short woman, but Ezra's six-foot-three height made him tower over almost everyone. "You wouldn't happen to know which quilt she was planning to donate?"

He shook his head, then spied a quilt neatly folded on the chair nearest the door. He didn't recognize the blue, white, and yellow spread. Then again, he never paid attention to stuff like that. Quilts were usually in two places in the house—on a bed or draped over the couch. Not folded up on a chair. This had to be the quilt she was planning to donate. "Here," he said, snatching it off the chair. It felt soft. Old, even. For a tiny second he doubted his theory. But why else would the quilt be here? He handed it to Sarah. "I'm sure this is it."

Sarah took the quilt. "*Danki*, Ezra. Are you planning to come to the auction Friday night?"

"Wouldn't miss it." He went every year, and usually came away with some good deals. He enjoyed listening to the auctioneers, usually Amish men who took turns making the calls. A Yankee service was hired to manage the auction, but the Amish auctioneers did the bulk of the work.

Sarah smiled. "Tell *yer mamm* I'll talk to her soon."

"Will do."

After Sarah left, Ezra finished making his sandwich, his mind now turning to the cherrywood sideboard he needed to sand. He also thought about what he could donate to the auction. He gave something every year, usually a small piece of furniture or a wooden toy he'd privately worked on and donated anonymously. He gained a lot of satisfaction knowing the sale of his handcrafted items went to a good cause.

This year, though, he had nothing to give. He'd spent so much time working on his house, and there wouldn't be enough time for him to make something. He decided to take some extra money with him and make a cash donation. It wasn't a homemade item, but it was something.

# CHAPTER 3

An hour before the auction started, Hannah Lynne rushed inside the building at the Middlefield Market, basket in hand. She was late, and she hoped Sarah Detweiler, who was in charge of both the pick-a-prize drawings and the quilts at the auction, would still let Hannah Lynne make her donation—a set of matching cloth napkins and a table runner. She'd made them the week before out of fancier fabric than she would have normally used. But she liked the bright primary colors—lemon yellow, royal blue, and crimson red—cut into thick strips and sewn together to make a striped pattern. Just looking at her handiwork, neatly arranged in the off-white, square-shaped wicker basket she'd purchased to contain the items, made her smile.

She waited as Sarah finished talking to another woman who was helping her set up the pick-a-prize items and the small paper bags that went in front of them. Hannah Lynne usually bought a few tickets, but she'd never won anything.

As she waited, she glanced at her basket again and smiled. She was pleased with her offering and hoped it would garner a lot of tickets. She looked up, just in time to see Ezra standing a few feet away, looking at a wringer washer that would be auctioned off later.

She clenched the handle of her basket. She hadn't seen him since church the Sunday before last. He hadn't come to the Middlefield Market for two Mondays—or if he did, he hadn't stopped by her table.

Hannah Lynne turned her back to him, reminding herself that because she had agreed to let Josiah take her home from the next singing, she had no business thinking about Ezra Yutzy anymore. Never mind that her skin was tingling from him being so close by.

"Oh, hi, Hannah Lynne," Sarah said from behind her, putting her hand on Hannah Lynne's shoulder. "Did you bring something for the auction?"

"*Ya,*" she said, turning around. Disappointment shot through her when she saw Ezra was gone. Giving her head a quick shake, she focused on Sarah. "It's not too late to donate, is it?"

"*Nee,*" Sarah took the basket from her. "Oh. These are very . . . bright."

Hannah Lynne smiled as she nodded. "I liked the fabric a lot."

"It should be popular with our Yankee visitors." She set the basket in an empty space on one of the long tables that were already covered with a variety of small auction items, including homemade cookbooks, candles, quilted potholders, and crocheted layettes. The layettes were made of pastel yarns, of course. Hannah Lynne's donation stood out among the others.

"Do you need any help?" Hannah Lynne asked.

"*Nee*, but *danki* for offering." Sarah smiled. "We're just about ready."

Hannah Lynne told Sarah good-bye, then walked among the tables, looking at the smaller items for the pick-a-prize drawing, making mental notes about which ones she would try to win. Then she went to look at the quilts.

Several quilts were hung over a long clothesline, carefully secured with clothespins. Slowly she walked past the first two, examining the perfect stitching. She was a decent seamstress, but she couldn't create anything as beautiful as what had been donated today. A sign was posted near the quilts, explaining how they would be auctioned off. This would be a silent auction, where each bid would be written on a sheet of paper until the bidding time ended. She didn't intend on participating in this one. She had enough quilts at home. Besides, handmade quilts like these always went for a high price.

Then she froze. Her heart skipped more than one beat and she changed her mind about not bidding. She couldn't believe she almost didn't see it. She moved closer, her heart pounding. She had to have this quilt.

. . .

Ezra wandered around the interior of the market building, eventually making his way to the back where a large group of women and a few men had set up tables and stands selling all kinds of food—homemade pretzels, beefy hot dogs, freshly fried and glazed donuts, cream sticks, barbecue sandwiches, small bags of chips, and more. Right outside the building was another tent set up with just baked goods. He'd visit that one next. His stomach rumbled with hunger. Right now he was ready for a hot dog and a can of pop.

After he purchased his food, Ezra found a spot to stand along the perimeter of the room. As he ate, he observed the milling crowd. Amish, Yankees, even several groups of Mennonites had all arrived from nearby counties to enjoy the auction. There were a lot of families. He also saw a couple of young children who were probably recipients of the special needs clinic's services. One was a young Amish girl in a wheelchair. She looked to be about five years old. From the stiff posture of her limbs he could see she had cerebral palsy.

The other child was walking, but Ezra noticed the young boy's cleft lip, one that had been surgically repaired. His straw hat was tipped back on his head, revealing a hank of light blond bang across his forehead. He grinned, showing he was missing two front teeth. Ezra thanked God that the community had the resources to care for him, and any other children with special needs. Although he knew he shouldn't be prideful, he couldn't help but feel a spark of satisfaction deep inside that they were all coming together to take care of their own.

He polished off the hot dog as more people filed in, some perusing the auction items, others purchasing food, still others finding a spot in the stacks of bleachers that had been pulled out for seating. He never sat at these things, instead preferring to walk around the floor and interact with the auction.

He tipped his head back and finished his pop, threw away his can and napkin, and headed for the middle of the building where there was a thickening crowd around several of the items on display. Many of the women—Amish, Yankee, and Mennonite—were looking at the quilts. He spied the one his mother had donated. She hadn't said anything to him about it, so he assumed he'd been right in giving the quilt to Sarah that day.

Ezra squinted a bit, his gaze locking on Hannah Lynne. She was there, staring at it, her mouth partially open almost as if in a state of shock. Strange. He frowned. Was there something wrong with her? He rubbed his eyebrow as he walked over to her, noticing that her gaze never left the quilt. When he stood next to her, she still didn't move. He doubted she realized he was there.

"Hannah Lynne?" he asked, leaning over a bit so he could see her face.

She slowly turned to him and smiled.

His voice suddenly stuck in his throat. Her smile was always appealing. But for some reason her expression was different . . . and beautiful. He couldn't stop from basking in the unexpected glow of Hannah Lynne Beiler's gorgeous smile. It was as if he'd never seen her before.

She turned from him, looking at the quilt again. "It's perfect, isn't it?"

He swallowed, his mouth dry as a cotton sock. "What?"

"This quilt." She reached out and touched the fabric. "It even feels the same," she whispered.

He had no idea what she was talking about. And he didn't really care, at least not about the quilt. He was more concerned about the tickle in his belly, and the fact that he couldn't take his eyes off her—two things he'd never experienced before.

She opened her small black purse and pulled out a wallet. He saw her thumbing through the bills before snapping the wallet closed. Then she grabbed the pencil next to the piece of paper on the table in front of the quilt. She wrote on the paper, took a step back, and closed her eyes. Her lips moved as if she was saying a silent prayer. Then she opened her eyes, turned, and walked away . . . as if she'd never seen him at all.

He followed her with his gaze, pushing back his hat to scratch his suddenly itchy forehead. *What had just happened?*

"Excuse me."

Ezra turned at the sound of an older woman's voice. The gray-haired woman's bright pink-and-lime-green-striped sweater was almost blinding, and she smelled like she'd dunked herself in a vat of sickly sweet perfume. She gave him an annoyed look, and he realized he was standing in her way. He stepped aside, then turned to search for Hannah Lynne. But he couldn't see her. She had disappeared into the crowd.

He looked at the quilt again to see if he had made a mistake. No, it was the one his mother had donated. More women were admiring it now, but none of them seemed to be showing the interest or sheer joy Hannah Lynne had. She really wanted to win that quilt.

For some reason he would be hard-pressed to explain, he really wanted her to win it too.

Had she bid enough? As the main auction started and the women admiring the quilts dispersed, he had the crazy notion to check out the bids. Then he shook his head. What would happen if he found out, anyway? What would he do if she didn't have the winning bid?

How would Hannah Lynne feel if they didn't call her name?

He paused, scratching his forehead again. Why was he overly concerned about this, when he should have been paying attention to the auction? That was his primary reason for coming. He turned his back on the quilts and went to the crowd that had gathered in front of the auctioneer's platform. Right now a young Amishman, who couldn't be more than sixteen or so, was auctioning off one of the wringer washers. He was doing a fine job of it too.

Ezra was thinking earlier that he could use a wringer washer in his new house. He should bid on it.

Instead he turned away from the auctioneer and the men helping him keep track of the bids and scanned the crowd again. Where was Hannah Lynne? Why hadn't she stayed around to see if she had the winning bid? He walked back to the quilts and saw that the papers with the bids had been removed. The winner was already decided. He frowned. Later he could try to figure out why he cared so much, but right now he needed to find her.

Because for some strange reason, he knew he had to be with her when the winner of that quilt was announced.

. . .

Hannah Lynne paced outside the entryway of the Middlefield Market building. She hugged her arms as the cool night air enveloped her. All around she could hear the sounds of the auction—the late Yankee arrivals pulling their cars into the huge gravel parking lot, the faint whinnies of buggy horses as they waited for their owners to return, the rapid fire of the auctioneer's voice as he auctioned off the latest items. In years past she'd been in the thick of the auction, visiting with friends, munching on sweet, sticky glazed donuts, and enjoying the bidding.

But that was before she saw the quilt. Now her nerves were tightly wound, coiled, and ready to spring at any moment. She had to win that quilt. She felt so rattled she hadn't been able to stick around to see if anyone else had bid on it. She stopped her pacing and for the tenth time closed her eyes and prayed. *Please, Lord. I bid every cent I could spare. Please let that be enough. In fact, weren't you the one who prompted me to bring more money with me than I normally do?*

"There you are."

Her body jerked at the unexpected sound. Her eyes flew open and she saw Ezra standing in front of her, barely inches away. She lifted her head to meet his gaze. He was a half foot taller than she was, so she had to crane her neck to look into his eyes, something she didn't mind. But for some reason her brain wasn't registering that Ezra Yutzy was not only standing in front of her, he was speaking to her. All she could think about was the quilt.

"I was looking for you," he said.

Her eyebrows pushed together. "You were?" she asked absently. "Why?"

"Because . . ." He shifted on his feet, not looking at her. "Well, I, uh . . ."

The fog cleared from Hannah Lynne's mind and it finally sank in how close he was to her. Not to mention he had been *looking* for her. That was a first. But why was he backing away?

"Is something wrong?" she asked, still looking up at him. Once again, she felt the zing of attraction that happened whenever he was around. Great. So much for her plan to move on. How could she do that when her heart wouldn't cooperate?

"*Nee . . . nix* is wrong." But he kept moving farther away from her, as if she had some sort of contagious illness. "It's just . . ."

"This conversation is turning weird," she said. For once she didn't have time to moon over Ezra. She was sure they would be announcing the winner of the quilt and she wanted to be there. "I have to *geh*."

She pulled her gaze away from his and started to go inside the building, fully expecting to leave him behind.

To her surprise, he did the exact opposite and fell in step beside her. She glanced up at him, trying to read his expression, but his handsome face revealed nothing.

When they entered the building, a bulky, broad man wearing a Cleveland Browns baseball cap bumped into her. "Excuse me," he said as he brushed past, but he'd caught her off guard and she lost her balance. Before she could stop herself, she was leaning against Ezra.

His hand cupped her elbow. It felt warm. Strong. She looked up at him at the same moment he abruptly released her. "Sorry," he mumbled.

"It's okay." But it wasn't. None of this was. She should be ecstatic that Ezra was by her side. That he'd touched her, even if it was accidental. Instead everything felt wrong, like he was in her presence out of some unknown sense of obligation.

She forged ahead, hoping he wouldn't follow. She grimaced when he did. She stood in front of the quilt. The bidding had closed, and the paper with the bids on it was gone. Part of her was relieved she didn't know right away who won the quilt. She still had a little while to pray that hers was the winning bid.

Ezra stood beside her, but didn't say a word. He was ignoring the rest of the auction to stay with her, which didn't make any sense. Finally unable to take the awkwardness stretching between them, she turned to him. "What's going on, Ezra?"

"*Nix.*" He shrugged, giving her a lopsided smile that under normal circumstances would have had her toes curling, but instead set her more off balance than she'd been after the Yankee man had bumped into her. "I want to see how the quilt auction turns out."

"Really," she said, arching one eyebrow in doubt. She crossed her arms over her chest. "Any particular reason why?"

"Nope." He stared at the quilt and shoved his hands into his jacket pockets.

She gave a skeptical glance at his handsome profile. Was there possibly a man more perfect than him? He even smelled good, like soap and lightly scented shaving cream. Suddenly her eyes widened as she realized her wish was coming true—Ezra had finally noticed her. Sort of. At least he was standing near her. If she reached her hand out a few inches, she could graze his fingers with hers.

She didn't dare, partly because she wasn't that bold, but mostly because he would probably think she'd lost her mind. She curled her fingers into fists and kept her arms tight across her chest.

For the next ten minutes they stood side by side, neither of them moving, neither of them saying anything. But Hannah Lynne's annoyance grew. Did he somehow find out how she felt about him? Was he teasing her by standing beside her and being silent? If so, it was the weirdest teasing she'd ever experienced. Why wasn't he bidding on the main auction items? Surely he wasn't here because he wanted the quilt.

Or did he? She could see he kept staring at the quilt, except for the few times he glanced at the auctioneer's stand to see what new item was being auctioned off. Otherwise, he seemed highly focused on the quilt.

She didn't see his name on the bidding paper when she had written her bid. What if he bid on the quilt after she did? That didn't explain why he sought her out, but at that point she didn't care. If he placed a bid after she did . . . A tiny knot formed in her stomach.

"Why do you want the quilt?" she asked, sounding sharper than she meant to.

His head snapped toward her. "What?"

She pointed at what she hoped would be her quilt . . . although that hope was disappearing quickly. "There are six other beautiful quilts here. Why do you want *that* one?"

"I—wait, you don't understand—"

Alma Yoder, one of the women helping Sarah with the auction, came up beside them. "We're ready to announce who won this lovely quilt," she said, grinning. She took down the quilt, and Hannah Lynne watched as she folded it, then walked back to Sarah and two other women standing nearby.

Hannah Lynne chewed on her bottom lip, forgetting about Ezra. She prayed again that she would win. She had to. The moment she saw the quilt, touched the soft, well-worn fabric, she knew it was meant to be hers. The resemblance was too close for it not to be. She watched as Alma took the name of the winner to the auctioneer stand.

Hannah Lynne followed Alma's every move as she hung up the quilt in front. One of the Yankee men who owned the auction business held the microphone, giving some of the Amish auctioneers a break. Alma handed him the paper.

"We have the first winner from our quilt auction. This is for the blue and white—"

"And yellow," Hannah Lynne whispered.

"—quilt hanging on the line to my right." He pushed up his small, square glasses, which had been resting on the end of his nose. "The winner is . . ."

# CHAPTER 4

Ezra's palms were damp as the auctioneer took the paper from Alma. He glanced at Hannah Lynne and saw her top teeth pressed against her bottom lip. Her *pretty* bottom lip.

He yanked away his gaze and slid his palms against his pants. What was wrong with him tonight? He'd never been this off-kilter.

"The winner is . . ." the auctioneer said into the microphone.

He looked at Hannah Lynne again. She seemed to be holding her breath. Then he realized he was too.

". . . Sarah Detweiler!"

His heart dropped at the announcement. But that was nothing compared to the disappointment he saw on Hannah Lynne's face. She pressed her lips together and turned around. He followed her gaze to see Sarah smiling, happy that she now owned the quilt.

"*Nee,*" Hannah Lynne whispered.

Ezra had the urge to put his arm around Hannah Lynne and draw her close. His arm was actually itching to do it. He watched, helpless, as she gave the quilt one last long look, pasted a smile on her face, and walked away.

He had to do something. His gaze followed her as she headed for the exit. She was leaving without her beloved quilt. Although he had no idea why she wanted it so much, that wasn't the point. She was unhappy. More like devastated. He couldn't stand to see her like that.

He shoved his hands in his jacket pockets as he tried to think of something he could do to cheer her up. Then his fingers grazed the top of his wallet. He remembered the extra cash he'd brought with him. Without hesitating he went to Sarah, who had just received the quilt and was commenting to Alma about the precise stitching.

"Sarah," he said, surprised at the desperation in his voice. "Can I talk to you for a minute?"

She nodded and Alma stepped away. Sarah draped the folded quilt over one arm and looked up at him.

"How much did you pay for the quilt?" At her stunned expression he added, "If you don't mind me asking." He looked around, trying to catch a glimpse of Hannah Lynne. He didn't see her.

"Sure."

When she told him the amount his eyebrows lifted. "Wow," he said. "That much?"

"*Ya*. And *mei* bid was only two dollars more than the second highest one. A lot of people wanted that quilt. I also wanted to make a *gut* donation to the clinic so I didn't mind paying that amount. It's a wonderful quilt, so *schee*. Perfectly stitched. One of the finest I've ever seen. I'm surprised *yer mamm* was willing to part with it."

Ezra nodded as Sarah spoke, but he barely heard what she was saying since he was mentally counting the money in his wallet. He pulled the brown leather billfold out of his pocket and asked, "Can I buy it from you?"

Sarah's brow wrinkled above her plain, silver-rimmed glasses. "You want to buy back *yer mamm's* quilt? I can return it to her if she changed her mind."

"She didn't change her mind." He took in a breath. "I can't really explain the reason I need to buy it from you . . . I just do. I can pay you almost twice as much as you bought it for."

Her eyes widened. "What? No. That's too much."

He opened his wallet and pulled out all the money he had. "Here," he said, thrusting it into Sarah's free hand. "Is this enough to double what you bid?"

"Ezra, I said I'd give it to you—"

"I don't want the clinic to miss out on a donation, and you shouldn't have to make one if you aren't going to get the quilt. You can give half of this to the clinic and keep the other half to buy a quilt." He glanced at the quilt in her hand, then at her again. "Please?"

Sarah nodded, taking the money from his hand and giving him the quilt. Before she could say anything, he left, taking off in the direction he'd seen Hannah Lynne go.

. . .

Hannah Lynne kept her head down as she walked out of the market building, not wanting anyone to see the disappointment she couldn't keep off her face. She'd been so sure she would win the quilt. She was willing to pay almost three months of her butter money to own it, and it would have been worth every penny.

She stopped halfway to the part of the lot where the buggies were parked and took a deep breath. She knew her mourning was misplaced. She'd had an opportunity to own a link to the past, but it had gone to someone else, which meant it wasn't God's will that she have the quilt. And here she was, pouting about it, instead of going back inside and using her butter money to bid on something else. In the end, all the money went to a great cause. Wasn't that the important thing?

Hannah Lynne sighed. Acknowledging the truth didn't make her disappointment any less real. She swallowed it, choking down the bitter emotion. She couldn't leave. There were other items to bid on, and if she didn't win any of those she would donate her money. Reminding herself of the real reason she was here, she turned around—and smacked right into a solid, warm chest.

"Oof," Ezra said, taking a step back, his jacket open, exposing one of the shirts she liked best.

Mortified, Hannah Lynne looked up at him. "I'm sorry. I didn't realize you were behind me." She averted her gaze, trying to avoid looking at his blue-gray eyes, or his strong chin, or anything else she found appealing—which was basically all of him.

"*Nee.* I should be the one to apologize. I kinda snuck up on you."

She nodded, then tried to make her way past him to

the market building. Idly, she realized they had spent practically the last half hour together but had said next to nothing to each other. Which was nothing new. He couldn't have made it any plainer that he wasn't interested in her, not even enough to hold a decent conversation. Her eyes suddenly burned. The evening, which she had looked forward to earlier, was turning into an emotional disaster.

She took another step forward, only to be stopped.

"Hannah Lynne?"

She glanced at his hand resting on the fabric of her navy blue sweater, so large it looked like he could encircle her arm with his long fingers. Then she noticed he was holding something in his other hand. The quilt. She spun around. "What are you doing with that?"

"I . . . uh . . ."

"I thought Sarah had won it."

"She did."

"Then why do you have it?"

"Because . . . I bought it from her."

So she was right. He had wanted the quilt. Which was strange. His reason wasn't any of her business, but she couldn't deny a tiny bit of irritation at seeing him owning what she had wanted. Nor could she push away the idea that he was going to give it to someone. That was the only explanation that made sense. Ezra wouldn't buy a quilt for himself. But he would buy one to give as a gift.

The perfect gift for a serious girlfriend . . . or a future wife.

Ezra's staunch bachelor status was no secret, but

perhaps he did have a girlfriend, or even a fiancée. It wasn't uncommon for relationships to be private until a few weeks before the wedding. Although she'd vowed to release him from her heart, thinking of him getting married made her chest tighten.

"Congratulations," she said dully, unable to think of anything else to say. She started to leave again.

This time his hand squeezed her arm. A soft, gentle squeeze that sent shivers down to the tips of her fingers.

He dropped his hand and cleared his throat. "Here," he said, thrusting the quilt at her.

"What?" She stared at his outstretched hand.

"This is for you."

Puzzled, she looked up at him and blinked. "I don't understand."

He took her hand, gently stretched out her forearm, and draped the quilt over it. "It's *yers* now."

Hannah Lynne gaped at the quilt. She couldn't believe what was happening. He had bought the quilt for her? Images flew through her head—all the times he'd stopped by her table to buy her butter, how he had sought her out earlier, the long minutes he'd stood by her side, waiting for the winner to be announced. Her pulse thrummed. Did she dare believe he had feelings for her?

She looked up at him and saw his perfect mouth curved into an engaging smile that reached right to her heart. She was powerless to not smile in return, and when she did, his grin grew wider, lifting the dark freckle on the top of his cheek.

Warmth, along with a sensation she'd never felt

before, flooded her body. She did the only thing she could do—she threw her arms around his narrow waist and hugged him tight, resting her cheek on his chest, the quilt snug between her arm and his side. She could hear his heartbeat through his shirt, against her ear. She paused, enjoying his nearness, listening to his steady pulse.

She was so wrapped up in surprise and happiness that it took her a moment to realize his arms were still at his sides. *Oh, nee.* She jerked back, looked up, and felt her heart sink to her knees at the bewildered expression on his face.

"I'm—" The apology stuck in her throat, as if it were coated with a gallon of peanut butter. She stepped back, her face flaming, moving the quilt to her hands. Whatever his intention was in giving it to her, it definitely wasn't romantic.

He coughed into his fist.

She wanted to sink into the gravel parking lot. She had made a huge, embarrassing mistake, one that didn't help clear up the confusion whirling in her mind. She brought the quilt to her chest, wishing she could bury her humiliation in the cozy fabric. "*Danki,*" she said. But the word was lost as a car whizzed by Navoo Road and honked its horn.

He nodded. Shifted on his feet. Then turned to go.

"Ezra," she said suddenly, unable to let him leave until she had some answers. "Why did you give me this?"

"I saw how much you liked it." He shrugged, sticking his hands in his jacket pockets.

"That's it?"

"*Ya.* That's it."

"Then I have to pay you for it." She slipped the quilt onto one arm, opened her purse, then realized she didn't know how much she needed.

He shook his head. "You don't have to pay me back—"

"I do." She fumbled for the money out of her wallet. "How much did you pay for it?"

"Hannah Lynne—"

"How much?" Her voice was too loud and too shrill, but she couldn't help it. She'd embarrassed herself already tonight. What was a little more mortification? Besides, she wasn't going to be beholden to him.

He paused. Then told her the amount the quilt had sold for.

She tried to hide her shock as she pulled out every last dollar she'd brought to the auction. "I know it's not enough . . ." Her mind whirred with ideas for making more money—doubling her butter production and sales and . . . and . . . She scowled. Other than getting a job, she didn't know how else to make up the rest. A thought came to her. "*Yer haus.*"

"What?" he asked, sounding dumbfounded.

"I can help you with *yer haus*. Make curtains, clean the kitchen, scrub the floors—"

"Stop." He took a step forward and bent down so their eyes were on an even level. "Please . . . stop."

# CHAPTER 5

Ezra straightened, thankful Hannah Lynne had heeded his plea and stopped talking. He rubbed the back of his neck with one hand. Now what was he supposed to do? When he'd given her the quilt, she did what he expected her to do—light up like a Yankee Christmas tree. But then she stunned him into near paralysis when she hugged him. That was something he hadn't expected, or been prepared for. Feeling her arms around his waist, her cheek against his chest . . . his heart rate had suddenly had a mind of its own and started to race.

He couldn't have moved even if he had wanted to. Not that he'd wanted to, which gave him a moment's pause. Her warmth, combined with the prettiest smile he'd ever seen in his life, had shocked him. When she pulled away . . . he'd wanted to kick himself.

Not only had the smile disappeared, but disappointment had crept into her eyes, their true color washed away by the fluorescent lights in the parking lot. A soft, rich brown, fringed by long, thick eyelashes. The sparkle he'd seen in them a moment ago had dimmed—and he would do anything to bring it back.

She offered him money, which was bad enough. Now she was naming off chores she could do for him, as if she were his indentured servant. He'd given her the quilt to make her happy, not because he expected anything in return.

And that's where he'd made his mistake. Gifts always had strings attached, and in his haste he hadn't thought about the ones connected to this quilt.

"You don't have to help me with *mei haus*," he said, keeping his voice steady—a major challenge considering that for some bizarre reason his vocal cords were unstable. "You don't have to give me money, either."

"Then I can't take the quilt." She pushed it at him, shoving it against his chest with so much force he had to take a step back to regain his balance. "I appreciate the thought but . . ." She backed away. "I can't accept it."

Ezra glanced at the quilt. He'd just spent a huge amount of money—well-spent money, but a lot of money—for a quilt that up until recently had belonged to his mother. He didn't ponder the irony of that for very long, because all he could think about was Hannah Lynne's face. She'd gone from happy to disappointed in a split second, even though she was doing a good job of hiding how she felt.

Although he couldn't explain why, he wanted to see her happy. He needed to see her smile again.

"Okay," he said, taking a tentative step forward. "I could use some curtains in the *haus*. And the kitchen counters need a *gut* wiping." But she was not, under any circumstances, going to scrub his floors.

"I can also make you some more butter—"

"*Nee!*" he blurted, thinking of all the butter in his mother's freezer. "I mean, I think this is a *gut* arrangement." He handed her the quilt.

There was barely a hint of a smile on her lips when she took the quilt from him. Small, but he would take it. He relaxed a bit.

"I can come over tomorrow morning," she said. "Since it's Saturday."

"All right."

She told him the time she'd be there, and he made a mental note of it. Truthfully, he still wasn't comfortable with this. But he didn't want her giving the quilt back, so he nodded his agreement. "See you then," he said, ready to leave. *Very ready to leave.*

Hannah Lynne grabbed his hand and put the cash in his palm. Then she folded his fingers over it. "Don't forget this."

He looked down at her fingers touching his. He'd never noticed how small her hands were, or that she had such delicate fingers. He felt a whisper of air whoosh across his skin as she pulled away.

Ezra watched as she walked back to the market building. He waited until she was inside before he turned on his heel, crushing the gravel as he went to his buggy. He drove home in a daze, still trying to process what had happened tonight. Good thing his horse knew the way home.

Rather than spending the night at his parents' house, he had planned to sleep at his own place, getting up early in the morning to work on some roof repairs. His father had been kind enough to give him the day off from work. As he pulled into the driveway and looked at the dilapidated house, he felt a bit of embarrassment. The place was a mess, and tomorrow morning Hannah Lynne would see exactly how bad it was.

He parked his buggy, led his horse to the barn and settled him down for the night, then went inside the house. He climbed the stairs to his bedroom, not bothering to turn on a lamp. When he started to take off his jacket, he remembered the money she'd given him, pulled it out of his pocket, and put it in the top drawer of his dresser. Later he'd give it as another donation. Keeping it didn't feel right.

· · ·

The next morning, Hannah Lynne turned her buggy into Ezra's driveway. She was more than fifteen minutes early, but she couldn't stand pacing in her bedroom another minute. Her palms were slick as she held the reins and pulled her horse to a stop.

She studied Ezra's house. She'd seen it before. It was a nice size and had a lot of potential. She could see why he bought it. What she couldn't see was her being inside it. Yet here she was, cleaning supplies in a bucket on the bench seat next to her, a tape measure in her purse, and a sandwich and an apple in a plain paper bag for her lunch later.

At least when she'd told her parents she would be gone all day helping a friend clean, they hadn't asked any questions.

If there had been any other way to pay him for the

quilt, she would have. Her impulsively hugging him had weighed on her mind last night, especially as she carefully folded the quilt and put it on the top shelf of her closet. She wanted to avoid him for the rest of her life. The embarrassment was still fresh in her mind.

But the best way to get it out of her mind was to work, so she tethered her horse, grabbed her lunch and the bucket, and strode to the front door. She knocked on it. Once. Twice. When he didn't answer she turned the knob, surprised to find it completely turned and clicked.

"Hello?" she said, slowly opening the door and stepping inside. She immediately tripped on a loose board and fell forward, landing on her knees. "Ow!"

"Hannah Lynne?"

She heard thundering footsteps above her as she pushed herself to her feet. Ezra was scrambling down the stairs and at her side by the time she was upright.

"Are you all right?"

"*Ya*," she said, spying the apple rolling on the floor toward the back of the room.

He glanced behind him. "Floor is warped." Then he looked down. "And there are a few loose boards."

"I found out the hard way."

"I'm sorry."

She looked up at him as he shoved his huge hand through his thick hair. His chin was damp, as if he'd freshly shaved. Then she saw that his short-sleeved, light-yellow shirt wasn't tucked into the waist of his broadfall pants. It was also sitting a little crooked on his shoulders, as if he'd just thrown it on.

"I got here a little early—"

"I'm running a little late—"

They both stopped talking. She tore her gaze from him and looked at her palms. They were red, but the skin was intact.

"I'll get that board fixed soon," he said, sounding a little sheepish. "I never use the front door, so I haven't worried about it. I guess I should keep it locked too."

That was the most she'd heard him speak, at least directly to her. She waved her hand and retrieved her apple. "It's fine. I should watch where I'm going." She picked up the apple, rubbed it on her dress, and held it up. "See? No harm done." She noticed his gaze wasn't on the apple. It was centered on her. But she knew better than to read anything but concern into Ezra's look. She'd learned that lesson the hard way too.

"*Gut.*" He nodded. "I wouldn't want you to get hurt."

Her heart sighed. This was one of many reasons why she'd fallen for Ezra. He was *nice*. Very nice. And even though he didn't have any romantic feelings for her, he wouldn't suddenly change his personality and become rude. That wasn't in him.

"I'd cook up some breakfast, but the stove's out of commission," he said, stepping across another askew floorboard. He was barefoot, and she was certain now that she had caught him in the middle of getting dressed, a visual she definitely couldn't think about.

"I already ate." She picked up her bucket and forced her thoughts on the reason she was here. "And I'm ready to work. Just point me in the right direction." She even managed a smile. Maybe the fall had knocked the tension out of her, but she suddenly didn't feel nervous around him. Or awkward. It was nice to be in the same room with Ezra Yutzy and feel . . . normal.

Well, not exactly normal. But at least calm enough to appear that way.

"The kitchen?" he said, sounding unsure. He was gesturing with one lanky arm to an adjoining room.

She followed, aware that he was right behind her. When she entered the kitchen her jaw dropped.

The place was a mess. Electrical wiring was scattered on the floor, not connected to anything. Dust covered the countertops. The bare kitchen window was coated with a thin film of dirt and grease. But none of that caught her attention as much as the huge jagged hole in the drywall above the stove. "What happened there?"

He moved to stand beside her. "The hole came with the house. That hole and that one." He pointed to another hole in the wall on the opposite side of the kitchen. "There are several of them all through the place. Along with some graffiti." He let out a disgusted sigh. "I think there were squatters here at one point. The house has been stripped of copper."

"Is that bad?"

"It's stealing, that's for sure. I have to replace a lot of it for the plumbing." He went to the sink and opened up the cabinet doors underneath. "I can show you what I need to replace—" Suddenly he slammed the doors shut.

"What's wrong?" she asked.

"*Nix.*" He stood in front of the cabinet and forced a smile.

"You look like you're hiding something."

He shook his head. "Nope. Not me."

But he had a nervous lilt to his voice. There was something under that sink. Now she was curious. Very curious. She went to him and tried to sneak around. "Let me see."

He shook his head and blocked her way. "*Nee.*" But his tone had changed, from unnerved to teasing. "*Nix* to see here."

"I don't believe you." She looked up at him and smiled. "You're not a *gut* liar."

His lips parted, as if he was about to say something. Yet he didn't move. Just stared at her.

A familiar pleasant shiver went through her as their eyes held. Then her mouth twisted into a grimace. Just when being around him was feeling natural, she had to read something else into his look. She backed away. "Okay. I won't look under the sink."

"You promise?" He wasn't looking at her, his gaze strangely averted. But his question held complete seriousness.

"I promise."

He nodded. "Uh, after I finish . . . upstairs, I'll be on the roof if you need me. There are a few leaks that have to be fixed. I'll just go out the front door and then around to the barn to get *mei* ladder and tools. I don't want to get in *yer* way." He flicked a quick glance at her, then hurried out of the room. She could hear loud creaks as Ezra climbed barefooted up the stairs.

Hannah Lynne sighed and went to her bucket of supplies. There was so much to do in the kitchen she didn't know where to start. As she thought a few minutes about the best plan of attack, her gaze kept dropping to the cabinet under the sink. *Hmm.* It would be impossible to work, knowing Ezra was hiding something in there. But she'd promised she wouldn't look.

Such a dilemma. She inched toward the sink, curiosity overriding her promise. She'd apologize to him later. Besides, what could possibly be under this filthy sink that he wouldn't want her to see?

Hannah Lynne crouched down and opened the cabinet doors.

• • •

Ezra had barely finished dressing when he heard Hannah Lynne scream. He groaned. He should have checked under the sink before she arrived that morning. Better yet, she should have kept her promise. He headed down the stairs for the kitchen, steeling himself for what he knew was coming next: hysteria.

When he walked in she jumped in front of him. "Gotcha!"

He jerked back in surprise. "What?"

"Is this what you didn't want me to see?" She held her bucket in front of him, letting the handle swing back and forth in her grip.

He looked down. There it was, a dead mouse the size of a small rat. And here was Hannah Lynne laughing with glee as she dangled it in front of him.

"I'm not afraid of mice. Or rats. Or snakes." She grinned.

"*Mei mamm*'s terrified of them."

"So is mine." She leaned forward. "And *mei daed*," she said in a loud whisper. "But he'll never admit it." She looked up at him, still smiling. "I'm the resident rodent wrangler at *mei haus*. I was even before *mei bruders* moved out."

"Really?" He found himself grinning right back at her.

"*Ya*. Don't get me wrong, I don't love them. But I'm not afraid." She fluttered her eyes with exaggeration. "I don't need a big, strong *mann* to take care of them for me."

He leaned against the doorframe, enjoying the teasing. "Is that so?"

"*Ya*." She tilted up her chin, which was already lifted due to her having to look up at him. "You don't have to protect me."

Her words unearthed an unexpected emotion inside him. No, Hannah Lynne didn't need protecting. She was independent. He'd seen enough of that through casual observation. The fact that she could handle vermin without flinching shouldn't have surprised him. But what did was the sudden feeling that while Hannah Lynne Beiler didn't need protecting, if she ever did, he wanted to be the one to protect her.

The feeling knocked him off-kilter, and his shoulder slid against the doorjamb.

"Where should I dispose of the dearly departed?" she asked.

"The woods," he said, glad she didn't notice his fumbling. "Out back." He'd offer to do it for her, but he knew she'd refuse. Instead, he walked across the kitchen floor and opened the back door for her.

With a quick nod she scooted past him, her shoulder touching his bare forearm. He glanced down. The hairs were actually standing on end from the fleeting, light touch.

What was going on here? He was confused, but his confusion wasn't disturbing. It was . . . pleasant. He liked the teasing lilt of her voice when she spoke to him, the way she'd batted her eyes, pretending to be helpless. He enjoyed the flirting—

*Flirting?* Was that what was going on? Then he shook his head. Why would Hannah Lynne flirt with him? She was interested in Josiah. Plus she'd never shown any interest in him.

No, she was being nice. Funny. She had a good sense of humor. That didn't translate to flirting. He knew better than that. Putting the notion out of his mind, he left the kitchen and headed out the front door to repair the roof.

# CHAPTER 6

By lunchtime, Hannah Lynne had made some head-way in cleaning the countertops and cabinets, including the one under the sink. Fortunately she'd only found one more rodent, one that had been dead for a while. She quickly disposed of it, chuckling over Ezra's assuming she'd be afraid of a harmless mouse. Well, not harmless, as they could do plenty of damage if not taken care of in a swift manner. They were also a health hazard. But vermin weren't the only health hazard in this house.

She stood and arched her back. Sunbeams tried to penetrate the thick film of grease and dirt coating the window above the sink. She'd tackle that after lunch. Right now her stomach growled, and she went upstairs to wash her hands. At least that plumbing worked. She also refilled her bucket and then went downstairs to retrieve her sandwich and apple, setting the bucket on the floor.

As she pulled her wrapped sandwich out of the paper bag she'd put on one of the counters, Ezra walked into the kitchen. He'd been stomping around on the roof all morning. His shirt and pants were dirty, but his hands were clean. She noticed this as he put them on his trim waist and looked around the kitchen. *There must be a working pump outside.*

"Wow," he said, nodding his approval. "You've done a lot in here."

Hannah Lynne followed his gaze. She had worked all morning, but it suddenly seemed like she hadn't accomplished as much as he was giving her credit for. There was too much work to do in a day. Or a week, or a month, even. "Not as much as I wanted," she mumbled.

"I know what you mean." He blew out a breath. "It's going to take a long time to get this place livable." Then he shrugged. "It's all right, though. I'm not in any big hurry."

Which probably meant he didn't have a secret girlfriend in his life. If he did, he would want to get the house ready for the two of them as soon as possible. She started to smile, then realized that little tidbit of information didn't matter. Even if he didn't have someone now, someday he would find a girlfriend . . . and a wife. She was coming to understand it wouldn't be her.

However, that didn't mean she couldn't enjoy his company, which she definitely did.

"I watered *yer* horse," Ezra said as she unwrapped her sandwich.

She turned to him and smiled. "*Danki.*" Nice and thoughtful. *He's perfect.* She stifled a sigh so she wouldn't sound like a thirteen-year-old girl mooning over her latest crush—which was exactly what she was doing, minus the thirteen-year-old part.

"What's his name?" he asked.

"George Washington Junior."

His brow lifted. "Seriously?"

She nodded. "But we call him Junior."

"Okay, I'll bite." He moved closer to her. "Why did you name him after a president?"

"When I was six *mei mamm* took me to the library. We would *geh* there all the time, and one February they had a display for President's Day. There was a children's book with a young boy and a cherry tree on the cover. It was George's biography, and I read that book at least five times before *Mamm* returned it." She looked up at him. "I have *nee* idea why I was so fascinated. Neither does *Mamm*. About a month later *mei daed* bought George and said I could name him. So I did."

"And *yer daed* was okay with the name?"

"He said it was a mouthful, but kept it. He was right about it being too long, though, so I shortened it to Junior about a year later."

"Why not just George?"

"I don't know. I guess I like Junior better." She was about to bow her head to pray before eating, but she realized something was wrong. "Where's *yer* lunch?"

He took off his hat and set it on the counter. His hair was slightly molded to his head, and she wanted to reach up and fluff it out for him.

"I knew I forgot something," he said. "That's all right. I'll eat later."

"You can't *geh* the rest of the afternoon without lunch."

"Sure I can."

She carefully split her sandwich in half and offered

it to him. It was a bit messy, with peanut butter and gooseberry jam dangling over the sides. "Here."

He shook his head. "That's *yer* lunch."

"This is *mei* lunch." She held up one half. "This is *yers*." She pushed it toward him again.

He eyed it dubiously, and she couldn't blame him. It didn't look like the most appetizing sandwich. Finally, he accepted it. "Hang on," he said, dashing out of the room. She heard his footsteps upstairs, then after a few minutes he was back in the kitchen. "Here," he said, handing her a can of pop. "I have these stashed up in *mei* room."

She accepted it, grateful since she had also forgotten something—a beverage. They both paused, eyes closed, and prayed before eating.

He leaned his upper thigh against the countertop, his hip rising just above it. His legs were so long they seemed almost endless. "I can't remember the last time I had peanut butter and jelly."

"I have it all the time." She took a swig of pop. "Peanut butter is *mei* favorite. I'm not real picky about what flavor of jelly."

Since it didn't take long to eat half a sandwich, they both finished quickly. After taking a long drink of his pop, Ezra looked at her. "I'm curious about something."

"What?"

"Those sayings on the butter wrappers. What made you come up with that idea?"

Hannah Lynne lifted her shoulders, trying not to show her delight that he noticed her effort. "I thought it would be a nice little extra for *mei* customers. The regulars seem to appreciate it."

He nodded, but didn't say anything else. She looked at the apple. There were no knives, or any other silverware, in the kitchen. Considering he was repairing the roof, he needed the nourishment more than she did. She handed him the apple, expecting him to refuse it. To her surprise, he didn't.

Even more to her surprise, he took a bite of the apple and handed it back to her, as if sharing the same piece of fruit was the most natural thing in the world. "Got to get back to work. I have a couple more holes to patch." He turned and walked out of the room.

She stared at the apple—more specifically, the bite he took out of the apple. He wasn't making it easy to forget her feelings about him.

• • •

Ezra hammered down a piece of flashing, squinting against the sunlight glinting off the metal strip. He was primarily a carpenter, but his father and grandfather had been able to do almost anything with their hands, from building houses to plumbing, and they'd handed those skills down to Ezra.

But his mind wasn't on the roof. Or even his house. As the sun shone brightly overhead and a chilly fall breeze whirled around him, the only thing on his mind was the pretty *maedel* in his kitchen. Pretty and quirky. Who knew she not only could handle mice, she also loved peanut butter. And George Washington. Not to mention her thoughtfulness toward the customers who bought her butter. He chuckled. Hannah Lynne was definitely an interesting girl, and unlike any other female he'd ever met.

He forced himself to focus on his task, because tumbling off the roof wasn't on his to-do list today. Once all the holes in the roof were repaired, he slid down the ladder and went back to the kitchen, wondering what Hannah Lynne had accomplished this afternoon.

Who was he kidding? He just wanted to see her again—closer than when he'd seen her get clean water from the pump in the backyard.

Ezra smiled as he quietly entered the room. Her back was to him as she scrubbed out the sink, the tie of her white apron drooping a bit at her waist. She wore a light blue dress, the hem brushing against the back of her calves, which were covered in black stockings. She wasn't a thin girl, but she also wasn't stout. More like curvy . . .

He yanked his gaze from her, heat rising from his neck to his face. What was he doing, staring at Hannah Lynne like that? Yet it took every bit of internal strength not to look at her again.

She turned and dipped a sponge into her water bucket, then squeezed it out and continued to scrub. She'd been working all day, and her efforts showed. The window above the sink gleamed. The cabinet doors were no longer covered in dust, and the light honey-stained wood shone. The countertops were warped and would need to be replaced, but that hadn't stopped her from tackling the dirt in the corners.

And she was doing all this for a quilt.

He wondered why the quilt was so important to her. His curiosity almost drove him to ask, but he pulled back. Her reason wasn't his business. Today she'd done enough work to pay for the rest of the quilt— which he still wished she would have freely accepted from him.

"Hannah Lynne," he said, surprised at the low, husky tone of his voice. He cleared his throat as she turned around.

"I'm almost done with the sink," she said, wiping the back of her hand across her forehead. "I thought I'd work on the floor next."

"*Nee,*" he said, going to her, recalling his vow that she wouldn't scrub his floors. "You've done enough today."

"But there's still plenty of daylight." She turned around and faced him, the back of her waist leaning against the sink. "And there's so much more to do—"

"For me to do, not you." He took the sponge from her hand. Then he reached around and squeezed it into the sink behind her. A thoughtless move, because if he had taken a moment to think before he acted he would have realized he would be very close to her. Close enough to hear her breathing, to see the sheen of perspiration on her forehead that she'd unsuccessfully tried to wipe off. He could smell her hair still tucked neatly under her *kapp*, the clean scent cutting through the mingling odors of cleaning products, dust, and stale air. If he leaned down he could easily touch his lips to hers . . . and found himself wanting to.

He dropped the sponge and took a step back, then several more as he scurried away from her.

"I'm going home," he said curtly. More curtly than he'd intended, but he couldn't help himself. He couldn't look at her for a moment, then finally got the guts to meet her eyes.

They were wide. Surprised. And so very, very beautiful.

"Okay," she said, sounding unsure. She turned to retrieve the sponge. "I'll dump the water outside—"

"I'll take care of it." He grabbed the bucket before she had a chance to, water sloshing on the sides and spattering his pants. But he didn't care. He had to get out of that room. He had to get away from her.

When he stepped outside the air cooled off his face, but not his emotions. At twenty-seven, he'd never dated anyone. He quit going to singings years ago because of the expectation to find someone. Not a single girl had caught his eye or captured his interest, not that way. That included Hannah Lynne.

Until now. Which didn't make sense. He'd seen her all the time. At church. At the market. She was as familiar a presence to him as anything else in his life. And when she wasn't around, he had never given her a second thought.

*And then I saw her looking at that quilt. Lord, what is happening here?*

He heard the back door open and he quickly tossed out the water. Hoping his face didn't look as hot as it felt, he turned and handed her the empty bucket.

"*Danki,*" she said, taking it from him. Her cheeks

were red, too, but that was to be expected, considering the amount of work she'd done in the kitchen. "I can come back next Saturday. I'll make sure to bring a broom. Plus I didn't get a chance to measure for the curtains."

"That's okay," he said, his words coming out in a rush. "You more than made up for the quilt."

She eyed him. "I don't think so. That quilt cost you a lot of money. More than a little scrubbing and rodent wrangling is worth."

"I said we're square."

His heart pinched at the flash of hurt in her eyes. Wow, could he have been any more surly? Yet the thought of her coming back, of them spending the day together even though they were both working, unnerved him.

Even worse, it confused him . . . because a huge part of him would like for them to work together again. *And again* . . .

But that wasn't fair to her. Or Josiah, who Ezra hoped realized what a lucky *mann* he was.

"Okay." She spoke the word in a low, almost imperceptible tone. "Junior and I will be on our way." Without saying anything else she walked over and untied her horse. Soon Hannah Lynne and the equine version of the country's first president were gone.

He went back into the house, the back door slamming behind him. He leaned his forehead against a dirty wall, trying to get a grip on his emotions. It was a long time before he could.

# CHAPTER 7

T hat evening after supper, Hannah Lynne sat on the edge of her bed and stared at the quilt still on the top shelf of her closet. She wanted to take it down, but she was afraid to. On the shelf it was safe. Nothing would happen to it there. It wouldn't be ruined.

Like her day with Ezra had been.

She didn't know how it happened. They were getting along so well. Lunch was *gut*, if not sparse, and he was in such good humor when he had last come into the kitchen. Then he had moved closer to her . . .

Her breath hitched at the memory of him standing inches from her. The scent of hard work and sunshine had permeated his clothes and skin, filling her senses. Nothing in her life had felt as right as being within inches of touching Ezra Yutzy, so close she thought she'd heard the rapid tempo of his pulse.

But that must have been her own racing heart she'd heard, because before she knew it he was practically on the other side of the room and couldn't wait to get rid of her. Had she done something wrong? Said something? Or maybe she'd let her true feelings slip out in a secret glance or quick draw of breath. Ezra wasn't stupid. And he wasn't interested in her. Why she couldn't get that to stick in her head, she didn't know.

She turned and flopped onto her bed, cupping her chin with her hands. What she did know is that she had to tell Josiah he couldn't take her home from the next singing after all. Being around Josiah didn't give her a fraction of the pleasant feelings she got from just looking at Ezra. She was hopeless, but she wasn't cruel, and stringing Josiah along was wrong.

Trying to get both men off her mind, she pulled out her book of inspirational quotes, searching to pick out a few for her next batch of butter wrappers. But the quotes reminded her of the conversation over lunch with Ezra, and she shut the book. Holding it against her chest, she closed her eyes and prayed.

*Lord, what am I supposed to do? I can't completely ignore him for the rest of* mei *life. How do you* un*love somebody?*

Because after spending the day with Ezra, she knew what she felt wasn't infatuation. It had to be love. If it wasn't she wouldn't feel this intensely. She wouldn't still remember the sting of his words. *I said we're square.* That was the same as saying he didn't want her help. Didn't want to be around her anymore.

Didn't want her.

She opened her eyes and sighed.

. . .

"Did you get a lot of work done on the *haus* today, *sohn*?"

Ezra looked up from his supper of meat loaf, gravy, mashed potatoes, and glazed carrots and nodded. "Got the holes patched in the roof."

"*Gut*." His father drank from his glass of water. "Do you need any more time off?"

Ezra pondered the question. He'd told Hannah Lynne he wasn't in a hurry to get his house finished. At the time he'd said the words, they were true. But suddenly an overwhelming urge to finish the place came over him. He didn't know where it came from. His parents had never said anything to make him feel like he needed to be out on his own. Living here was convenient for everyone—he was close to work, he helped his parents with the chores, he contributed to paying the living expenses, and in return he had a roof over his head and food in his belly. He'd been satisfied.

Now he felt dissatisfied. More than he'd ever been in his life.

"*Ya*," he said, swirling the potatoes around on his plate. "I could use a few more Saturdays off, if you can spare me." He turned to his mother. "As soon as I can get the plumbing going, I'll be moving out."

His mother set down her fork. "You will?"

Ezra nodded. "I know it seems sudden—"

"Not really," his father said dryly.

"—but I think it's time."

*Mamm* nodded slowly. "If you're sure. Just remember, you always have a place here."

"I know." He squeezed her hand. "I appreciate it."

They continued eating in silence for a few moments. Then *Mamm* said, "I talked to Sarah Detweiler today.

She said the auction was a huge success." She turned to Ezra. "She also told me how you paid her to get *Grossmutter*'s quilt back."

Ezra frowned. "Huh?"

"The quilt you gave Sarah for the auction." *Mamm* speared a shiny, sweet carrot slice with her fork. "That was *Grossmutter* Keim's quilt. Now, don't pretend you didn't overhear me telling *yer daed* that. If you hadn't, why would you have bought the quilt back for me?"

He stared at his mother. "Why didn't you say anything about this before?"

"I figured it was God's will that the quilt be in the auction. It's been packed in *mei* hope chest for years. On a whim I decided to get it out and clean it. But when I found out it was in the auction, I didn't want to pull it out. I was sure it would get higher bids than the quilt I had intended to donate. And I know *yer grossmutter* wouldn't have minded since the proceeds of the sale went to a *gut* cause."

He nodded. That's why he'd never seen it before. He smiled as he remembered his *Mamm*'s mother. She died when Ezra was ten, but they'd had a special bond. She'd make his favorite butter pecan cookies for him whenever he asked, and she called him by a special nickname. He never knew what it meant, but whenever she said the word it felt like he was wrapped up in a warm blanket on a freezing winter day. He still missed her.

"So where is the quilt?"

Ezra froze.

"I'd like to drape it over the back of the rocking chair. That's what I intended to do with it, but then you gave it to Sarah for the auction." She smiled at Ezra. "And that was fine. It's just nice to know it's now back in the *familye*."

His smile slipped from his face. His mother looked so happy, as happy as Hannah Lynne had been when he'd given her the quilt. His grandmother's quilt, now he knew. His mother should have said something. Then again, this was just like her, to assume God was in the details, including little—and big—misunderstandings.

"She only made that one quilt," his mother continued. "She started several others, but she never finished them."

The meat loaf in his stomach rebelled.

"Maybe because the first one she made was so beautifully done." His mother raised an eyebrow. "Or it was because she had twelve *kinner* and very little time for quilting."

"Why were you the one to get the quilt?" Ezra asked.

"I'm not sure. I know when she made it she said she wanted me to have it. I'm the oldest, so that makes sense. I should have taken it out years ago, but . . ."

Ezra saw her swallow, and he sank lower in the chair.

"I didn't want anything to happen to it." She brightened, a carrot still poised on her fork in midair. "Later on I realized that was silly. *Mutter* would have wanted me to enjoy the quilt, not keep it boxed up."

"It's at *mei haus*," Ezra blurted, causing even his father, who had checked out of the conversation at the mention of the word *quilt*, to give him a sidelong look. "I accidentally left it there." Great, now he was lying to his parents.

"Oh, *nee*." *Mamm* sighed. "I'll have to wash it again after it's been over there."

"*Nee* need," Ezra said, mustering a half-grin. "It's not dirty, I promise."

"*Gut.* Bring it as soon as you can." She smiled again, and her blue-gray eyes sparkled. "I guess the quilt was meant to stay in our *familye* after all."

He stared at his nearly empty plate, dazed. What was he going to do now? He had no choice—he had to get the quilt back from Hannah Lynne. Not only did it belong to his mother, it meant a lot to her. How could he tell *Mamm* Hannah Lynne not only had it but he'd sold it to her? Never mind he wasn't going to keep the money. It still sounded greedy. Heartless.

Thoughtless. He pinched the top of his nose.

"Ezra?" his mother said. "Do you have a headache?"

"*Ya*," he said, lying again. "Just came on."

She started to rise. "I'll fix you some peppermint tea. That will help."

He nodded, and she went to the stove to get the kettle. His mother had dozens of tea recipes, a variety of concoctions to cure almost any ailment. But tea wouldn't solve this dilemma. He'd made a mess. Now he had to clean it up.

He just hoped Hannah Lynne could forgive him.

• • •

Hannah Lynne had just dozed off when she heard a knock on her bedroom door. She hadn't meant to fall asleep so early, but she'd been so tired from the day's work, and from dealing with the turmoil in her heart, that once she'd laid down on her bed, she'd conked out. She was still wearing her dress and *kapp*, although she'd taken off her stockings and shoes. Rubbing her eyes, she got up off the bed and answered the door. "*Ya, Mamm?*" she said to her mother, her voice still thick with sleep.

"Were you expecting company tonight?"

Hannah Lynne shook her head. "*Nee.* Why?"

"Ezra Yutzy is here to see you. He's waiting downstairs."

Hannah Lynne gripped the door handle. She blinked, wondering for a moment if she were sleepwalking. "Ezra?"

"*Ya.*" Her mother took a step back. "He said it was important that he speak to you."

"Tell him I'll be right there." Hannah Lynne willed her pulse to slow. Ezra could be at her door for any number of reasons—she might have left something at his house, for example. Or maybe he wanted to apologize for being so short with her when she left. She could see him doing something thoughtful like that.

She smoothed out her dress, checked her *kapp* to make sure it was in place, and noticed that one thin lock of hair had escaped during her sleep. She should properly secure it, but that would mean undoing her *kapp* and redoing the bobby pins, and she didn't want to keep him waiting. She tucked the lock behind her ear, put on her stockings and shoes, and headed down the stairs.

When she reached the bottom step, she saw Ezra

standing in the living room, next to her father. Or rather towering over him. They were talking, probably about cows, since that's pretty much all her father ever liked to talk about. Ezra nodded and listened politely, but she could see the strain around his mouth. Uh-oh. That wasn't a good sign.

"Hi, Ezra," she said, walking toward him. She put her hands behind her back and forced an even tone. "What brings you by?"

"We'll be in the kitchen if you need anything," *Mamm* said, her announcement as subtle as a dog howling at the moon. She tugged on *Daed*'s shirt, and he followed.

When her parents were gone, she raised her chin to look up at Ezra. Now he looked almost sick, like his stomach was upset. Her awkwardness disappeared as concern took over. She stepped forward and placed her hand on his arm. "What's wrong? Is there something I can do?"

His Adam's apple bobbed up and down, but his gaze remained steadily on hers. "*Ya*. There is something you can do."

"Anything." She moved closer to him, all sorts of tragic scenarios going through her mind. He was in pain, and she wanted to take that from him. To hug him like she had in the parking lot at the Middlefield Market. A sweet man like Ezra didn't deserve to be hurt like this. She lowered her voice. "Tell me what you need."

"I need the quilt back."

# CHAPTER 8

Ezra stifled a groan at the shock on Hannah Lynne's face. "Excuse me?"

"I need the quilt back." Oh, this was painful. He dug into the pocket of his jacket for the money she'd given him at the auction. He'd stopped by his house to get it, and the musty smell of the rest of the house hadn't yet overwhelmed the clean scent coming from the kitchen. Which made him feel even more like a heel. How could he put a price on the work she'd done today?

*Dear Lord, how can I take the quilt from her?*

His fingers touched the bills in his pocket at the same moment he looked into her eyes. He stilled. Whatever spark had started between them earlier that day—or at least on his part—was not only still there, it seemed to grow, warming his belly and his heart. Her *kapp* was a little crooked, and a strand of hair was tucked behind her ear. She still smelled as wonderful as she had in his kitchen, and her skin took on a creamy tint in the low light of the gas lamps in the room. She was so beautiful he could hardly breathe.

Then she grimaced as he brought out the money.

When he held it out to her, Hannah Lynne's sweet face contorted into an angry expression he hadn't known she was capable of.

"I have to buy back the quilt," he said, holding out the money to her. "If you could get it for me—"

"Why?" She crossed her arms over her chest. "Why do you need the quilt?"

He pressed his lips together. Was it even possible to explain why? He wasn't sure he could, at least not in a way that made sense. He was standing there, holding out money that was really her money, to buy back a quilt that he'd bought for her that belonged to his mother and was made by his favorite grandmother. No matter how he looked at it, he was at fault. It was his dumb mistake.

One he didn't want to admit to Hannah Lynne.

"Does it matter why?" He thrust the money at her, more irritated with himself than with her. "I just need it back."

She looked at the money and shook her head. Her eyes narrowed. "You said we were square."

"Would you just take the money?"

"*Nee*! You want *mei* quilt."

"Technically it was *mei* quilt," he countered.

"That was before you gave it to me," she answered back hotly. "Remember? You didn't even want me to pay for it."

"That was before."

Her hands dropped to her sides as she took a step toward him. "Before what?"

Her voice was raised, and he matched his level to

hers. "Before . . . never mind." He bent over until their gazes were even. "Why do you want the quilt so badly? You never told me."

"You never asked."

"I'm asking now."

She paused, her eyes never leaving his. "It's none of *yer* business."

"So it's okay for me to tell you, but you not to tell me?"

"That doesn't make any sense!"

He tossed the money on the nearby coffee table and moved closer to her. "None of this makes any sense!" He was thoroughly angry right now, and he had no idea why. He couldn't take his eyes off her. The lock of hair had escaped from behind her ear and hung against her cheek. She blew at it from the corner of her mouth, but it fell right back in its original place, drawing his attention to her cheek, then to her mouth.

Ezra could feel his pulse pounding in his ears. He couldn't take this—whatever *this* was—anymore. So he did the only thing he knew to do—he grasped her by the shoulders and kissed her.

• • •

*Ezra is kissing me. Ezra Yutzy is kissing me . . .*

Those words were somewhere in the back of her mind, which wasn't working quite right as Ezra drew her against him and continued to kiss her. But just as soon as she started to kiss him back—at least she thought she was kissing him back, but she really didn't know since she'd never been kissed—he dropped his hands from her shoulders and pulled away.

She looked up at him, her eyes wide and her chest expanding further with each breath she took. How long had she wanted Ezra to notice her, to like her? She'd never even dreamed of kissing him. Well, at least not that often.

It was wonderful and confusing and—

"I'm sorry," he said.

*Hurtful.*

He moved away until his backside hit the door. He thrust it open and darted out of her house, as if his pants and hat were on fire. The screen door bounced shut behind him, and the cool night air flowed over her heated body.

She touched her fingers to her lips. He kissed her, and he regretted it.

"Hannah Lynne?"

She turned at the sound of her mother's voice. "*Ya,*" she ground out, her voice sounding like crushed gravel.

"*Yer daed* and I thought we heard yelling." She went to Hannah Lynne. "Are you okay?"

*Nee.* She was *not* okay. "*Ya.* We just had a disagreement. A friendly one." The smile she gave her mother was so tight she thought her skin would crack. "Because we're . . . friends."

Her mother nodded and returned the smile. "I didn't realize you and Ezra knew each other that well."

"We don't." She was realizing she didn't know him at all.

"*Yer vatter* and I are going to bed," *Mamm* said as *Daed* entered the room. He gave Hannah Lynne a tired wave and started climbing the stairs. "See you in the morning," *Mamm* added, then followed him.

Hannah Lynne stayed in place, her lips still tingling, the front door still open. The night air sifted through the mesh screen. She could hear the crickets and cicadas starting up their nightly melodies, punctuated by the intermittent sound of a hoot owl. She shivered, but still she didn't move.

Ezra had kissed her and she had no idea why. But despite being irritated with him—and now plainly angry—she wouldn't have traded those few seconds for anything.

She shivered again, and the chill brought her to her senses. She shut the front door and started for the stairs, noticing the money on the coffee table as she passed by. Terrific. Now she had to see him again. She couldn't keep both the money and the quilt—and she definitely was not parting with the quilt. She scooped up the bills and went to her room.

After she shut her bedroom door, she put the money on her dresser. She tucked the stray hair back over her ear and went to the closet. The kiss was forgotten for a moment as she looked at the quilt. Why would a *mann* want a quilt that much? *Why won't he tell me why?*

She reached up and retrieved the quilt, then unfolded it on her bed. She kneeled in front of it, her fingers grazing over the old, soft fabric with reverence. It wasn't the same quilt. She knew that. But it was close enough. Memories came back, along with tears as she remembered a time long in the past, when she was a child of seven. A bratty child her great aunt Edna was watching while her mother was in the hospital with an attack of appendicitis.

*Hannah Lynne was mad. She missed her mother, and Aenti Edna was mean. Her brothers didn't have to stay with Aenti, so why did she? She wanted to be home, to play in the barn and be around the cows. Not stuck inside while her aunt made her wash dishes. When Hannah Lynne had asked for macaroni and cheese for lunch, Aenti Edna made her eat liverwurst. Hannah Lynne hated liverwurst. When her aenti wasn't looking, Hannah Lynne had taken her glass of grape juice and poured it all over the pretty quilt on Aenti Edna's bed. That would show her.*

Hannah Lynne cringed, as she always did when she thought about that time. Her father had picked her up before her aunt had discovered the quilt. By then the grape juice had hours to seep through and stain the fabric. Which it did, ruining what Hannah Lynne later found out was an engagement gift to her aunt from her uncle, who had died in a farming accident two months earlier.

It didn't matter that Hannah Lynne was only seven when she ruined the quilt. Or that her aunt had forgiven her, and that she and Hannah Lynne had ended up very close up until her aunt's untimely death from ALS four years ago. Despite the ugly stains on the quilt, her aunt had still used it. She'd cuddled Hannah Lynne with it when she was ten and had a fever from the flu. She displayed it in the living room during the holidays, not caring that people saw the damage Hannah Lynne had caused. Whenever anyone asked what happened to the quilt, *Aenti* Edna shrugged it off, telling everyone that she wasn't as careful with it as she should have been. No one, including her mother, had known what Hannah Lynne had done. Her aunt and uncle had no children, and near the end of *Aenti*'s life, when she could still talk, she told Hannah Lynne that she had loved her like a daughter.

After *Aenti* Edna was buried, Hannah Lynne had gone with her mother to pack up the house. When Hannah Lynne couldn't find the quilt, her mother admitted they had hidden it in the casket. "It was her last request," her mother had said, tears glistening in her eyes. "That quilt was always her tangible connection to Abel. She wanted it with her when she was buried."

Hannah Lynne hadn't understood how an object could hold so much emotional value. Until she saw this quilt. Tears slipped down her cheeks as she picked up the quilt and wrapped it around her shoulders, the way *Aenti* Edna had done when she was a little girl. It was like her aunt was there, sitting next to her, ready to bring her chicken soup when Hannah Lynne felt well enough to eat.

How could she part with it? How could anything replace the feeling she had right now?

She glanced down at the quilt, looking at the binding. Her aunt's quilt hadn't been so finely stitched, but the pattern, small squares of quilted yellow-and-blue baskets on a white background, was similar. Her aunt's quilt had only been yellow and white. And purple, once Hannah Lynne had finished with it.

Guilt still nagged at her, not as strong or intense since it had faded with time and maturity. But she doubted she'd ever get over what she'd done. Just like she'd never stop missing *Aenti* Edna.

Running her finger down the edge of the quilt, she felt something irregular in the stitching. She paused, and peered at it. Sure enough, the stitching at the trim of this part of the quilt was different. She moved the area closer to her lamp so she could see more clearly. Even squinting, it was hard to make out what she thought were words. Two words. One she recognized immediately. She sucked in a breath.

*Ezra.*

The other one next to it she didn't know, even though she could make out the letters. *Amor.* Ezra Amor? That didn't make any sense. Amor wasn't an Amish last name, and Ezra was the only Ezra she knew in her district. Surely it wasn't a coincidence that he wanted a quilt that had his name stitched on it, the letters so tiny and perfect that she doubted she would have ever seen them if she hadn't felt them first.

Her shoulders slumped. How could she keep the quilt now? And why didn't he just tell her it really belonged to him? Somehow it ended up in the auction by mistake. It would be like Ezra not to pull it from the auction, but to pay for it so the special needs clinic would still get the money.

Then why would he turn around and give it to her? None of this made sense. It was too late to talk to him now. She'd have to see him tomorrow. But church wasn't the right place to talk, and she was sure he would avoid her anyway. Besides, she had to tell Josiah her plans to spend time with him had changed. Then she'd drive to Ezra's parents' house in the afternoon.

The memory of his kiss came to the front of her mind. While she was finding out about the quilt, she would find out why he kissed her too. She was done hiding her feelings for him and puzzling over his odd behavior. By the time they were finished talking, she would have answers—whether she liked them or not.

She turned off her lamp and lay down on the bed, the quilt still wrapped around her body. As her eyes closed, her fingers continued to touch Ezra's name.

. . .

On Sunday afternoon, Ezra went out to the carpentry shop. He couldn't work, but at least it was an escape from his father's loud snoring as he napped on the couch and his mother's more delicate snoozing as she leaned back in her chair. At least they had stopped asking him how he was feeling after he'd feigned a stomach upset to avoid going to the service that morning.

The scent of sawdust and fresh wood hit him as he opened the door, then closed it behind him. Outside the weather threatened rain, and gray, dull light shone through the windows, leaving the room dimly lit. He could turn on one of the gas lamps, but he didn't bother. He started to pace.

He'd left his hat in the house, and he fisted his

hands through his hair. Fatigue dragged at him. Last night he'd barely slept, kept awake knowing he was caught between two women he cared about. One of them he loved and the other one . . .

The memory of Hannah Lynne's sweet mouth made him pick up the pace. His heart clenched at the thought of upsetting her. But hadn't he done exactly that yesterday? Then he took advantage of the situation by kissing her. He still didn't know why he did it, just that he had to. And because he was such a *wonderful* person, he apologized for it, when he wasn't sorry at all.

Ezra rubbed his eyes as he walked the length of the woodshop, his shoes kicking up the sawdust he and his *daed* were never able to sweep completely off the floor. Hannah Lynne obviously had some sentimental attachment to the quilt that he wasn't aware of, and that she didn't want to share. But his mother had an attachment, too, an important one. Sure, he could probably go to her, explain his blunder, and she would chalk it up to God's will. Yet that wouldn't be fair to her. This was his error, one he had to fix . . . and he had to break Hannah Lynne's heart to do it.

At the sound of the door opening he stopped his pacing, which had him ending up in the back of the shop. "*Daed?*" he said as he turned around.

"*Nee.*" Hannah Lynne walked into the shop. Alone, without the quilt. She continued to walk toward him, while he continued to be stuck in place. She stopped when she was a few feet from him. Her *kapp* was straight this time, her hair combed and parted neatly and mostly hidden underneath the white head covering. Her hands were clasped in front of her, but her gaze remained steady. Calm. Bold, even.

"Ezra," she said, her chin lifted. "I saw you coming back here as I drove in. We need to talk."

# CHAPTER 9

The first thing Hannah Lynne noticed after she spoke was Ezra's hair. It looked as if he'd used an eggbeater instead of a brush that morning. Some of the ends were standing straight up. His hair was thick and wavy, and he looked a little wild. Maybe more than a little wild, since his blue-gray eyes were wide open and wary as he looked down at her.

Then he spoke. "Hannah Lynne, about yesterday—"

She held up her hand. "I don't want to talk about yesterday. I want you to tell me about the quilt." She took a step toward him. "The truth, this time."

He ran his hand through his hair, and now she could see how it had gotten so disheveled. "The truth is, I'm an idiot." He gave her a wry smile. "And all of this is *mei* fault."

Hannah Lynne listened as Ezra told her about accidentally giving the quilt to Sarah Detweiler for the auction. "What I didn't know was that the quilt was made by *mei grossmutter*. When *mei mutter* found out from Sarah that I had bought it back, she was relieved." He sighed. "That's why I need the quilt. It belongs to *mei familye*."

She nodded. "I know." She took another step forward, and she was glad to see he didn't move away. "What I don't understand is why you gave it to me?"

His hand went to his hair again, but he pulled it away and rubbed the back of his neck instead. "When I saw you looking at that quilt," he said, his low voice dropping even lower, "I could tell how much you liked it. It was almost as if you . . ." He glanced away.

"As if I what?"

"As if you loved it." He met her gaze again. "Because of that, I knew you had to have it. I didn't want something as unimportant as money to keep you from something you loved."

Her bottom lip trembled, and she took one more step closer to him. "Why didn't you just tell me that yesterday?"

"Because . . ." His eyes turned the color of dark slate and he seemed to search for the words. "I should say it was because of *mei* pride. It wouldn't let me admit I'd messed up." This time he took a step toward her. "But the real reason is because I didn't realize until now . . . right this minute . . ."—he bent his head closer to her, his voice lowering more than she'd thought possible— "that *yer* happiness means everything to me."

If her body had been made of ice she would be a puddle by now. His words, combined with the sincere tone of his voice and the darkening of his eyes, made her feel more wonderful than any dream she'd ever had of Ezra Yutzy. Questioning the why and the when and the how that brought them to this place, to this realization that there was an undeniable attraction and connection between them, would be a waste of time. And where Ezra was concerned, Hannah Lynne was tired of wasting time.

They moved toward each other in unison. They stopped a few seconds later, also at the same time. And at the same time, they reached for each other's hands, and held tight.

"Hannah Lynne?" Ezra said, his eyes never leaving hers. "I need to ask you something."

"Okay." Her pulse raced as it always did when she was around him, but this time the feeling was different. Relaxed. Peaceful. As if she was destined to end up here with him, his warm hands holding hers. It took a beautiful quilt to get them to this point, an heirloom that had an important, yet separate connection to them both.

He leaned closer. "May I kiss you again?"

Before she answered, she ran the tip of her index finger over the prominent freckle on his cheek.

"Why did you do that?" he asked.

"Because I've always wanted to."

He smiled. "You didn't answer *mei* question. Is it okay if I kiss you? I want to do it right this time."

She nodded . . . and the kiss she received was more than right.

. . .

The next morning before she went to the Middlefield Market to set up her butter stand, Hannah Lynne stopped by Ezra's parents' house. She pulled into the driveway, brought her buggy to a stop, and looked at the quilt neatly folded on the seat beside her. She sighed and ran her hand over the soft fabric one last time.

She picked up the quilt and got out of the buggy. Ezra would probably be in his workshop by now. She smiled dreamily as she remembered the kiss—and several more after that—he'd delighted her with yesterday. She'd returned home floating on fifty clouds of sheer bliss.

However, she wasn't here to see him, as much as she wanted to. She was here to give his mother back her quilt. She knocked on the door, and a few moments later *Frau* Yutzy opened it.

"Hannah Lynne, this is a surprise."

Ezra's mother smiled, and Hannah Lynne wondered if Ezra had said anything to her about what happened between them yesterday. She hoped he hadn't. She didn't mind if his mother or anyone else knew about the change in their relationship, but she did want a little private time to savor the reality that she and Ezra were now a couple. She hadn't even told her own parents yet.

*Frau* Yutzy opened the door wider. "*Kumme* in. Would you like some *kaffee*?"

"*Ya*," Hannah Lynne said. Once inside, she held out the quilt to *Frau* Yutzy.

"I thought Ezra had this?" his mother said. "He told me it was at his *haus*."

Uh-oh. Maybe she should have consulted Ezra before bringing the quilt. She thought about telling her the long convoluted story, but she quickly changed her mind. "Ezra wanted me to give it to you," she said

simply. Which was true . . . she was just leaving out
some details.

*Frau* Yutzy gave her an odd look before accepting
the quilt. Then she smiled, holding it close to her body.
"*Danki*," she said softly, then started to lay it on the
chair near the door, only to pause. "I'm going to put
this in *mei* room," she said. "*Geh* ahead and make *yer-
self* at home in the kitchen. I'll be there in a minute."

Hannah Lynne walked into the Yutzys' kitchen,
the strong scent of coffee hitting her right away. She
looked at the table, imagining Ezra and his parents
eating meals there together. Her mind wandered to the
thought of her and Ezra eating at their own table in his
house . . . then drew her thoughts up short. No need to
ponder that possibility right now.

She glanced in the corner of the kitchen and noticed
a large cooler on the floor. The lid was open . . . and
naturally Hannah Lynne was curious. She glanced at
the kitchen door, then crept over to the cooler. She
would take only a little peek. Maybe the contents
would give her some insight into what kind of food
Ezra liked.

She gasped when she looked inside. The cooler was
full of butter. *Her* butter.

"How do you like *yer kaffee*?"

Hannah Lynne spun around, stepping away from
the cooler. "A little sugar," she said, going to the table
and pretending she hadn't been snooping. She sat down
as *Frau* Yutzy poured their coffee before joining her at
the table.

At that moment Ezra walked into the kitchen. His

eyes lit up as he met Hannah Lynne's gaze. "Hi," he said, his deep voice sounding shy.

"Hi."

They looked at each other for a long moment, long enough that she forgot *Frau* Yutzy was there.

"I forgot about the wash," Ezra's mother said suddenly, rising from the chair. "I need to get it out soon so it will dry. Ezra, would you mind keeping Hannah Lynne company until I get back?"

Ezra glanced at his mother. "I'll be glad to," he said, his gaze returning to Hannah Lynne.

When his mother left, Hannah Lynne asked, "Does she know about us?"

With a shrug Ezra went to Hannah Lynne. "Maybe. I didn't say anything to her, though." He leaned down and kissed her. "I didn't expect to see you here. Although I'm not complaining."

"I stopped by on the way to the market to give the quilt to *yer mamm*. She put it in her room."

He sat next to her. "Probably the safest place for it."

Hannah Lynne chuckled. "Probably."

"Yesterday she told me there's a story behind the quilt," he said, taking her hand. "After you left and I went inside, she was just coming down from the attic and started talking about it again." He looked down at their hands clasped together. "It's a pretty amazing story."

Hannah Lynne leaned forward, eager to hear it.

"The quilt is actually mine," he said. "*Mei gross-mutter* even stitched *mei* name on it."

Nodding, Hannah Lynne took a sip of her coffee,

still keeping her other hand snugly nestled in Ezra's. She already knew this, of course, but she continued to listen.

"*Mei grossmutter* also stitched another word on the quilt. *Amor.*"

"What does that mean?"

"It was her nickname for me," he said. "Her family was originally from Romania, and she married an Amish man in Lancaster. Then they moved to Middlefield. *Mei grossmutter* had stopped speaking Romanian and spoke only English and *Dietsch*, except for one word. *Amor.* It means *love.*"

She squeezed his hand. "That's so sweet."

He nodded. "Apparently *Mamm* found a letter yesterday, one that had been misplaced for years. She didn't know *mei* name was on the quilt until she read the letter." He swallowed, and looked into her eyes. "That quilt was not just an inheritance for *mei mamm*. It was *mei grossmutter*'s gift to me for *Mamm* to keep, for when I married and had *mei* own *familye*. She told *mei mamm* the secret of the names in the letter *Mamm* had somehow never read."

His gaze held hers, which made her thoughts wander again to the possibility of a permanent future with him. The love she saw in his eyes made her believe it was possible.

He released her hand. "I'm sure you have to get to the market," he said.

"*Ya.*" She didn't want to leave, but they both had to go to work. They stood at the same time, and he moved a step closer to her.

"Maybe I'll see you there later today," he said with a grin.

"Ezra, you don't have to buy any more butter." She tilted her head in the direction of the cooler. "I think you've got more than enough."

He leaned down, his lips near hers. "That's because I can't resist the *maedel* who makes it."

# EPILOGUE

## ONE YEAR LATER

Hannah Lynne fell back on the full-sized bed, her body sinking into the soft mattress, the skirt of her dark blue wedding dress bunching up slightly around her legs. She looked up at the ceiling and smiled, content. She closed her eyes, only to open them again when Ezra landed beside her.

"Finally," he said, taking her hand. He pressed it against his chest, which was covered in a crisp white shirt and black vest that made him look absolutely gorgeous. "Alone, at last."

She turned to him, her smile widening. Their wedding had been a few hours earlier, and while tomorrow they would do the obligatory visiting of friends and family, tonight belonged to them, in Ezra's house. *Their* house. They had finished renovating it together.

She released his hand and scooted up a little, glancing at her new husband's feet as they dangled a bit over the edge. "Maybe we should get a longer bed," she said.

"Someday." He sat up next to her and grinned. "It's

fine for now." He leaned over and kissed her cheek. "I have something to give you."

She watched as he scrambled off the bed and went to the hope chest at the foot of it. The chest was the engagement present he'd given to her five weeks ago. He'd made it himself, even carving a quote in the center of the lid. It was from the wrapper of one of the many, many, *many* blocks of butter he'd bought from her. *Being in love makes every morning worth getting up for.* At the time she wrote it down she had no idea how true those words were.

Her eyes widened as he pulled a quilt out of the chest. Ezra laid the folded quilt on Hannah Lynne's lap and gazed down at her. "It's back where it belongs. With both of us."

She could hardly speak. "I'd hoped . . . I didn't want to presume . . ."

"You knew it would be *yers* again." He sat down next to her on the bed and tweaked her nose.

She reached over and planted a soft kiss on his freckle, then leaned her head against his shoulder.

"There's something else," he said. He showed her the stitching on the quilt, where his name and *Amor* were. "Can you see it?" he whispered.

On the other side of *Amor* were more carefully stitched letters. She smiled as she realized what they spelled.

"*Mutter* tried to match *Grossmutter*'s stitching."

"She came close." Hannah Lynne peered at her name, now a permanent part of the quilt. A tangible connection to her aunt, and now to the man she loved.

She gazed at him for a long moment. "I love you," she said, resting the palm of her hand on his cheek.

"I love you too," he said, leaning into her touch. "*Amor.*"

She pressed her lips to his, and as they kissed, he pulled the quilt around them both.

# ACKNOWLEDGMENTS

A big thank you to my editors Becky Monds and Jean Bloom and my brainstorming/critiquing partners-in-crime Eddie Columbia and Kelly Long. Once again, I couldn't have written this without you all.

# DISCUSSION QUESTIONS

1. Hannah Lynne and Ezra were brought together by several misunderstandings. Sometimes God uses the unexpected to make things happen. When in your life has something unexpected happened and you could clearly see God bringing those circumstances together?

2. The DDC Clinic is a real special needs clinic in Middlefield, OH. The auction in this story is also a real auction (although I took a few fictional liberties with the actual quilt auction). Is there a cause in your life that is important to you? How do you and your community come together to support it?

3. Do you have a special heirloom that you treasure? What is it and why?

4. If the quilt mix-up hadn't happened, do you think Ezra and Hannah Lynne would have eventually revealed their feelings for each other? Why or why not?

# THE MIDWIFE'S DREAM

KELLY IRVIN

# GLOSSARY

*ach:* oh

*aenti:* aunt

*boplin:* babies

*bruders:* brothers

*daed:* father

*dawdy/daadi haus:* grandparents' house

*Englisch/Englischer:* English or Non-Amish

*fraa:* wife

*freind:* friend

*gelassenheit:* fundamental Amish belief in yielding
    fully to God's will and forsaking all selfishness

*Gmay:* Church District

*Gott:* God

*groossdaadi:* grandpa

*groossmammi:* grandma

*gut:* good

*haus:* house

*jah:* yes

*kapp:* prayer covering or cap

*kinner:* children

*lieb:* love

*mann:* man

*mudder:* mother

*nee:* no

*rumspringa:* running-around period when a teenager
    turns sixteen years old
*schweschder(s):* sister(s)
*suh:* son
*wunderbarr:* wonderful


*The German dialect spoken by the Amish is not a
written language and varies depending on the loca-
tion and origin of the settlement. These spellings are
approximations. Most Amish children learn English
after they start school. They also learn high German,
which is used in their Sunday services.

*To my daughter, Erin, whose dream was always to be a mother. You're doing a great job, sweetie! Love always.*

Wait for the LORD;
Be strong and take heart
And wait for the LORD.

PSALM 27:14 NIV

# Featured Jamesport Families

## Cyrus and Josephina Beachy (Deacon)

| | |
|---|---|
| Iris | Carl |
| Joseph | Louella |
| Rueben | Abigail |
| Samuel | |

## Jeremy and Bertha Kurtz

| | |
|---|---|
| Nathanael | Mahon |
| John | Jason |
| Avery | Mary |
| William | Mark |
| Salome | |

## Bartholomew and Rachel Shrock

| | |
|---|---|
| Liam | Micah |
| Annie | |

### Aidan and Bess Graber

Joshua

# CHAPTER 1

The baby boy slid into Iris Beachy's hands so fast a person might think he was late for supper. He opened his mouth wide and declared his dislike of his new surroundings with a loud wail.

"Hello to you too, sweet one." Her best friend's new son weighed at least ten pounds. He arrived with a full head of dark hair that stood up in wet spikes around his red, wrinkled face. Iris chuckled and held him up for Rachel and Bartholomew Shrock to see. "He's a full-grown man. Better set him to work chopping wood."

"He's here. Our boy's here, *fraa*." Bartholomew left his wife's side to take a closer look. His big grin split his face over his long brown beard. "He's a giant."

"Built like his *daed* for sure." Iris suctioned fluid from the baby's nose and mouth with a syringe. He didn't like that at all. The wail turned to an aggravated howl. "Hush, hush, you're fine. It's a good thing you've done this before, Rachel. He had plenty of room to squeeze out without any tearing."

Twice before. Fortunately, Rachel's mother had taken little Annie and Liam to her house at the beginning of the six hours of labor that started on a cloudy February afternoon in which the Missouri sky spit ice and snow at passersby as if to taunt them for daring to venture outdoors.

Iris wiped the baby off and looked him over from top to bottom. His skin was pink, his toes and fingers perfectly formed, his legs and arms strong. She laid him in the old blanket Rachel had placed in the cradle by the bed. They would save the tumbling block crib quilt Iris made for later when he was dressed. She placed a clip on the cord and cut it.

"Your *suh* has a healthy set of lungs."

She handed the squalling baby to Rachel, who sank back onto the pillows and tucked her new baby into the crook of her arm. His cries subsided seconds later. "He's built like Bart, but he looks like me. Don't you think?"

"He looks like my *groossdaadi*. No teeth, all hair." Bartholomew leaned over Rachel and tickled his son's cheek with one huge, callused index finger. "Micah. We'll name him Micah."

Rachel smiled up at them. Bartholomew's hand moved from his baby to his wife's cheek. She held it there with her free hand. The look her friends exchanged brought a lump to Iris's throat. She ducked her head and dealt with the afterbirth.

*Be thankful for Rachel and Bartholomew's blessing. Be joyful. Be thankful. Be content.*

Iris reminded herself, as she always did, of God's blessing in giving her this role in the Jamesport community. She'd delivered six babies on her own since Laura Kauffman retired as the *Gmay* midwife. Many more under Laura's tutelage. To be able to bring her friends' babies into the world was a gift. God allowed her to be present when a new life bounded into her arms and began this journey in the world.

*Thank you, Gott.*

Even if He hadn't fulfilled her one and only dream. That of her own family. A husband and her own babies. Not yet, she amended. On His time, not hers. OnO She gathered up the bloody towels and sheets. She refused to lose faith. Not when her friends married and had their babies. Not when her twenty-third birthday passed.

Plenty of time, her mother kept saying. Plenty of time.

"It's dark out already. I better do my chores." Bartholomew headed for the door. "I'll let you women do what you do. Iris, I'll hitch up the buggy and bring it around front so it'll be ready when you are."

Iris cleared her throat of that annoying lump. "I won't be long. The road will be bad and getting worse."

Fortunately, the Beachy farm was only a stone's throw from the Shrocks'. Perfect for visiting back and forth. Perfect for watching Annie and Liam grow and change. Now Micah. The annoying lump returned. Iris made a pile of the bloody towels and stood. "Micah is a fine name."

"I told Bartholomew we couldn't pick Ephraim because I know you want that name for one of your boys." Her tone airy, Rachel smoothed Micah's blanket. "It would be too confusing when they get together to play."

Leave it to Rachel to hop over all the parts in between. Finding that special friend. Courting. Marrying. "You can use the name for your next one."

"You'll need it. Don't you worry." Rachel patted the bed in a sit-with-me motion. "You have lots of time. Look at it this way, when you get married, you'll be too busy having your own *boplin* to deliver other people's. You'll miss it."

Rachel was a good friend. She'd just given birth and she chose to focus on how that made Iris feel. She always knew what Iris was thinking. All the way back to when her *daed* became the deacon and he started taking care of *Gmay* business. Then *rumspringa* and the singings. And Aidan. Iris settled onto the bed and began to re-braid Rachel's hair. "You're a mess."

"Don't change the subject."

"No point in talking about it. *Gott*'s will is *Gott*'s will."

Rachel kissed Micah's forehead. His eyelids fluttered. He went back to sleep, lips puckering as if he were sucking. "You are the kindest, nicest, sweetest person I know, Iris Beachy. And no man would say you're hard on the eyes. Your turn will come. I promise you that."

"You're sweet, but you can't promise me anything."

"Mahon Kurtz likes you."

"He has a funny way of showing it."

"He knows you're still in love with Aidan. He's waiting until you're ready."

"Am not."

"Are too."

"Don't be silly." Iris tugged at Rachel's chestnut hair.

"Aidan asked me to marry him. I said no. Not the other way around."

"Ouch. Not so hard." Rachel pushed Iris's hands away from her head. Even with her skin blotchy, hair sweaty, and nightgown stained and wrinkled, Rachel was the pretty one. At sixteen, Bartholomew asked her to ride home with him after their first singing. They never looked back, marrying two days after her nineteenth birthday. "Because you're wise beyond your years. Aidan loves Bess, and you knew it before he was willing to admit it. Mahon is waiting for you to give him a sign you're ready."

"You see what you want to see."

"What does Salome say?"

Salome was the other still-single woman in the gaggle of girls who'd once been inseparable. She taught school and waited for her special friend. She was also Mahon's sister. "She thinks her brother is short a few tools in his toolbox. He's busy working the farm with his *bruders* now that his *daed* is retiring. And when he's not, he draws pictures and looks at the stars."

Rachel giggled. "So draw him a picture."

"Don't laugh. It's not like our paths don't cross at church and at every frolic and every school picnic."

"You like him. You know you do."

She did like him. In a warm, content, he'll-always-be-around sort of way. She'd simply never thought of him in that light. He was Salome's goofy brother who wore glasses and knew the names of all the constellations in the sky before he learned his multiplication tables.

"He needs to know you're interested back." Rachel smoothed Micah's wild hair. He sighed, the sweetest, most tender sound imaginable. "Most men do."

"If he's not interested enough to approach me first, then I reckon it's not meant to be."

"Admit it." Rachel scooted up on the pillow. Her face had that same fierce expression it did when she accused her little brother of eating her lunch at school. "You won't do it because you're mad at *Gott*."

"Am not."

"Are too."

"I think we've had this conversation already."

Rachel laughed. Micah frowned and sputtered. She shushed him. "Go home, *freind*."

"Do you want something to eat first?"

"I'll get it in a while. Help yourself if you're hungry." Rachel pulled the quilt up so it covered both her and Micah. "I'm going to enjoy lying here with no little ones tugging on my skirt or asking me for a cookie or needing a diaper changed for a while longer. Bart will be hungry after he finishes the chores. We'll eat together."

Rachel would be back on her feet making breakfast in the morning, and Iris would get a good night's sleep before doing her own chores. She glanced out the bedroom window. The icy panes reflected the kerosene lamp back at her. The days were short this time of year. "*Mudder* will have left a plate warming on the back of the stove for me. She'll be sitting by the fire, waiting."

"That's where you get your sweetness—your *mudder*." Rachel grinned. "Definitely not from your *daed*."

"*Daed*'s different at home." Rachel was teasing, but

Iris couldn't help but defend her father. "His bark is worse than his bite, always has been."

To others, Cyrus Beachy might be a stern deacon who taught baptism classes. But at home, he was still a big, overgrown teddy bear to her. The man she'd climbed all over as a little girl, the man who tickled her until she shrieked on cold winter nights after she beat him three times in a row in checkers. The man who read stories to his children every night before presiding over their prayers.

She wanted a husband who would be a father like that. Aidan would've been that kind of husband. She gritted her teeth and administered a silent scolding as she always did when these thoughts wiggled their way into her brain. Aidan belonged to someone else now. "I better get going."

"Talk to you soon."

Rachel's sleepy voice trailed after Iris as she tugged on her wool coat, mittens, scarf, and bonnet. Her satchel in one hand, she trudged out into a biting wind that took her breath away. Icy snowflakes pelted her cheeks as she slipped and slid down the porch steps and slogged toward the buggy Bartholomew had retrieved as promised. Sable snorted, whinnied, and stamped her feet as if to say *hurry up*. Iris ducked her head and grabbed her bonnet to keep it from flying away.

Minutes later she turned the buggy onto the highway and headed for home. Her hands and feet were frozen and her nose numb. It had been a long day. The urge to doze overwhelmed her. Her stomach rumbled. She snapped the reins, and Sable picked up speed. Home, a grilled-cheese sandwich, a hot cup of tea, and bed, in that order. The buggy's wooden wheels skidded under her. "Whoa, whoa. Take it easy, girl."

Only a mile more. One more mile. The wind whipped through her coat as if she wore nothing. An engine revved behind her. Who else was silly enough to be out on the road in this weather? She eased toward the shoulder. A horn blared. She swerved still closer to the edge, afraid to go too far for fear of landing in a ditch she couldn't see under the heavy blanket of snow.

The horn honked again and again in an irritating refrain. She twisted in her seat. Headlights blinded her. "*Ach*, okay, okay." She pulled over a little more, halted, and threw her hand up in the air to wave them on.

Instead of passing, the *car*—or was it a truck— pulled in behind her and stopped. The engine idled in a weak *put-put-put*.

She strained to see the black form behind the lights. A pickup truck maybe.

A door opened. Words were exchanged. English. The door slammed.

Sudden heat rushing through her, Iris gripped the reins. She couldn't outrun a car in her buggy. She heaved a breath and licked chapped lips. Her whole mouth was dry. "Who is it? What do you want?"

The headlights illuminated a form that moved toward her. Her heart hammering in her chest, she squinted.

A man strode toward her.

# CHAPTER 2

Iris couldn't see his face. He wore a dark hat. A dark coat, black pants, black boots. A Plain man? Why would a Plain man be in a car that pursued her on an empty country road on this icy cold night? Her heart whipped itself into a frenzy of off-kilter beating. The taste of metal in her mouth made her gag. She swallowed against the acid taste. "Who is it? Speak up."

"It's me. Mahon."

Her heartbeats fought to resume their normal rhythm. The *whoosh* of adrenaline leaving her body left her weak. Her lungs ached with the effort to breathe. A rush of anger followed, warming Iris from head to toe. She hopped from the buggy and trudged toward him. Her rubber boots, a size too big, sank into the snow, halting her forward progress, which served to aggravate her more. "What are you doing following me in a car? Are you driving? Why did you honk at me?"

She paused for air. Plain women did not talk to Plain men this way. Even if it was Salome's little brother. Iris's breath puffed white in the dark night. The rush of cold air burned her lungs. Her heart beat in her ears like a huge drum.

"You're needed."

Mahon let the words hang in the air as if they made perfect sense, as if they answered every question. He offered no apology for scaring the living daylights out of her. Iris blinked. Had he said he needed her? Or had she imagined that?

"Turn off the headlights. I can't see."

"There's no time. You're needed." He jabbed one thumb over his shoulder. He wore no gloves. Some days men weren't the brightest of animals. "We were headed to your house. What are you doing out here in this weather?"

"Delivering Rachel's baby . . . Why am I answering your questions? What are you—"

"Hurry up! We're freezing." Salome's sharp school-teacher voice pierced the darkness. The headlights disappeared, leaving them in the darkness of a country road with no lighting. "The heater in this thing only works part of the time. I think Jessica's water broke just now."

Iris closed her eyes and opened them, hoping they would adjust to the dark. "Salome?" Not only was Mahon in this English car, but so was his sister. And who was Jessica? Iris could see the vehicle now, a light-colored van. Tan or brown. A man sat behind the wheel. A stranger. "Get out here and tell me what's going on."

"*Ach.* It's too cold." Salome hung out the passenger door window. She pulled the scarf wrapped around her neck up over her bonnet with one hand. "We've got a lady in here who's expecting. We'll explain the rest at your house, I promise, but we need to get there before this baby comes. Jessica thinks it's coming soon."

A baby. Why hadn't Mahon said that? "I'll meet you there. Go on ahead. *Mudder* will help until I get there."

Her father wouldn't be happy about Salome and Mahon bringing strangers to his door, but Cyrus Beachy would never turn away a person in need. Iris plunged through the snow as fast as her boots would allow, hoisted herself into the buggy, and waited for the van to pass. The engine rumbled and whined before settling into a hit-and-miss putter. The wind blew the nasty smell of gas fumes and burning oil in her face. They would arrive long before she did, but her mother would know what to do. No longer tired or hungry, Iris urged Sable into a canter. Fifteen minutes later she pulled in next to the van, which blocked the hitching post in front of her house. Sable was a patient horse. He would wait for one of her brothers to stable him—if she didn't wait too long to ask.

She ran up the steps, skidded across the icy porch, and tugged open the door.

Two English teenagers sat on the couch by the fireplace, a tattered blue gym bag on the floor at their feet. Mahon sat across from them in the straight-backed chair wiping condensation from his black-rimmed glasses. It had been years since she'd seen him without his glasses. He glanced up at her entrance. His eyes, normally a brilliant blue behind the lenses, looked softer and warmer. He and Salome could be twins. He nodded and stood. "This is Quinn and Jessica from Iowa."

The girl was rail thin except for her swollen belly. She wore a wool navy peacoat not large enough to button across her stomach. Someone—probably *Mudder*—had placed a blanket over her shoulders. Her porcelain skin, huge blue eyes, and curly blond hair that hung to her waist gave her the look of dolls Iris had seen in the toy store windows in St. Louis. She wore no makeup. Tiny earrings like purple jeweled flowers adorned her ears and one side of her nose. The boy had wispy brown hair on his lip and chin that didn't match the darker hair cut close to his head. A single diamond stud flashed on his right earlobe. His eyes were bloodshot. He tucked a cell phone into his jeans pocket and put an arm around Jessica in a protective gesture.

"I'm Iris."

"I know." Quinn's tone stopped short of belligerent. "They said you could help Jess. Are you a nurse?"

"A lay midwife. I deliver babies."

"We don't have much money." Jessica offered this fact in a high, tight voice. "We don't have insurance."

"I wouldn't take your money—"

"I'm more worried about whether you know what you're doing," Quinn broke in. "Did you go to medical school?"

"I apprenticed—"

"She knows." This time Mahon interrupted her. He plopped his glasses on his nose. "That's why we brought you to her. We could always go into town."

"No."

They both spoke at once. Quinn's tone definitive, Jessica's less certain.

Iris glanced at Mahon. He shrugged. "Your *mudder* is getting a room ready. Salome is in the kitchen making hot cocoa with your *schweschders*."

"I thought she was about to deliver."

"Your *mudder* says no." His tone was apologetic. His face, with its chipmunk cheeks, was red. He stood and walked past her, his stride swift as if he couldn't wait to escape. No Plain man wanted to discuss these things with a woman not his *fraa*. "I didn't ask for details. I'll put up your horse and the buggy."

She caught his woodsy scent as he passed. "Bundle up."

What a silly thing to say. Of course he would bundle up. They'd known each other since they were old enough to catch tadpoles in the pond and make mud pies for pretend frolics. It had never been awkward between them, never been a boy-girl thing. More of a brother-sister thing. Until her friends planted the seed. Had his done the same? This wasn't the time or the place to find out. Iris waited until the door closed behind him. Then she went to Jessica and knelt in front of her. "Can I touch you?"

The girl nodded. Iris placed her hand on the girl's black-and-red plaid flannel shirt pulled tight over her belly. A minute ticked by. Another. And then another. "When are you due?"

"Not for three more weeks." Jessica glanced at Quinn as if seeking permission to speak. He shrugged. "That's why we thought we had time to get to Texas. I was gonna find a doctor there. I even have my bag packed and ready."

She motioned to the gym bag on the floor. The knob of her delicate wrist stuck out under the frayed sleeve of her shirt. "I brought a nightgown for the hospital and diapers and formula and some bottles and a pacifier—even an outfit to put her in."

Formula and bottles. "You don't want to nurse your baby?"

Jessica wrinkled her nose. "I know it's good for her, but I still have to finish school, and I probably have to get a job for after school, and I can't be carting her around with me everywhere."

Who would care for the baby while Jessica went on with her life? That was none of Iris's business. "It's a girl?"

"That's what the doctor said. We saw her in the sonogram and everything. She was mostly a blob, though."

"What else did he tell you the last time you went to see him?"

"*She* said Jess needed to eat more. She wasn't gaining enough weight." Quinn snorted. "She eats like a horse."

"Do not."

Iris smiled at the girl. "You're eating for two."

Jessica nodded and leaned back. Iris waited. Quinn smelled of cigarette smoke. Jessica's scent was flowery, like lilacs. Quinn sat rigid and unmoving, while Jessica's face grew whiter. Her lips trembled. Finally, muscle contracted under Iris's fingers.

"Oh no. Not again." The girl gasped. She grabbed Quinn's free hand and gripped so tight her knuckles turned white. She sat up straight. Her mouth gaped open. "Ow, ow, ow."

"Breathe, breathe through it." Iris kept her voice gentle. She stroked the girl's other arm. "Relax into it."

The contraction subsided. Jessica sank back into her chair. "See, it's getting close. My baby's coming."

"It's not time yet."

"That's what the other lady said." Quinn snorted. "I thought when the water came out, it was time for the baby to come."

"The contractions are still far apart."

"But they hurt so much." Jessica sniffed and wiped at her face with the back of her coat sleeve. "It feels like it's killing me. I can't do it. What if I can't do it?"

Iris had seen this before with other first-time mothers, but never this young. She wanted to ask Jessica how old she was, but she bit back the question. That also was none of her business. "You can. I promise. Women do this all the time. All over the world since the beginning of time. We'll get some cocoa to warm you up. If you want to walk around for a little bit, that might help move things along."

"Walk around?" Quinn tightened his arm around Jessica, his look suspicious. "Aren't you supposed to get in bed?"

"No. Unless you're tired and want to rest for a while."

"She hasn't been sleeping good."

"You wouldn't either if you had a watermelon sitting on your bladder and had to pee every five seconds." Jessica's voice crept higher with each word. "You wouldn't sleep if your back felt like you'd been lifting fifty-pound bags of potatoes all day."

"It'll all be over in a few hours." Quinn swung his gaze toward Iris as if seeking reinforcement. "You'll be fine."

"It might be a little longer than that."

"We have to get on the road."

"There's no rushing a baby." Iris stood. "I'll see about the cocoa."

She grabbed her satchel and fled to the kitchen where she found her little sisters, Louella and Abigail, vying for Salome's attention while she poured cocoa into mugs and added miniature marshmallows.

"Iris! Iris, an *Englisch* lady is in the front room." Louella, who was eight, beat six-year-old Abigail by a hair's breadth in their mad dash across the room. "She's having a *bopli*."

"I know." Iris took turns kissing each girl on the top of their *kapps*. "Where's *Daed*?"

"Isaac Borntrager died." Louella held out a sticky hand full of crushed marshmallows. "Want some?"

"*Nee*, but it is nice of you to offer." *Daed* would help Bishop Freeman Borntrager prepare for his father's funeral. The man had lived to the great age of eighty-nine, but recently he'd taken to bed with a terrible cough. Her little sister was matter-of-fact about the situation.

"Can you sit at the table and drink your cocoa while I talk to Salome?"

They could, so she took their mugs to the table and settled them in. Then she turned to Salome. "Tell me everything."

"He had pneumonia."

"I know, bless his heart. He lived a *gut* life. Tell me about our visitors."

"They ran away from home. That's what I think." Salome sipped her cocoa and winced. "Hot."

"Stop drinking hot chocolate and spill the beans. How did you end up in their van?"

Salome leaned on the counter and wrapped her hands around the mug. "Mahon walked out to help *Daed* with the chores and saw them sitting in the van with the engine running. He asked if they needed something. Quinn said he needed help for his wife."

"I don't think she's his wife."

"Me neither, but he said they're driving to Texas. He has a job there and a place to live. He said so and she just kept nodding."

"Why didn't Mahon give them directions to the medical center in Chillicothe?"

"He tried. Quinn said there was no time."

"Her contractions are still ten minutes apart, even now."

"I know that now." Salome shrugged. "I reckon they've never had a baby before."

"I hope not." Iris poured more water into a pot on the stove and turned up the flame. Then she opened her satchel and pulled out the tools of her trade that needed washing. "They don't seem prepared to be parents at all."

"What did *Mudder* say?"

"She hugged the girl and asked Quinn if he wanted some venison stew."

That was *Mudder*. Unflappable.

"He said he wasn't hungry."

Iris turned. Her mother stood in the doorway, a pile of sheets in her arms. "The girl looks like she could use a meal, but he said no before she got a chance." *Mudder* frowned at the memory. Her first instinct was always to feed people. Especially if they needed fattening up. "I put fresh sheets on your bed and covered it with the plastic one. I don't reckon you'll be sleeping tonight."

"*Gut*. It'll probably be awhile before she delivers, but it's nice to be ready."

*Mudder* deposited her load on a chair by the table, then trotted over to the stove. She stuck her hands above it. "It's cold in there, but she'll warm up once she gets going. She's walking around in circles now in the front room. She said you told her to do it. Her friend asked me why he can't get on Facebook out here."

Iris's chuckle mixed with Salome's. Mother surely had no idea what Facebook was. "Did you tell him we have no Internet access?"

"Stop laughing. I know what Facebook is."

Both Iris and Salome knew from *rumspringa* experience that a cell phone signal could in fact be had on the farm. Quinn could likely make a phone call if he needed to or send a text, but there was no Internet service. Of course, *Daed* wouldn't like him chatting on the phone in the house.

"I hope this isn't causing you too much trouble." Salome set her mug on the counter and went to stand by the woman she sometimes called *aenti*, other times *Mudder*-number-two. "We didn't know what else to do."

"I don't consider it trouble, helping strangers in need." *Mudder* patted Salome's arm. "It's what Jesus did. It's what the good Samaritan did."

"Do you think *Daed* will feel the same? *Englischers* having a baby in his house?" Iris watched the expression change on *Mudder*'s face as she rubbed her wrinkled hands together to warm them. "Will everyone feel that way?"

She didn't have to specify. They knew she meant Freeman.

"I'm going there in a few minutes. I'll tell him myself."

"In this weather?" Iris shook her head. "You shouldn't be out there. You have a cough already."

"I'll be fine. Rueben will take me. They'll need help with the preparations."

Death notices. Food. Cleaning. The viewing. Building the coffin. It wouldn't have to be big. Freeman's *daed* had shriveled in his old age, a wizened little man with big ears, sparse hair on his head, and a beard that reached his waist. He wouldn't take up much space. The cold, hard earth in the cemetery would be difficult to pierce. Iris shivered. "Take care."

"You too." *Mudder* slid her coat from the hook by the back door and shrugged it on. "That girl is small and she's scared and she has no idea what she's in for. It'll be a long night."

"The baby will be here by midnight, I reckon."

"Babies come on their own time."

# CHAPTER 3

Mothers are always right. Iris glanced at the wooden clock shaped like a log cabin hanging on her bedroom wall. Midnight had come and gone. The hands crept toward one. Jessica sat on the side of the bed, her hands gripping the rumpled sheets on either side of her body. Her toes, with nails painted bubble-gum pink, curled into the piece rug on the floor. Sweat soaked her tangled hair, her eyes were red-rimmed from crying, and snot ran from her nose. Her shoulders heaved as she sobbed. Quinn had collapsed on the floor across from her, his back to the wall, long legs sprawled in front of him. He clutched his phone as if somehow he could wring help from it.

Her back to Jessica, Iris slipped over to his side and squatted.

"Try rubbing her back and shoulders."

"No way." He shot a panicked look at Jessica. "She doesn't want me messing with her. You heard her. She bit my head off. She blames me for all this. Like she wasn't even there."

"It'll help if she relaxes. We're on the homestretch. She needs you."

"Oh no, oh no, oh no."

Iris pivoted. Her face contorted, Jessica plopped sideways on the bed and curled up in a ball. "I can't take this anymore. I can't take it."

"Yes, you can." Iris straightened and moved to the bed. She took a washrag from a basin of water sitting next to the kerosene lamp, wrung it out, and wiped Jessica's face with gentle strokes. She handed her a tissue. "You're almost there. You're doing great."

The girl's ragged sob said she didn't agree. She rolled to her other side and rubbed her belly. "Have you ever had a baby?"

"No, but I've delivered plenty." Iris eased onto the mattress and massaged the girl's thin shoulders. She worked her way down Jessica's knotty spine. "Babies mostly come on their own. They just need a little help."

"Did the mother ever die?"

"Not one. No babies either."

Laura had prepared Iris for that. It happened rarely, but it happened for reasons only God understood. So far she'd been spared the anguish. Iris worked her way back up the spine and across the shoulders. Jessica uncurled a little. Her head lolled forward. "That feels good. I'm so tired."

"I know you are. Tell me about yourself. How old are you?"

"I turned sixteen on Christmas Eve."

Sixteen. The age Plain girls and boys began their *rumspringa*, a time of courting and seeking a special friend. The time before making the decision to be baptized. She glanced at Quinn. His head lowered, he used his thumbs to tap out something on the screen. Texting. She'd like to pluck the phone from his hands and toss it in the snow outside the window.

"How long have you and Quinn been together?"

"Since seventh grade."

"A long time."

"He's my soulmate. I knew it the first time he kissed me after our basketball team won state and he made thirty points."

"Where's your school?"

"I'll do that." Quinn stood next to her. His hand brushed hers away. He put both hands on Jessica's shoulders and squeezed. "I texted my cousin. He says he's got room for us. We just have to get there."

"It hurts. Oh, it hurts." Jessica's voice rose. She screamed. "I hate this. I hate you. I hate your cousin."

Quinn stumbled back. "Do something for her! You're supposed to help her."

"I'm sorry! I didn't mean it. I love you, Quinn. I love you." Jessica sobbed. "Help me, help me."

"You'll be okay, babe, I promise." He glared at Iris. He had tears in his eyes. His Adam's apple bobbed. "Do something."

"It's okay. Jessica, you're doing fine. You're almost there." Iris moved to the foot of the bed. She patted Jessica's knee and lifted the sheets. She took another peek. "It's time to push. Quinn, you can help."

He looked as if he wanted to be anywhere in the world except in that bedroom. "You don't need me. You're the midwife."

"Quinn, help your wife deliver your baby girl. Now."

"She's not my wife."

"But this is your baby, isn't it?"

He wiped at his face with the back of his hand. "Yah, it is." He gripped Jessica's shoulder. "I didn't mean that in a bad way, babe. What do I do?"

"Get behind her. Encourage her."

He did as he was told. Iris moved into position. "You can do this, Jessica. Give it all you have. Just think, in a few minutes you'll see your baby."

Jessica screamed again and again, but she pushed. For a skinny girl, she had great lungs and plenty of muscle. The contractions ripped through one after another now. Four pushes and the baby's head crowned. Iris gently rotated her shoulders. "Give another big push. A big push now."

The shoulders slid out. Then the rest of the body. Jessica and Quinn had an itty, bitty baby girl. Her eyes were closed. Her mouth gaped, but no sound came out.

Iris cleared her nose and throat. "Come on, sweet thing, come on."

Seconds ticked by. "Come on, sweetie." She rubbed the baby's belly and patted her back.

"She's not crying." Jessica sat up. "Why isn't she crying?"

The baby's arms flailed. Tiny fingers rolled into fists. Her eyes opened. Finally, she wailed.

Quinn tottered one step in Iris's direction. Shaking his head, he stared down at the baby. His mouth dropped open, and he bawled almost as loud as his new daughter.

# CHAPTER 4

Iris shifted the dirty sheets into one arm and closed her bedroom door with a shove of her elbow. She stood in the dark hallway for a few seconds, enjoying the silence. *Thank you, Gott, thank you.* She leaned her head against the door. The wood was solid and cool against her warm forehead. *Thank you.* She never doubted for a second God was good, but some days— and nights—were hard. These English kids, barely able to navigate life, were now responsible for a baby. Iris had cleaned up the little mite, watched while Jessica diapered her, and convinced her to try nursing. That didn't last long. Both nodded off to sleep after a few minutes. Quinn mostly stared out the window, even though it was dark and he could see nothing. She left him with a quiet good night he barely acknowledged. She wanted the responsibility he so obviously feared, but it had been denied her for reasons she couldn't fathom. She took a deep breath of cold air and straightened.

She would not ask the question. She simply would not. *Why, Gott?*

Shaking her head at her own prideful audacity, she

strode through the hall to the stairs. God must be so disappointed in her inability to trust in His plan for her. If she never married, never had children, she would accept it as part of a bigger plan she couldn't see but would come to know. She was not, as Rachel put it, mad at God. She was certain that was not allowed in her *Gmay.*

She might not like it, but she would be an obedient believer. A cheerful believer. She started down the stairs, repeating the words in her head, ignoring their grubby tarnish after forty-eight hours straight of delivering babies. "I just need to sleep."

"Who are you talking to?"

Iris lurched to a stop. She grabbed the bannister with her free hand. Mahon sat at her father's desk against the wall under the bannister. His hat lay on the desk next to a pad of paper, the one her *mudder* used to write to her pen pals. His big hands covered the top sheet. He stared up at her, looking much like a child caught stealing a still-warm apple pie from the windowsill.

"What are you doing here still? I told you to go home." She glanced around the front room. A fire blazed in the fireplace. "Is Salome here too?"

"*Nee.* Your *bruder* took her home." Mahon tore the top sheet from the pad, wadded it up in a tight ball, and tossed it in the wastebasket next to the desk. He stood and stretched his head from side to side. He rubbed his neck. He had thick, curly brown hair. "The *bopli* is *gut*?"

"In this weather?" Mahon had nice hair. She shouldn't

be thinking about Mahon's hair. It was just that she hardly ever saw it. "Which *bruder*?"

Mahon smiled, a slightly lopsided smile that made him look less like Salome and more like his father. "Joseph. Rueben went with your *mudder*. Samuel and Carl went to bed when your *schweschders* did."

Mahon could be counted on to keep track of everyone. To keep little ones safe and bigger ones in line. She tromped down the remaining stairs and headed for the kitchen and the laundry room. "*Jah*, the *bopli* is *gut*. Small, but she has all her fingers and toes and a healthy cry. The *mudder* is fine too. Giddy with relief. The *daed* almost fainted."

"They'll get the hang of it." The tread of his boots told her Mahon followed. "It stopped snowing a couple hours ago, but I figured I should stay around. It didn't seem right to leave you alone here with strangers I brought into your house."

Joseph took Salome home. Did that mean they were courting? Salome hadn't said a word. Joseph often disappeared in the evenings, but a sister didn't ask questions. If something was going on, neither would want to make Iris feel bad in the wake of Aidan and Bess's marriage. She didn't feel bad. She was thrilled for her friend. Joseph was a hard worker, faithful, kind, and the joker of the family. He and Salome might be well suited to each other.

The rest of Mahon's statement registered. "I'm not alone." As the oldest of seven children, Iris didn't remember a time when she'd ever been alone. "Didn't Reuben come back from taking *Mudder* to Freeman's?"

"He did, but he went to sleep."

Mahon's yawn echoed in the laundry room.

Laughing, Iris dumped the sheets next to a pile of shirts and dresses. Nine people in one house made for a long laundry day on Mondays. "Sounds like you should do the same." She turned in time to catch him with his glasses in one hand and rubbing his eyes with the other. He looked up at her. He did have nice blue eyes. Right now, they were sleepy eyes. "You'll have chores to do in a few hours."

"I'll sleep when you do." The words hung in the air for a few seconds. Red scurried across his clean-shaven face, coloring chipmunk cheeks. "I mean . . . I didn't mean . . . You'll sleep here and I'll go home and sleep. I mean—"

"I knew what you meant." Iris grinned at him. "You're the one who's addled from lack of sleep. Do you want some hot tea before you go?"

"That just might hit the spot."

Iris brushed past him and went to the kitchen. She made tea while he sat at the table and watched. He didn't seem to need conversation. Or maybe he was afraid of what might come out of his mouth after that last gaffe. Inhaling the aroma of cinnamon and spice and everything nice, she smiled as she set the mug on the table. She pushed the teddy bear plastic bottle of honey toward him. He smiled back and squeezed a generous dollop into his tea and then another and another.

"Would you like a little tea with your honey?"

"*Mudder* says my sweet tooth is part of why I'm so

sweet." His face colored all over again. "I should just shut up."

His *mudder* was right about him being sweet. Even though he was the younger brother, he'd kept watch over Salome growing up when they went to the pond to swim or fish. He shared his cookies with them and carried Iris to the house the time she sprained her ankle falling out of the pony wagon the day after her tenth birthday. He never told on them when he saw them coming back from a party at the Rankins' farm during their *rumspringa*. "How's your *daed*? I haven't talked to Salome in a while."

He stirred his tea, his expression somber. "He and *Mudder* will move into the *dawdy haus* this spring."

"Nathanael and his *fraa* will take the big house?"

"And run the farm with my other *bruders*."

"You're not happy about it?" Iris sipped her tea. The aroma of cinnamon reminded her of the tea her *mudder* made when Iris had a cold. All she lacked was the scent of fresh lemon. "You and John get along like puppies from the same litter. You always have."

"It's not that." He cupped the mug in his hands and blew on the hot liquid. "There's John and Nathanael and Avery and William."

"You do have a bunch of older brothers." At twenty-three, Mahon was number five of the Kurtz boys. Only Jason and Mark were younger. He and Salome had one other sister, Mary, who was sixteen. "But Avery has the harness shop."

"He found himself a decent living." Mahon nodded,

but his gaze wandered to the kitchen windows. "Me, I don't like being inside."

"Which is *gut*, since you're a farmer."

"I like farming." He yawned so wide his jaw popped. "It's just tough to making a living these days, especially with my *bruders'* families depending on the income."

She couldn't hide her smile at his attempt to cover another yawn. "Do you want to do something different?"

"I would like to make some of my own decisions about how to do it, that's all. To do it better."

"There's a lot of that going around." Iris had listened to plenty of similar discussions among her brothers and her father at the supper table. "My *bruders* and *daed* don't always agree either."

"*Daed* says it's pie in the sky, like the stars I'm always looking at. He says I should get my head out of the clouds and pay attention to what has always worked. It's not like I want to run off and buy a tractor or hook up electricity." His voice deepened, became gruffer. "But we do the same thing, generation after generation. It's what we do. How we stay who we are. Keeping the world at arm's length."

He stopped and drew a breath. His Adam's apple bobbed.

"You only want to provide for your family better."

He nodded. "Now land is hard to come by and there are too many of us. I want to make a decent living on my own so I can . . ."

"Can what?"

"Pie in the sky, that's all." He ducked his head, then

raised it so his gaze met hers. He shook his head. "That's a discussion for another day."

He wasn't talking about farming anymore.

A spiral of heat drifted through Iris, warming her cheeks and her hands. The kind she hadn't felt in a long time. "You better get home. Dawn will be here before you know it."

"You should be the tired one."

"I'm always wide-awake after I deliver a baby." She dabbed at a drop of honey on the table with her finger. "It never stops being a mystery. It never stops being a gift."

"*Gott* is *gut*."

She lifted her gaze to his. "He is."

He smiled. She smiled back. Nothing goofy about that smile. He had full lips and even, white teeth. Why was she thinking about his lips? The heat intensified. She grabbed her mug and lifted it to her lips. Liquid slopped over the edge and burned her fingers. "Ouch."

"You're getting punchy." He stood. "I better go."

She didn't want him to go. The thought startled her. "It's so cold and dark. Be careful."

"Worried about me?"

She hesitated.

"Don't answer that. Joseph said I could borrow a horse." He paused next to her chair. His hand brushed her arm for a split second, a move so swift and so soft she might have imagined it. "I'll try to get it back here sometime tomorrow. I want to check on you anyway."

She touched the place where his fingers had been, then followed him to the front room. "Why?"

He stuck his arm in the sleeve of his wool coat. "I told you, I feel responsible for them. I brought them here."

"I'm the midwife. Where else would you take them?"

"Into town, I guess. Will your *daed* say it was a good choice?"

"He will." She was sure of it. She knew her *daed*. "We don't turn people in need away from our door."

He buttoned his coat. "We'll see." His gaze remained fixed on her face as he tugged open the door. An icy blast of winter air blew through Iris. It did nothing to cool her. She must be coming down with something. "We'll see about many things, I hope."

The door closed. Iris remained in the middle of the room, staring at it, debating whether she shared the sentiments his eyes suggested.

# CHAPTER 5

The feathers tickled. Iris wiggled under the weight of the blankets and quilts on Abigail and Louella's bed. She didn't want to open her eyes. Not yet. Her eyelids were too heavy.

Tickle. Tickle. She wrinkled her nose and slipped her hand out into the frigid morning air to scratch it. Too cold. Icy cold. She rolled on her side and curled up. To her delight, she didn't encounter the warm, space-hogging body of either sister. For little girls, they certainly took up more than their share of the bed. If they were up, it surely meant dawn had broken. Time to roll out of bed. On the other hand, a few more minutes wouldn't hurt. *Mudder* would understand. She always got breakfast when Iris had a late night.

Tickle. Tickle.

"Stop it."

"The baby's crying."

"What?" She forced her eyes open. Morning sunlight coming through the bedroom window made her squint. A short, blurry figure stood by the bed, silhouetted in the light. "Huh?"

Tickle, tickle.

Iris's sight adjusted. Abigail crawled onto the bed. The mattress creaked. The little girl's pudgy fingers trailed down Iris's nose and across her cheek. Her middle, lower teeth were missing so she tended to lisp when she talked. She smelled like peanut butter and looked as perturbed as a six-year-old with freckles and auburn hair could look. "The *bopli* is crying."

Iris propped herself up on one elbow. She had to think a minute. Rachel's baby? No. Jessica's baby. She probably *was* crying. Newborn babies did. "Why are you telling me?"

"There's nobody else to tell. *Mudder* and *Daed* are still at Freeman's."

"Where are Jessica and Quinn?"

"I don't know. I asked Samuel. He says he hasn't seen them." The little girl shrugged. "I ate a peanut butter cookie, but I'm hungry. Can you make pancakes? Louella is trying, but I think she put too much milk in the batter."

"Coming."

Iris struggled into her dress. She would deal with her hair later. She raced down the hall to her bedroom. The wails were loud and insistent. The baby was hungry. She rapped hard on the door. "Jessica? Quinn? Time to get up. Can't you hear the baby crying?"

No answer. The cries wound themselves around Iris's heart and squeezed. How could anyone hear a baby cry and not want to hold her and hush her and rock her? She turned the knob and shoved the door open. "Jessica? Quinn? Your baby—"

The room was empty. Except for the baby, who had

been laid in the wooden cradle Iris had positioned by the bed before leaving them to sleep. Iris rushed to its side. The baby was wrapped in a faded, nine-patch crib quilt with purple, pink, and lilac squares. The quilting was beautiful, intricate, and hand-stitched. The white cotton batting on the backside had yellowed with age and had a ragged stain that looked like coffee or tea. She scooped up the baby and tucked her in her arms. "You poor thing. Are you feeling neglected?" She sank onto the bed and rocked back and forth. "You're fine. I've got you. I've got you."

The baby's face turned a deep reddish-purple from exertion. She beat her tiny fists against the air and demanded satisfaction. "I know, I know," Iris crooned. "You poor thing. Where is your *mudder*?"

She examined the room, searching the corners with her gaze as if Jessica or Quinn might be hiding in the shadows. The scruffy gym bag still sat next to the cradle. It was open, the sides flopping down, revealing an array of plastic baby bottles, cans of formula, disposable diapers, baby wipes, and a few outfits—frilly dresses not warm enough for a winter day. Iris tucked the screaming baby against her shoulder and patted. "Oh my, oh my, you sweet thing. You need a diaper change and a good feeding."

A folded piece of notebook paper had been attached to the bag strap with a safety pin. Iris struggled to unpin it with one hand. Finally, she gave up and ripped it off, tearing one corner. She managed to unfold it and smooth it out on top of the heap of sheets and quilts.

Dear Iris,

 Her name is Lilly Marie. Grandma was right. We can't keep her. We thought we could, but now that she's here, Quinn and me know it's not gonna work. Quinn says we can come back for her after we get settled and get jobs and I finish high school. You know a lot about babies. I'm not afraid to leave her with you. You'll take good care of her. I'll come get her as soon as I can. I promise.

 Keep track of how much you spend on diapers and formula. I'll pay you back. I promise. Quinn says this note can be like an IOU.

 Talk to you soon.

                              Promise.
                              Jess


 Iris continued to rock. Her throat ached. She rocked harder, but Lilly kept crying. Maybe she knew her mother and father were gone. Maybe she missed the scent of her mother and the warmth of her womb. *IOU one baby.* "I'm so sorry. I'm so sorry," she whispered. "She'll be back. She says she'll be back."

 They'd entrusted Iris with this baby. Whatever possessed them to do that? What circumstances or sequence of events led to abandoning a baby in the home of strangers? Inhaling the scent of baby spit-up and wet diaper, she tilted Lilly back and examined her face. A few curly wisps of blonde hair graced her soft scalp. Her eyes hadn't decided yet what color they would be. The shape of her face and her rosebud lips made her look like her momma. Not much of Quinn and his dark, brooding looks in her. "Hello, Lilly. It's nice to meet you—again."

Lilly wailed.

"I know, I know." Iris laid her on the bed and unwrapped the beautiful crib quilt. Someone had stitched it with love many years earlier. She made quick work of changing the diaper. "We'll find you some warmer clothes, little one, and cloth diapers. *Mudder* may have some tucked away in her chest or we can borrow from Rachel. She'll have saved Annie's clothes in case she has another girl."

Iris had prayed for a family of her own, but not like this. Not the abandoned baby of another woman. Still, who was she to argue with God's plan? And wasn't Lilly better off with someone like Iris who knew about babies and who had family to help? Or was that her own pride and desire talking?

Maybe this was simply Quinn and Jessica's plan. God surely frowned on abandoning babies. They were gifts from Him.

"*Ach*, Lilly, what am I to do?"

*Gott, what do I do? Show me the way.*

"What is all this caterwauling?"

Iris started. "*Daed.* You're here."

"I am. I came to take care of chores." He strode into the room in the bowlegged walk he'd passed on to his boys. "Where are these *Englischers* who spent the night in my house?"

"They're gone." She held out the note, pleased that her hand didn't shake. "They'll be back, though. Jessica promises."

*Daed* adjusted his wire-rimmed spectacles, the frown over his gray beard deepening as he read. The wrinkles in his forehead pinched at that spot over the bridge of his nose between bushy, matching eyebrows. His gaze met hers, his blue eyes piercing. "They're two teenagers who most likely ran away from home. They left a baby only a few hours old in the hands of strangers. You believe that promise?"

"I know if I were her *mudder*—"

"You're not."

Iris swallowed hard against the bitter bile in the back of her throat. She picked up Lilly and hugged her to her chest. *Daed* didn't mean to be cruel. He didn't have a cruel bone in his hefty body. "I know, but I've watched many *mudders* with their newborn *boplin*—"

"And not one of them has run off and left that *bopli*, has she?"

"Nee."

"We need to find them. We can't be responsible for their child."

"Mahon and Salome will help." She grabbed the gym bag and handed it to *Daed*. "She needs to eat."

He took the bag and followed her out the door to the stairs. "They certainly will. They meant well, but bringing these people into our house wasn't a good idea."

"You would turn them away in the snow and ice? She was having a *bopli*."

"Are they *mann* and *fraa*?"

She couldn't lie. *"Nee."*

"What kind of example does that set for your *schweschders* and *bruders*?"

"She was having a baby."

"I know." His growl softened to a low rumble. "And now we have a baby. If they can't be found, we'll have to get the *Englisch* authorities involved."

"Daed—"

"How will she be fed?"

"They left formula and bottles. The *mudder* provided for her."

"The *Englisch* way." With a snort, he clomped down the stairs. "Formula costs a lot. Feed her and then go into town for more. We don't want the poor thing starving in the meantime."

His bark was worse than his bite. But his tone left no doubt. He was serious. What English "authorities" would be involved with an abandoned baby? Was it really abandonment if Jessica and Quinn left the baby with someone like Iris? If they told someone at the sheriff's office, Jessica might never get her baby back.

"We'll figure it out." She held Lilly closer. "I promise."

# CHAPTER 6

Sweet, sweet silence. Iris tiptoed from the cradle nestled between the table and the wood-burning stove across the kitchen to where her mother washed breakfast dishes at the sink. Fed, burped, and freshly diapered, Lilly had succumbed to sleep after a few lingering, halfhearted sobs. *Daed* left the house to go back to Freeman's. Likely he would share the latest news with the bishop. Freeman would offer counsel. He might think it best to call the sheriff's office. In the meantime, Iris planned to take good care of this newcomer, as she would any other guest in their home.

*Mudder* glanced up from the cast-iron skillet in her hands and smiled. "Finally—"

"Shhh!" Iris put her index finger to her lips. "You'll wake her."

"She'll get used to sleeping through anything around here." *Mudder* chuckled and handed the skillet to Iris. "No point in babying the *bopli*."

"Very funny." Iris kept her voice low all the same. She picked up a towel and dried the skillet. "I need to go to Salome's. Do you think you can take care of her for a few hours?"

"I think I can handle it." *Mudder* made quick work

of a pot and laid it in a plastic drain on the counter. "Do you really think you can catch up with them? I reckon they've gotten pretty far down the road, and you don't even know what direction."

"Quinn said they were headed to Texas, but they would have to stop in town for some supplies for Jessica." Heat toasted Iris's cheeks. Even talking to *Mudder* about these things was awkward. "We don't know what time they left either."

"Samuel said the truck was gone when he went to feed the animals." *Mudder* dried her hands and went to the table. She picked up a rumpled piece of paper. "What do you know about this?"

Iris peered over her shoulder. It was a drawing in pencil. The artist had a delicate touch. The details were fine, the wrinkles in her dress, the stains on her apron, the tendrils of hair that had escaped her *kapp*, her long chin. Iris didn't own a mirror, but she'd seen herself in mirrors many times. Her mind replayed the previous evening. Mahon at the desk, his hands over the tablet. The swift move to crumple the top sheet and toss it in the wastebasket. "That's me, isn't it?"

"Any idea how this got in our wastebasket?"

"Mahon was sitting at the desk last night."

"Why would he draw a picture of you?"

Why indeed? Heat curled its way up her neck and across her cheeks. "Did *Daed* see it?"

"*Nee*, I was cleaning the front room, and I emptied the basket." *Mudder* crumpled the sheet. She marched to the stove, opened the door, and tossed it in. Flames consumed it in an instant. "I knew he sketched. His *mudder* mentioned it."

"Nothing wrong with that."

"Animals, landscapes, and the like, *nee*." *Mudder* bent over the cradle and adjusted the quilt around Lilly's chin. "Leaving portraits of you lying about is another thing. We don't abide by pictures of ourselves. It's vain and leads to idolatry."

A sermon Iris had heard many times. During *rumspringa*, she and Salome took their pictures in a booth in town. Black-and-white strips of half a dozen silly poses, arms around each other, tongues sticking out, laughing so hard, their mouths hung open. *Mudder* found the strip. The lecture lasted twenty minutes and the photos disappeared into the fire, the paper curling and crackling in the flames. "He threw it away."

"But he drew it." *Mudder* went back to her dirty dishes. "What's done is done, I reckon. As long as you understand why I burned it."

"I'm not one to think highly of myself." Her tone was far too sharp for a daughter addressing her mother. She softened it. "I'm sorry. I'm tired."

"And worried, I suspect. Worrying helps nothing."

"*Daed* wants Quinn and Jessica found or Lilly turned over to the authorities. I don't even know what authorities it would be."

"Your *daed* will figure that out with Freeman. He wants what's best for the *bopli*." *Mudder* made quick work of another pot and laid it on the counter. "So do you, I reckon."

"Jessica is so young. I'm not sure she can be a *gut mudder*."

"But you can?"

"You don't think I can?"

"I know you *will* be. When the time comes. But this isn't your time."

"If it ever comes." The words were out before she could corral them. "I mean—"

"I know you're impatient. You're uncertain." *Mudder* examined a plate, then dunked it in the tub that held rinse water. "I can understand that, but there's no hurrying *Gott*'s plan. His timing is different from our own."

"Maybe it's not a matter of hurrying the plan. Maybe the plan doesn't include me being a *mudder*."

"You talk about being a *mudder*, but you don't mention being a *fraa*."

That would require a *mann*. She dried the pot and returned it to its spot in the cabinet. How could she explain the vacant space in her heart? She no longer ached for Aidan. Knowing he loved another had closed that door forever. "I feel as if I'm waiting for something. I've been waiting forever."

"Or someone?" *Mudder* scooped up silverware from the bottom of the tub and began to scrub. "Like someone who draws pretty pictures of you."

"*Mudder!*" Mahon had been bored, nothing more. Iris cast about for another topic. "I know it's been a few years, but do you have any cloth diapers stored away? Or any of Abigail's baby clothes?"

"I have a few things tucked away." *Mudder* tugged

the towel from Iris's hands. She patted her fingers dry, a faraway look on her lined face. Iris knew what she would look like when she reached middle age. Fine wrinkles framed her *mudder*'s blue eyes. Gray had overtaken her blonde hair. Her figure grew rounder with each child and each passing year. "The baby's crib quilt is very pretty, for sure."

Iris followed her mother's gaze to the cradle. "It's old. The colors have faded, and there's a stain on the back."

"It's strange . . ." *Mudder*'s voice faded away. She dropped the towel on the counter. "I have something to show you."

After a last peek at Lilly, who slumbered with one fist against her tiny mouth, the other hidden under the quilt, Iris scurried to catch up with her mother, who headed for the back hallway and the bedroom she shared with *Daed*. There, she flipped up the clasps on a massive trunk at the foot of the bed. Iris had never seen it open. She used to ask as a child, but *Mudder* never let her look inside.

"What is all that?"

"Originally this was my hope chest. Now it's mostly full of quilts and keepsakes. A few things my *mudder* gave me." *Mudder*'s voice had an odd tremor in it that Iris had never heard before. She smoothed her hands across a baby's lilac nightgown, then held it up. "This was your sister Molly's."

"I don't have—"

Iris stopped, compelled to silence by the pain etched on her mother's face. She looked much older for a split second. She looked like *Groossmammi* Plank before she passed.

*Mudder* laid the nightgown back in the chest with the care reserved for something precious and irreplaceable. "Molly was our first *bopli*. Your older *schweschder*. She only lived a few hours."

She plopped onto the bed and picked up an envelope yellowed with age. Her head bent, she turned it over and over. Finally, she lifted the flap and showed Iris the contents. A single, small lock of wispy, auburn hair. Her fingertips, callused from years of gardening, laundry, and sewing, caressed the tendrils and then returned them to the envelope.

"I didn't know." Iris eased onto the bed next to her mother. "You never talked about her."

"Some of *Gott*'s gifts are fleeting." *Mudder* shrugged. "My pea brain isn't big enough to understand them all. She was here. Then she wasn't. No point in dwelling on it. You came along a year later."

She patted Iris's hand. Her fingers were warm and sturdy. "I'm glad you stayed around."

It was as close as her mother ever came to expressing affection through words. Iris cleared her throat. "Me too."

She had had a big sister. Her life would've been so different with an older sister to share a room, to share secrets, impart wisdom, make mistakes with, and learn from them together. They might have teased their brothers together, gone to singings together. Molly would've known what to do about Aidan. Big sisters knew these things. They might have bickered over which side of the bed to sleep on or whether to have the window open or closed on a fall evening or who would wash and who would dry the dishes. Life would've been different. "No one knows? There's no marker at the cemetery."

"We were visiting your *aenti* Esther in Haven." *Mudder*'s voice cracked. She reached for a tissue from the box on the table next to the bed. "I was sick after the birth. We stayed almost a month. We buried her there. It was a long time ago."

"But it still hurts."

"*Boplin* are *Gott*'s gifts. Their days with us are in His province. Still, my prayer for you is that you never have to know how much."

*Mudder* placed the envelope back in the chest, nestled in the folds of the nightgown. She bent over and lifted a pile of quilts. "Here it is." She laid a crib quilt in Iris's lap. "A nine-patch quilt."

The same pattern as the one Jessica left for Lilly. The colors were different. Black blocks framed the outside. The inner blocks were purple, a pale lavender, and black. It was old as well, but someone had cared for it better. "Where did this come from?"

"It's been handed down, *mudder* to *mudder*, for generations on my family's side." *Mudder* patted the quilt. "I intended to give it to you when you had your first baby. That's the way we've always done it."

"So *Groossmammi* gave it to you when you were expecting Molly."

"*Jah.*"

"It would've gone to her?"

"It would have, but instead it'll go to you."

Iris ran her hand over the pieced cotton blocks. The quilting, done by hand, was perfectly stitched. She held it out to *Mudder.* "It's not time. Keep it until it's time."

"I wanted you to know I have faith. It's more than a quilt that warms a baby on a winter night. It reminds us that behind our faith and community, family is most important to us."

"I know."

"Don't lose faith because of what happened with Aidan."

It was the closest her mother had come to speaking of her courtship with Aidan. "I loved him for a long time."

"But you knew in your heart that he was meant for another. When we marry, we are yoked for life. You don't want to give that gift to the wrong person." *Mudder* wrapped her arms around the quilt and held it to her chest as if wrapping it in a hug. "You were wrapped in this quilt on your first day on earth. It kept you warm. It let you know you were loved. You are still loved. And one day you will find your mate."

Iris managed a smile. "If I don't marry, there's always Louella."

"Wait upon the Lord." *Mudder* cleared her throat and smiled back. "In the meantime, I think I have a small stack of Abigail's clothes in here somewhere." She pulled back a folded full-size quilt to reveal more nightgowns. "I guess I wasn't quite ready to let go of them. Just in case."

In case Abigail wasn't the last. There would always be room in the Beachy house for one more and in a mother's heart. "I'll take them to the laundry room."

*Mudder* laid the crib quilt back in the trunk. "It'll be here when you're ready."

Iris nodded. No need to tell *Mudder* she'd been ready for years now.

# CHAPTER 7

*G*ott had a way of providing. Iris studied the two drawings. Others in the *Gmay* might not think much of Mahon's skill as an artist, but it was a God-given gift. Perfect likenesses of Quinn and Jessica stared back at her. When Mahon heard that the couple had left their newborn daughter at the Beachy home and disappeared before dawn, he had agreed to help. It took him less than five minutes to sketch the two pictures with Iris peering over his shoulder at the table in the Kurtzs' toasty warm kitchen that smelled of baking cinnamon rolls and simmering beef stew. He caught Quinn's dark, handsome features and Jessica's elfin quality in the shape of her chin, upturned nose, and large eyes.

"You draw well." Her mind's eye pictured the rumpled sketch *Mudder* had tossed in the stove earlier in the day. Iris picked up the drawing of Quinn. The tuft of brown whiskers under his bottom lip spoke of the desire to look older. The beard wouldn't grow no matter how hard he tried. "It's not just how he looks, but how he is."

Mahon glanced at his mother, who stooped to pull

the cinnamon rolls from the oven. He shrugged and laid his pencil next to a thick, rectangular sketch pad. "It's just something I do in my spare time. Anything to help you find them."

A *harrumph* from the vicinity of the stove told Iris that Bertha Kurtz was listening. Iris slid into the chair across from Mahon. She flattened her hands on the rough pine to keep from reaching for the sketch pad. Curiosity killed the cat. "It's raining now and the snow has turned to slush. Not much to do in the way of chores."

"I know. I was waiting to return the horse until it lightened up." He picked up the pencil and stuck it behind his ear. "It's a mess out there. I should drive you into town. We can talk to a few folks, see if anyone saw them or talked to them."

"Maybe they told someone where in Texas they're headed."

"Sounds like something Salome should do with Iris." Bertha turned from the stove, potholder mitts still on her hands. Her wrinkled cheeks were rosy from the heat. "I reckon your *daed* will need help with something before the afternoon is over."

"Salome won't be home from teaching until late." Mahon's tone was respectful, but firm. "Cyrus wants this taken care of. He has concerns."

Iris waited. Her heart did a crazy one-two-one-two beat that made her catch her breath. Because of the baby, not because of the prospect of spending an afternoon with Mahon. Their conversation the previous evening had replayed in her head, keeping her awake for more than an hour after his departure, despite her exhaustion. That touch. Had she imagined it? Rachel had planted the seed. It was the power of suggestion, nothing more. The power of suggestion made her warm despite icy temperatures outside. That was all.

"He's right about that." Bertha frowned. She wouldn't disagree with the deacon. No member of the community would. "See to it that you're back in time for evening chores. Your *daed*'s back is out of whack again."

"We'll take your buggy since it's already hitched." Mahon stood, sketches in hand, and headed for the door. "You can drop me off on the way back."

"We should take this." Iris picked up the sketchbook and scooted away from the table. "In case you need to draw something."

It sounded lame in her ears. Because it was lame. Mahon grabbed his coat from the hook by the back door. The look of discomfort on his face said he thought so too, but he shrugged and nodded. He put on his coat and held out his hand. "I'll take it."

"I can carry it. You'll be driving."

His anxious gaze fixed on the sketchbook, he chewed on his lower lip for a second. "I'll be back before supper, *Mudder*."

Bertha sniffed. "Don't track mud in the house when you do get here."

A few minutes later they were on the road to Jamesport under a gloomy, gray sky that threatened to open up and drench them. Iris held the sketchbook in her lap with both hands. It was important to Mahon, which made it seem heavy and substantial to the touch.

She studied the fields as they rolled by, searching for a topic of conversation. Patches of snow shone white against the muddy earth spattered with rain. The weather? The baby? She couldn't stand it anymore. "Can I look at your drawings?"

She opened the book before he could reply. The first few sketches were landscapes. Missouri in spring. A horse pulling a buggy on a road that wound past an open field, a red barn in the distance. Roses on a trellis outside a front door, complete with a welcome mat on the porch. An oak tree and an unoccupied tire swing. The strokes were fine and sure. The drawings contained as much detail as a black-and-white photograph, like memories caught and suspended in time.

"I wish you wouldn't."

"Why? They're beautiful."

Iris turned the page and found her own likeness staring up at her. She sat in a lawn chair, a glass of something in her hand. Her head was thrown back as if she were laughing. She looked up at someone who stood just beyond the page. She glanced at Mahon. He scowled straight ahead. A pulse beat in his jaw.

"I'm sorry." She shut the sketchbook. The *clip-clop* of horse's hooves in the muck filled the silence for several seconds. Half a dozen thoughts whirled through her head. He'd captured her image at a singing or a picnic. A happy, carefree moment. Such moments seemed long ago. For him, too, perhaps. But he'd never approached her at a singing. She always left with Aidan. Mahon's presence barely registered in those days. "Why do you draw me?"

"I draw other people."

"Other women?"

He didn't answer. The squeak of the wooden wheels as they spun in the muck punctuated the question. The wind whistled through the bare branches of the sycamore and elm trees that lined the road. It cut through her wool coat. She shivered. "I didn't mean to pry."

"My *daed* says drawing doesn't serve a purpose. He says it's like daydreaming, filling up time with doodles." He cleared his throat. "He's never mean about it. He only wants me to understand. It's not like making furniture, which is useful and can be beautiful too. Or the crib quilts you make for the babies. The quilts keep them warm, but they're pretty too."

He'd noticed her crib quilts. She set that observation aside to study later. It sounded as if he'd heard this lecture many times. "But you still draw."

"It doesn't interfere with my chores." Mahon's glance sideswiped hers. His face turned a deeper hue of scarlet than the cold warranted. He snapped the reins as if to hurry along this never-ending ride. "I think while I do it. I puzzle things out. I record memories. It doesn't hurt anything."

He stumbled over the words as if searching for the right ones to explain something he feared she would never understand. But she did. While she pieced and quilted the crib blankets she, too, puzzled over life's strange twists and turns. She imagined the lives the babies would have, what they would look like, the world they would inherit in years to come. She, too, tried to understand that which couldn't be understood. What did farmers think about during those long afternoons when they tilled the fields? What did *Mudder* think about as she toiled over load after load of laundry or pulled weeds in the morning sun on a spring day? Was it any different? *Daed*—and the bishop and the minister— would argue the end results were. Food from the fields and the garden, clean clothes, quilts, useful products unlike these sketches that served no other purpose than to memorialize a moment in life. "*Gott* made beautiful flowers. It doesn't seem they serve much purpose other than to make us smile and tell us spring is here."

"I'm sure they serve other purposes." His expression softened and he smiled. "They provide food to the bees."

"I'll give you that one."

The silence was more companionable then.

She longed to open the sketchbook again. Is that what her mother meant by pride? What Freeman talked about in his messages on Sundays—personal vanity, idolatry. The sin of worshipping one's self. All that in an innocent sketch of her laughing. Or maybe it was the call of the forbidden, like the keggers during her *rumspringa*. She'd been so anxious to gulp down that red cup of beer. Then, when Salome wasn't looking, she'd spat it out and rushed in search of water to drown the nasty taste. The English farm boys had scoffed at her queasiness.

"Why don't you want me to look at the sketches?"

"My whole life I've been told not to get carried away with it. To drop the pencil and go do something worthwhile."

"I used to get that when I read books instead of darning."

"But you didn't feel . . . compelled to read."

"*Nee*, I just like it." She grinned, thinking of her early foray into Nancy Drew mysteries, eventually replaced by Miss Marple and Hercule Poirot. Lives so different from hers and worlds apart. Vocabulary too. "I keep a book in my room and go to bed early."

His chuckle sounded rueful. "I share my room."

"You didn't answer my question."

"I don't draw other women."

"Why do you draw me?"

He snapped the reins. "Giddy-up." As if he couldn't wait to reach Jamesport. "It passes the time."

"The time until what?"

"Until you're ready."

Maybe she should ask him to draw *her* a picture. "Ready for what?"

"I don't remember you asking so many questions." He glared at her. "Me."

One syllable could be worth a hundred drawings, if it was the right syllable.

She wasn't cold anymore. In fact, she considered removing her mittens and her coat.

"You asked." He growled deep in his throat, like an old barnyard dog awakened from a nap. "I'm waiting for you to get over Aidan Graber, come to your senses, and see we're meant to be together."

# CHAPTER 8

*Come to my senses?* Heat scorched Iris's ears. The burning on her cheeks had nothing to do with the icy-cold wind. She inhaled and counted to ten. Three times.

"You asked." Mahon sounded as aggravated as she felt. "More than once."

How dare he? *Get over Aidan.* "What are you talking about?"

"You forget I live in the same house as Salome. I spent as much time with you as her when we were *kinner.* I watched you leave with him after the singings. I watched your face when you watched him at Caleb's funeral. I saw your face when he married Bess. All this time I've waited for you to see what's on my face."

He'd found the words after all.

"Well, well . . . I don't . . ." Iris sputtered. "You never . . ."

"You did ask."

Iris laid the sketchbook between them. His words hung in the air. Rachel was right about everything. Mahon's feelings came as no surprise, truly, so why was she so stunned? The depth and breadth astounded her. He'd held his peace for a long time. Now the words rushed out like a torrential river that bowled her over. "I don't know what to say."

"Don't say anything. Do me that favor."

To say nothing would be unkind. Yet his declaration put him far ahead of her on this path. He couldn't expect her to race to meet him at the end. "It's not fair."

"What's not fair?"

"You could've tried." As if she would've had eyes for anyone other than Aidan in those days. Now she wasn't being fair. No other words came that would help her explain the tumult in her heart and head. "You could've said something."

"Your heart was—*is*—with someone else."

"No. It's not. Not anymore. Granted, it was at one time, but I've made my peace. I turned him down."

"He asked you to marry him and you said no."

She turned her face toward the fields. Shame coursed through her. Did everyone know of her heartbreak? What passed between her and Aidan was private. Like having a leg amputated and experiencing phantom leg pain. "How do you know this?"

"Salome and Mary talk when they do their sewing at night. They forget I'm around."

The sound of the rain-engorged creek gurgling past her on the cool spring evening on which Aidan had proposed assailed Iris's ears. The way the rocks had smacked the water when she made them skip better than he did. Frogs croaked. A mockingbird trilled. Her heart beat in a ragged, painful tribute to what she knew was coming. "I had to say no. He didn't *lieb* me."

"Another woman might have said *jah*, thinking he would grow to *lieb* her."

"In three years, he never kissed me." She bent her head and stared at her hands, her voice a whisper. Mortified, she cringed and put her hands to her burning cheeks. Had she said those words aloud? "You don't want to hear this."

"I'm glad."

Her hands dropped. She swiveled and glared at him. "Why?"

The childish, chipmunk face disappeared, replaced with a man's fierce stare. His blue eyes were warm and liquid. His cheeks were red from the cold and emotion. He transferred the reins to one hand. His free hand landed on hers and squeezed, his grip hard, nothing like the soft brush of the previous evening. "It means your first kiss is reserved for the man who loves you." He let go and returned to the business of driving. "Me."

Her mouth gaped. Unable to think of a single word of response, she closed it.

They made the rest of the drive to the Jamesport Grocery Store in silence. Mahon pulled into one of the spots in front of the hitching post and tethered the horse. "They might have stopped here for supplies before heading out of town."

She owed him a response. The connection between her brain and her mouth was tied in a million knots. She nodded. He hopped from the buggy and looked back. "Are you coming?"

She nodded again. Shaking his head, he strode around the buggy to her side. He glanced around at the nearly empty street and then up at her. "Don't worry about it."

"I'm not worried." Her voice sounded breathless in her own ears. Her gaze fastened on his mouth. The power of suggestion? She had waited forever for that first kiss from Aidan. It never came. Mahon was right. It should be reserved for a man who loved her, whom she loved just as much. "Don't *you* worry."

"I've been waiting quite awhile. I'm used to it. I'm not going anywhere."

She studied him. He looked nothing like Aidan, who was tall and blond and had an angular face. But Mahon did have that same sense of loyalty. Aidan's love for a friend had kept him from courting the woman he loved. When Caleb died, Aidan had the opportunity to finally seek her out. Instead, he asked Iris to marry him because he felt an obligation after years of courting. Knowing his true heart, she'd sent him to Bess with her blessing. Mahon was waiting for her and only her. The thought was like needle and thread darning the rips in her heart. Still, no words presented themselves.

He smiled, a soft, tentative, knowing smile. "Except into the store."

She climbed down and followed him inside, where they found Kathy Myers behind the register. Snapping a wad of gum the size of her thumb, the teenager scratched the end of her pimpled nose and laid aside her cell phone. She took her time looking at the sketches. "Yep, I've seen him." She pointed to Quinn. "Right after I unlocked the doors this morning. He was waiting outside in a van. Parked right next to Mrs. Lumpkins's station wagon and Cheryl Reiner's pickup truck. They like to do their shopping early to beat the rush hour. Like we got a rush hour in Jamesport on a Thursday morning."

"Did he say anything? Like where he was headed?"

"Nope, and I never got a chance to ask." The bells over the glass double doors dinged. Kathy waved at Tillie Matthews, who waved back and headed toward the bread aisle. "You should show these to Dan Rogers."

"The sheriff's deputy?" An uneasy feeling churned in Iris's belly. "Why? Is he in town for something?"

"Mike called him." Mike was Mike Turner, owner of the grocery store. Kathy tapped Quinn's sketch with a fingernail painted neon purple. "After I called Mike to tell him this guy walked out of the store without paying for anything."

"He shoplifted. Are you sure?"

"He was carrying one of those green camouflage army backpacks." Kathy pointed at the overhead mirrors. "I watched him pick up a package of sanitary napkins, some chocolate donuts. A bottle of aspirin. Some OJ. Next thing I know, I'm ringing up Mrs. Lumpkins and I hear the bell. I look up and he's out the door. I ran around the counter and sprinted after him. He took off like a bat out of hell in a brown van that sounded like it was on its last leg."

Mahon turned around and leaned on the counter between the gum and mints rack and the rack of sales flyers. He scooted down to let Tillie pay for her bread and milk. "Is Deputy Rogers coming to town?"

"He's already here." Kathy waved Tillie's twenty-dollar bill in the general direction of the street. "He was on his way to the Purple Martin Café for a piece of Zeke's chocolate cream and meringue pie before he headed back to Gallatin."

Iris whirled, tugged a cart from the row by the doors, and headed for the baby food aisle. How could Quinn do such a thing? Desperation? He only needed to ask. They would've helped. How could he do this to Lilly? How could he do this to Jessica?

A father who could leave his baby girl behind could also steal, it seemed. He'd left Iris with the responsibility of feeding his child. She picked up a can of powdered formula. The cost of one small can made her mouth drop. At this rate her small savings from selling crib quilts at the craft sales would be quickly depleted. No matter. She would earn more this spring. She grabbed two big cans and set them in the basket, followed by three gallons of distilled water.

"You don't want to tell him, do you?" Mahon halted near the long rows of baby food in jars of every color. He picked up a jar of purple plums, then placed it back in its spot, the label turned out. "You're worried about what it means for the baby."

"If we tell him about Quinn and Jessica, we'll have to tell him about Lilly."

"We have to tell him." Mahon took over the cart for her and headed toward the counter. "A man broke the law and we know something about him."

"We don't even know his last name." Iris tugged her wallet from her canvas bag. She counted the bills inside it, once, then again. "We can't help them find Quinn and arrest him. He's Lilly's *daed*."

"He's also a shoplifter."

"Would Freeman want us to get involved?"

"We're already involved." They waited for Mr. and Mrs. Haag to finishing paying for their groceries. A lot of frozen meals. Sugar-free cookies. Banana pudding. And prune juice. "Not to mention, your *daed* wanted us to find them. A sheriff's deputy can do that easier than we can."

"And put them in jail."

"Just Quinn. Which would force Jessica to go home to her parents and take her baby with her."

Her expression puzzled, Kathy shoved a lock of bleached blonde hair from her eyes. "I didn't know you two were married, let alone had a baby."

"We don't."

"We're not." Iris's words collided with Mahon's.

Kathy's dark, finely plucked eyebrows rose and fell. "Okay, whatever you say."

Mahon parked the cart. "I'm going to the Purple Martin. Are you coming or not?"

A baby should have a mother and a father.

A series of bad choices had brought them here. That's what her father would say.

Iris followed Mahon down the street to the Purple Martin Café, home of the best chicken fried steak in town. The aroma of bacon frying mingled with the scent of freshly baked apple pie greeted her when she pushed through the glass double doors. Her stomach rumbled. Owner Ezekiel Miller hustled toward them with his usual enthusiastic wave. If he found it odd they had walked in together, he didn't show it. "Table or booth?"

Mahon shook his head. Iris followed his gaze. Deputy Rogers sat at the counter polishing off a huge piece of chocolate cream pie crowned with golden, brown-tipped, puffy meringue.

About fifteen seconds into Mahon's recitation, Rogers laid down his fork. Thirty seconds in, he tugged a slim notebook from his shirt pocket and began to take notes. He asked a few questions about the van, Quinn's and Jessica's descriptions, where they were from and where they were going, all of which Mahon answered. Rogers sat in silence for a few seconds after Mahon finished.

"Can I keep these?" He pointed to the sketches.

Mahon nodded. Iris tried to read the deputy's expression. A word from her Agatha Christie novels came to mind. *Inscrutable.*

He leaned forward on his stool, looking past Mahon to Iris. "They didn't specify where in Texas?"

Iris shook her head.

"Neither one of them offered a last name or said where they came from?"

"They told Mahon they were from Iowa. That's all I know."

"And they left their newborn baby with you?"

"*Jah.* Yes."

Frowning, Deputy Rogers scratched his forehead with his index finger. "A shoplifting baby abandoner. This day just gets better and better."

"Are you going to take the baby?" To her chagrin, Iris's voice squeaked. Her *daed* would not want her inserting herself into a sheriff's investigation of two *Englischers*.

Deputy Rogers shoved his empty plate back and picked up his coffee cup. "That wouldn't be for me to say. I'll talk to the children's division and the juvenile office." He shook his head. "Either way, a judge has to make the order. Unless a kid is in imminent danger. Then we can put them in temporary protective custody until the judge reviews the case and makes a ruling."

Iris breathed.

"Are your parents willing to be responsible for the baby—at least for now?"

Iris nodded. She would take care of Lilly, but it was her parents' house.

Deputy Rogers dropped a dollar tip on the counter. He scooped up his bill and the two sketches. "I've known your parents for a long time. I reckon that baby is in good hands—better than she would be with those kids. They qualify as temporary protective custody in my way of thinking. Before anything regarding permanent custody of the baby can be decided, we have to find the parents."

Lilly would be in good hands—her hands. "How do you find people when you don't even have last names?"

"The sketches will help. We'll put out a BOLO— that's a "be on the lookout"—and send the sketches to other law enforcement agencies. We'll use social media. Believe me, we have our ways." He stood and headed for the cash register at the end of the counter. "I'll go by and talk to your parents before I head back to Gallatin. I want a look at the baby and the bag they left. If you think of anything else, let me know."

Iris nodded once again, but her mind repeated the two most important words he'd said. *Permanent custody.*

# CHAPTER 9

Sleep. Sweet, elusive sleep. Maybe the sponge bath would relax Lilly enough to make her nod off. Iris rubbed her burning eyes and picked up the towel. Avoiding the spot where her belly button would one day be, she patted the baby dry. She'd been careful not to get it wet. So many things to think about with a newborn. Especially this tiny one who was a decent eater but seemed to have her days and nights mixed up. Cry and eat at night. Nap, cry, and eat all day.

"You're nice and clean after your first bath." Iris dressed her in a lilac nightgown she plucked from the bag of hand-me-downs Rachel had given her when she went over to check on the new mom and baby Micah. Both were doing well. Micah slept a lot. Lucky Rachel. "See how sweet you look in your nightie. And you know what that means? That means it's time to sleep. Can you do that for me?"

Lilly cooed and then burped, a loud, brash sound much too big for such a small baby. A stream of white, stinky formula spit-up followed. Iris sighed. "Just be that way, Lilly Marie."

Thank goodness for hand-me-downs. The next nightie was a soft blue cotton. Her arms heavy with fatigue, Iris redressed Lilly and wrapped her in the nine-patch quilt Jessica had left behind. Something from her real mother. It took more than blankets or blood to make a true mother. A true mother rocked her baby in the middle of the night. She patted her back when she had a tummy ache and nursed her when she was hungry. She didn't run to Texas while others slept. "Do you have a tummy ache, my sweet? Am I giving you too much formula?"

She didn't know anyone who bottle-fed so she had no one else to ask. Lilly didn't answer. She didn't wail either, which was a good sign. Iris settled into the rocking chair she'd moved into her bedroom, along with the cradle. "You're fed. You're clean. You have a fresh diaper." She began to rock. "Now you sleep. It's night. We sleep at night. Now close your eyes and sleep."

Lilly's head bobbed, but her eyes were wide open. She'd slept through Deputy Rogers's visit the previous afternoon, according to *Mudder*, who said *Daed* did all the talking. Yes, they would take care of the baby. No, they didn't know where the parents had gone. The deputy went through the gym bag and scoured the bedroom where they had slept, with hardly a word before telling them the same thing he'd told Iris and Mahon. If they thought of anything else, let him know.

"What else could there be?"

Lilly wrinkled her tiny nose and sighed at Iris's entirely rhetorical question, but her eyes remained open.

"*Ach, bopli, Aenti* Iris needs to sleep."

Aenti *Iris*. Would she ever be more than an aunt? Mahon's words spoken in the buggy reverberated in her mind. *Waiting for you to be ready*. Mahon didn't think of her as someone's aunt. He drew sketches of her. Beautiful sketches. Despite the cool air in her bedroom, a wave of heat engulfed her. The trip home from Jamesport as the dusk began to gather had been spent rehashing everything Deputy Rogers said at the restaurant. Neither had broached the subject of the sketches or Mahon's declaration. He hopped from the buggy at his house with a promise to return *Daed*'s horse as soon as he could and a backward wave. Just like that.

She closed her eyes for a second, remembering his smell of burnt wood and the way he bit his lip as he worked on the sketches. The way he cocked his head to one side and then the other as he studied his work, his dark eyes intent and critical. The sound of his voice when he said he was waiting for her. As if he couldn't quite catch his breath.

Why hadn't she said anything? It had been cowardly to leave him hanging. She didn't know what to say. To acknowledge his feelings was to make room for the possibility that she might also have feelings for him. That those feelings might grow. That she might have to explore again the path that left her wide open to pain and anguish.

"I'm not mad, *Gott*. I'm not." She spoke aloud, letting her voice drift toward the rafters. He already knew what she thought, what she felt, how she hurt, how she feared. God knew it all. So why didn't He do something? "Sorry, *Gott*. Sorry."

She'd spent her whole life learning the lessons of *gelassenheit*. Yielding to *Gott*'s will.

No one talked about not liking it. What did a person do with those feelings?

*I'm waiting for you.*

Mahon was waiting for her. How long would he wait? He said he was used to waiting. That he wasn't going anywhere. She could trust those words. She could trust him, couldn't she? The memory of his hand on her arm, the feel of his warm fingers—farmer's fingers that wielded a pencil with a deft touch. Touching her. She closed her eyes. To open herself up to Mahon, to trust him, was to trust God.

God was waiting for her too.

To yield to His plan. She was tired of going it alone.

"Is that how you feel, *bopli*?" She snuggled the baby closer. "You look tired. Like me. We both need to sleep."

"Sleep, baby, sleep." She sang, first in German, then in English, trying to blot the sound of Mahon's voice from her head. It was a deep voice, deeper than Aidan's, even though Aidan was a bigger man. Mahon was solid, barrel-chested, compact. A farmer who liked to draw. A farmer who read the stars the way she read books. He intrigued her. She'd known him all her life, and now it turned out she didn't know him at all. *"Grandpa tends the sheep, Grandma brings in the skinny cows."*

Lilly gurgled.

*"Jah*, it's a funny song. I don't know why they're skinny cows." She shook her head. All these thoughts spun round and round in her head. They had no place

to go. She could tell no one. Not Rachel with her three little ones and her happy life. Not Salome. Mahon was her brother. She might tease him, but she loved her brother. "It doesn't matter. You need to sleep. I need to sleep."

Lack of sleep explained her silly thoughts. Not cracks in her good-girl façade. She held what she most wanted in her arms, but this baby did not belong to her.

Lilly babbled and swung her tiny fists. "You are a sweet thing, *jah*, you are."

The baby's mouth opened wide, closed, and formed what looked like a smile. "You smiled at me, didn't you? You smiled!"

Everyone said newborn babies didn't smile. *Mudder* would say it was gas. Iris knew differently. Babies often smiled at her after she delivered them. She was the first person to greet them in this strange, new world with its cold and dark shadows. She shared a special bond with every child she delivered. Iris touched Lilly's soft check and snuggled her closer to her chest. "You are loved, my sweet, you are cherished."

All babies should know that and feel it. Iris rocked a little harder. Her eyelids felt heavy, her arms limp. She didn't dare fall asleep before the baby did. She swallowed the lump in her throat. "How about 'Jesus Loves Me'?" Lilly might not understand about Jesus' love now, but one day she would. Did Jessica believe in Jesus? Iris didn't allow her voice to falter at the thought. Lilly's eyelids dropped. Her hands stilled.

*Thank you, Jesus.* Iris softened her voice to a low whisper. Lilly's eyes closed. *Thank you, Jesus.* She held

Lilly's warm body, limp in sleep, close to her chest and inhaled the sweet scent of her hair, the scent of hope, of possibility, of dreams that can come true. "Sweet, sweet *bopli*."

"Hey, there you are."

Iris jumped at the sound of Salome's voice. "Hush, hush," she whispered. "I just got her to sleep."

"Sorry." Shoulders hunched, Salome moved into the room in an exaggerated tiptoe. "Put her down so we can talk."

*Mudder* was right, as usual. Lilly would learn to sleep through anything in this house. "I'm tired." Iris eased from the chair. Holding her breath, she lowered Lilly into the cradle and stepped back. "I thought I would go to bed too."

"It's early." Salome shivered. "I'm cold. Let's go in the kitchen and make some hot tea."

Early for someone who was getting uninterrupted sleep. "One cup and then I'm going to bed."

Salome grinned and led the way down the stairs and through the front room. *Mudder* wrote letters at the desk, her head bent over the paper. She didn't look up. Their giggles boisterous, the girls played checkers with Carl. *Daed* sat in the rocker by the fireplace, *The Budget* newspaper in his lap. His glasses were tucked into the sparse hair on his head. Ethan Shrock, Bartholomew's brother, sat in the chair across from him. Both men smiled as Iris passed on Salome's heels. Ethan raised his hand and waved. Neither said a word.

"What are you doing out so late on a cold night?"

Iris paused halfway through the room. Salome continued her beeline for the kitchen with barely a glance toward the other visitor. "Is everything all right with your family?"

"*Gut, gut.*" Ethan's gaze—which could only be described as hopeful—meandered toward Salome's back disappearing into the kitchen. "We—I needed to talk to your *daed.*"

*Daed* simply nodded. He wore his deacon face. His lips would be sealed unless Ethan let the cat out of the bag. Which he obviously didn't intend to do.

"What is Ethan doing here? Do you know?" She followed Salome into the kitchen where she filled the kettle with water and placed it on the stove. Her mind was fuzzier than an old blanket. "I haven't been getting much sleep."

"We'll get to that. You looked tuckered out." Salome busied herself setting out mugs and teabags. "Motherhood is hard."

"I'm not the *bopli*'s mother."

"I hope you remember that."

"What are you talking about?"

Salome turned and faced Iris. "It would be easy to get attached to such a sweet little thing."

"She's a baby who needs loving. It's not her fault her parents took off."

"No word from Deputy Rogers?"

"Not yet. It's barely been twenty-four hours." Iris plopped into a chair at the table. She kept waiting for him to show up at the door to take Lilly away. Which made every moment she was responsible for this small, fragile life more bittersweet. "I'm sure it's like hunting for a needle in a haystack."

"Lots of nooks and crannies between here and the Mexican border." Salome opened a plastic container and selected a large chocolate chip cookie from its contents. "What will they do if they don't find them? They don't even have a last name to try to find other relatives."

"I'm not exactly sure. Something about a children's division and a judge." Iris rubbed a spot behind her right ear. Her head ached. "He said something about permanent custody."

"Ethan asked me to marry him."

It took a second for the abrupt change of subjects to register. "Ethan?" This explained his presence in the Beachy living room. "When?"

"Last night." Her nose crinkled, eyebrows lifted, and forehead creased, Salome laid a cookie on a napkin. She held it out to Iris from an arm's length away. Was she expecting a sudden explosion? "We told your *daed* tonight. He said he'll talk to Freeman tomorrow after the funeral. The announcement will be made Sunday."

"That's *wunderbarr*." Despite her best effort to ward it off, a new ache spread down Iris's throat into her chest. She swallowed against it, stood, and held out her arms. Salome walked into the hug. "You never said a word."

"It's silly, I know." Salome's arms tightened around Iris. Her voice dropped to a tearful whisper. "I wanted to tell you before it was announced."

"I thought it might be you and Joseph."

"Silly you! Joseph? That would be like kissing my *bruder*."

*Like kissing Mahon.* The thought did cartwheels in Iris's head. *Stop it. Concentrate.* This was Salome's moment. "Joseph took you home the other night. The thought crossed my mind, that's all. Why didn't you talk to me about Ethan before?" Iris took a step back and peered into her friend's face. "You knew I'd be happy for you, right?"

"I knew you would be because you're that kind of friend, that kind of person. It's just that you and I are the last ones, and I know how hurt—"

"It doesn't matter." Iris forced a smile. The last ones in their group to marry. "Ethan is like Bartholomew. A *gut* man. You will be a *gut fraa* to him. I'm happy for you. I can't believe you kept it a secret."

Salome swiped at her face with her sleeve. "It really started about the time you broke it off with Aidan. I didn't want to add salt to the wound. Besides, courting is private."

"Except between friends." More than a year had passed. Aidan married Bess. Salome never said a word. Neither did Rachel. She had to know about her brother-in-law. How tender they must think her feelings. How fragile they must see her. Had she moped around that much? Friends and family should feel free to share their happiness. "I'm fine. Perfectly fine. I promise. I assume Rachel knows."

"*Jah.* I want the two of you to be my witnesses."

Iris hugged her a second time. "It would be an

honor." Watching her friend marry would be a special day she would never forget. "Where will you live?"

"With his parents until he can build our house on a piece of Bartholomew's property. Just on the other side of Rachel's house."

Just down the road from the Beachy homestead. She would watch Salome's babies grow and play with Rachel's. They would bake and do laundry and cook together. They would piece the crib quilts and quilt them together. Just as they did now. God willing, there would be babies. Iris would deliver them. "And teaching? Who'll take over at the school?"

"It's for the *Gmay* to decide." Sadness crept into Salome's face. "I will miss it. I *lieb* teaching and my scholars. I think one of the Schultz sisters would make a *gut* teacher."

She took the tea kettle from the stove and poured steaming water into the two mugs. The calming scent of chamomile filled the air. Iris closed her eyes for a second, inhaled, and sighed.

"There's that sigh." Salome carried the mugs to the table, only slopping a tiny bit. "*Ach*, hot, hot. The sigh that says you're sad."

"It says I'm tired." And puzzled over God's plan for her.

"So, you went into town with Mahon." Salome set a mug in front of Iris and settled in a chair across from her. "What did you talk about?"

"Nothing in particular."

"Then how come he was so grumpy when he got home? He went out and chopped wood for two hours."

"You needed the wood, I reckon."

"Spill it, Iris."

"He draws pictures of me."

Salome paused, cup halfway to her lips. She lowered it to the table. "Like portraits?"

"Like black-and-white photographs." Iris nodded. "They're beautiful."

"*Daed* wouldn't like it."

"Mine either."

"Still, it says something about his feelings for you. You know it does."

Iris sipped her tea. It was scalding hot. Maybe that would pass as an explanation for the red that surely ran rampant across her cheeks. "He told me he's waiting for me."

Salome's face lit up in a grin. Mahon's grin. "I knew it. I knew it. He told you when you went into town."

"He said he would wait until I'm ready."

"My *bruder* finally stepped up." Salome hooted. "He finally grew up and admitted he likes you. And you like him back, don't you?"

"Courting is private."

"Which means you're courting." Salome clapped her hands. "I knew it. *Gott* is *gut*."

One conversation and a touch on the arm did not courting make. Iris took the cup to the counter. "The funeral is tomorrow. *Mudder* and *Daed* are helping, so I'll have to take the girls. The boys will get there on their own. I really need to get some sleep now."

Ethan stood in the doorway, a silly grin stretched across his face. He towered over her, the spitting image of Bartholomew. He would be good for Salome, a sturdy place for the butterfly to land after swooping from one flower to the next. "I just came to see if everything is all right."

"For sure." Iris managed another smile. "I'm happy for you. Treat her right or I'll lock you in the outhouse."

He shifted from one boot to the other and ducked his head. "For sure."

"It's a true blessing. I mean it."

"We'll look forward to your day as well."

Ethan and Mahon had worked many frolics together. They hunted and fished together. What did he know? "I'm going to bed."

Salome's and Ethan's mingled laughter followed her out the door and up the stairs.

# CHAPTER 10

Aheart can be lifted at a funeral, even one held in a March wind that whipped bare tree branches, bending them to the ground. Iris tucked the quilt around Lilly's face and trudged toward the Borntrager home. The folded playpen hoisted between them, Louella and Abigail followed, their high-pitched chatter like birdsong. Isaac Borntrager had lived a long and full life. He would rest easy now. No tears were shed at the cemetery. None would be shed now as guests from across states gathered to eat and fellowship in his memory. Iris dropped a quick kiss on the sleeping baby's forehead. They didn't have many assurances, but the circle of life was one.

"Let me get the door for you."

Cold that had nothing to do with the wind swept through Iris. She forced her gaze up. Aidan pushed the screen door open and smiled down at her. "I saw you from the window. You have your hands full."

Their paths had crossed plenty of times in the last year. She saw him at church, at frolics, at weddings, including his own.

But they never talked, not just the two of them. He

looked good, as always. Tall, lean, broad-shouldered. Sandy-brown hair and blue eyes that could pierce to the bone or drown a person with their unexpected flood of emotion. She shifted the bag on her shoulder. Traveling with a bottle-fed baby meant a full bag, but not more than she could handle.

"How are you?" Before he could answer, she squeezed past him, careful not to brush against his bulky winter coat. "I hope it's warmer in here than it is out there."

"I'll help the girls with the playpen."

A few minutes later he was setting up the pen in a bedroom. The girls had abandoned Iris for ham sandwiches and brownies. "I heard about the *Englischers*." He straightened and studied his handiwork. The pen had seen better days. All seven Beachy children had used it. "Any word on their whereabouts?"

*"Nee."* She settled her bag on the floor and laid Lilly on the bed to unwrap her blankets. Her eyelids fluttered and then closed. She should be tired. She'd been up half the night alternately feeding and fussing. "I reckon they're some place in Texas by now."

"And left you holding the bag, so to speak."

"The *bopli, jah*." She tucked the quilt around the sleeping baby and faced him. "She's a sweet baby. The *mudder*'s note said she would be back for her."

"But you're hoping she doesn't come back."

"That's a terrible thing to say, Aidan Graber."

"I didn't mean it that way." He edged toward the door. "I just meant you *lieb* your *boplin* and you won't see one of them neglected or abused. It's one of the things I . . . like . . . respect about you."

"Most people wouldn't want to see that."

"Except one who leaves her with strangers."

"She thought it was best for this baby. That I might do better than she could. She had Lilly's best interest at heart."

Sometimes best wasn't easiest. Often it wasn't.

"You will be a *gut mudder.*"

Their gazes met. The silence stretched. He tilted his head and gave a small shrug.

"*Gott* willing." She managed a quick nod. "I know."

"There you are." Bess stuck her head through the doorway. She held her son, Joshua, on her hip. The chunky two-year-old, with his almond-brown eyes and hair, was the spitting image of his father, Caleb. What a precious gift of remembrance from Bess's first marriage. "Henry and Timothy are looking for you, Aidan. Something about going hunting Saturday."

"Sounds like a *gut* idea to me."

Aidan strode toward the door. Joshua held up his pudgy arms. "*Daed, Daed.*"

A grin spread across Aidan's face. He took Joshua from Bess, held him high until the boy giggled, then wrapped an arm around his waist so he faced outward on Aidan's hip. Aidan and Bess exchanged a look that made Iris duck her head and study the nine-patch quilt. A family heirloom from a family Lilly might never know. Someone had quilted every piece with loving stitches, thinking of the baby it would warm as she did. Who was she? Lilly's great-grandmother? A great-aunt? The ache in Iris's heart had nothing to do with Aidan. Not Aidan the man. It had to do with what he represented. Her dream of stitching a crib quilt for her own baby. To be a *fraa* and a *mudder*.

Aidan was no longer the man to fulfill those dreams. Her heart had let him go. She took a breath and released it, delighting in the sense of relief that flooded her. Time had healed that wound. Her head and heart were now together in knowing she had been right to let him go. Lilly's eyelids fluttered again. This time they stayed open. She stared up at Iris and batted her tiny fists.

"Sweet thing, you're awake." Iris scooped her up. "Did you have a nice nap?"

*Mudder* and the other women were serving food. She should help. Lilly would like the kitchen and its toasty warmth. So would Iris. She turned. Aidan was gone, but Bess still stood in the doorway, half in, half out of the bedroom. Her expression was equally uncertain.

"I wanted to ask you something."

"Here I am." Iris picked up her bag. "I was headed to the kitchen to help with the food."

"Me too."

Bess didn't move. She was a sweet, loving woman who made Aidan happy. He deserved to be happy. So did Bess, who'd lost her first husband in a buggy-truck accident after only a year of marriage. "What was your question?"

Bess stepped into the room. Her normally rosy face was wan. She put her hand to her mouth and cleared her throat. She smoothed her hands over her apron as if smoothing nonexistent wrinkles. "She's a tiny thing. What's her name?"

"Lilly Marie . . . something. I don't know her last name. She came early. She usually sleeps all day and fusses all night."

Bess trudged to the bed and sat. She blew out air so hard the tendrils of hair that had escaped her *kapp* fluttered. "Joshua did that for the first few months. I thought I would never sleep again. He had reflux— you know, he spit up all the time and it irritated his throat. And he had food allergies. I had to be careful what I ate."

"This one is bottle-fed. I wonder if that has something to do with it. Maybe the formula doesn't suit her." Iris rocked Lilly in her arms. It was apparent Bess didn't come to talk about reflux and spitting up. "Are you all right? You look peaked."

Bess wiggled. Her fingers plucked at the cotton material. "If you don't want to do this, I understand. It seems strange to ask you, but it would be strange not to ask you."

"Do what?"

"Deliver our baby." She put her hand to her mouth for a second, then let it drop. "I'm in a family way."

Plain folks didn't usually talk about being pregnant. Iris didn't pretend not to understand why Bess felt it necessary to bring it up now. "I'm happy for you. Really. This is *gut*."

"I wanted to tell you before it became obvious. To give you fair warning."

"That wasn't necessary." Iris wiped spit-up from Lilly's chin and stared into eyes that were leaning toward blue now. The baby gurgled and hiccupped.

"You don't have to be concerned about my feelings. I'm fine. Really, I am. I promise."

She was as surprised as Bess, surely, to find this was true.

"I'm glad." Bess patted the spot next to her on the bed. "Sit down. You look tired. You look like a new *mudder*."

Iris took her suggestion.

"Can I hold her?"

Iris nodded. Her arms were tired, yet they didn't seem to want to comply. Bess slid her hands under the baby and tugged. Iris forced herself to let go.

"Do you look like your *mudder*?" Bess tickled the baby's face. "You're so tiny. I don't remember Joshua ever being this tiny."

Lilly wailed.

Bess rocked and cooed and soothed. Lilly's cries grew louder. Shaking her head, Bess handed her back. "She wants you."

The thought shouldn't warm Iris's heart, but it did. She bent her head, hoping Bess didn't read her face. "Shhh, shhh, baby. Shhh."

Lilly's wails subsided.

"She's attached to you, poor thing." Bess stretched. Her hand went to her mouth. She sighed. "I don't remember so much morning sickness with Joshua either."

"*Jah*, I will deliver the *bopli*." Iris would be there at this special moment in Bess and Aidan's life, the birth of their first child together. The thought didn't rankle as it would have once. Instead, she felt joy on their behalf. She touched Lilly's cheek. They were blessed to have each other and to be a family. Lilly should have that too. If not with her own parents, then with Iris's family. "We'll talk in a few weeks."

"*Gut.* That's settled." Relief spread across Bess's face. "Aidan always talks about how kind you are."

"Aidan talks about me to you?"

"You gave him a gift. He'll never forget that. He wants you to be happy." Bess got to her feet, hand still on her stomach. "I'll never forget it. I know how short life is. I hope you find your special friend soon."

Iris didn't answer. Mahon's face as he said, *I'm waiting for you* floated in her mind's eye. Courting was private.

# CHAPTER 11

Maroon, navy, lilac, beige. The colors pleased Iris. Her head bent close to the kerosene lamp despite its heat, Iris laid out her diamonds, dark material cut on sixty-degree angles, along with triangles in the beige, that would create the blocks for her tumbling block crib quilt. This would be Bess and Aidan's gift upon the birth of their first child. She hummed "Trust and Obey" as she picked up her threaded needle and sewed together the first set. She would use another shade of blue for the border.

The wood in the fireplace snapped. The smell mingled with that of the kerosene. Tree branches, tossed by a fierce March wind, scraped the side of the house. March had come in like a lion, as usual. She loved night sounds. Everyone slept. Finally. Even Lilly slumbered in the second cradle *Daed* had lugged up from the basement. She smiled at the memory of his gruff willingness to perform these small tasks for the baby. Even Freeman had stopped to tickle her cheek after church. A gesture that released the floodgates. Everyone wanted to have a look at the *Englisch* baby.

The days had taken on a rhythm. Lilly slept better at

night. She didn't spit up so much. Iris helped more with the chores. *Mudder* cared for the baby while she made her rounds to a few expectant mothers. Rachel's Micah continued to flourish. The Plank twins were putting on weight. Hannah Yoder would deliver any day now. Visiting with "her" mothers kept Iris busy, and her own mother loved having Lilly to herself. Louella and Abigail bickered over who would hold her and who would feed her. A nice problem to have.

No one talked about what would happen next. She glanced over at the cradle. Lilly had her fist tucked against her mouth, sucking on her fingers in her sleep. She had such a look of peace on her face. Such trust to sleep knowing someone looked after her.

What would she think when that day came and Iris tried to explain she wasn't her real mother? What her real mother had done. How could she break a child's heart like that? Maybe she could simply be her mother. After all, wasn't loving a child ninety percent of parenting? Providing food, clothing, and a roof over her head meant little to a child who wasn't loved.

Love wove together family and home, no matter the circumstances.

A soft knock broke the silence. She stilled her needle and listened. Maybe it was the wind. A more insistent knock. Her fingers went to the hollow of her throat. Her pulse pounded. Jessica and Quinn? So be it. She marched to the door and swung it open.

Mahon stood in the doorway. Rain dripped from the brim of his hat. His coat was wet. Mud caked his boots. "It's raining."

Iris looked beyond him. "So it is."

"It wasn't when I left the house. Spring has sprung, it seems."

"Took you by surprise."

"*Jah*. From the look on your face, you too."

He took her by surprise. His unwavering interest. His solid presence.

"Can I come in?"

She stumbled back. "I was sewing."

"I was hoping you were up reading." He glanced around. "And the others weren't."

"They're not much for reading."

He unbuttoned his soggy coat and slid out his sketch book. He laid it on the table without mentioning it. "I know we can't take a buggy ride, but I thought we could talk."

A buggy ride. Her mouth went dry. She licked her lips. "Would you like some hot cocoa?"

"How's Lilly?"

"Growing. She smiled at me the other night."

He grinned. "Can I see her?"

Iris pointed to the cradle, close but not too close to the fireplace. "She's sleeping."

He trod as lightly as a muscle-bound, hardworking farmer could toward the cradle. "She has Jessica's look."

"I'll make the hot chocolate. You dry off."

Her heart did jumping jacks as she heated the milk in the pan and added cocoa, sugar, and vanilla. She scrounged around in the cabinet until she found the last few marshmallows the girls had left. With hands that shook, she carried the mugs to the front room. Mahon sat in the rocking chair. He had the sketch pad in his lap and his pencil in his hand. He didn't look up.

She set the mugs on the table and went to look over his shoulder. His strokes were quick and sure. The soft line of her cheek. The tiny tuffs of blonde hair. The long lashes. Rosebud lips. The nine-patch quilt. "You've caught that peaceful look on her face. I'll remember that when she's awake and fussing."

He tugged the sheet from the pad and held it out. "For when they take her home."

Writers used the phrase "heavy heart" for a reason. Hers suddenly weighed twenty pounds. Her throat ached as if she'd acquired a cold in the last few minutes. "You think they will?"

"I think you shouldn't get too attached." He took back the sketch and laid it aside with the pad. "I'm aware such advice comes too late. I know how hard it will be to let her go."

"No one could hold her and not become attached." Iris picked up the sketch and touched Lilly's face with one finger. "Who holds any baby and doesn't become attached?"

"Someone with a very cold heart or someone who is herself a child?"

"Young girls raise babies every day."

"Maybe she was unduly influenced by the father."

"What if they don't come for her? What then?"

"Decisions will have to be made."

By her *daed* and Freeman and the *Gmay*. By a judge. By everyone but Iris. She wanted to pick up Lilly, keep her safe, even if that meant running away with her. That would only make Iris like her parents. Runaways. She would never do that.

No matter how much she wanted to keep this baby safe forever.

Iris laid down the sketch and turned to the fireplace. She warmed her hands over the flames and tried to arrange her face in some semblance of a woman who could accept whatever fate God planned. She heard and then felt Mahon's presence next to her. His hand slid across her palm until his fingers fit between hers. He lifted her hand to his mouth and kissed it. Her muscles trembled as if each one played its own sweet note. "What are you doing?"

He dropped her hand and touched her jaw so she would turn to face him. His eyes were the color of sky and happiness and ocean. She'd never seen the ocean. Until now. The waves lapped, faster and faster. He inclined his head. His lips touched hers for a second, then withdrew. She started to protest, but his lips returned and covered hers. This time she put her hands to his chest in hopes he wouldn't move.

He tasted sweet and perfect.

His was the kiss she'd always wanted. She simply hadn't known it.

It had been worth waiting for all these years. From a friend who could be trusted with her heart.

He stepped back. "You were worth waiting for." His voice was a hoarse whisper. "I hope you know that."

Their timing was in perfect sync.

Lilly chose that moment to screech. They both

jumped. Iris smacked her hand to her chest. Her heart beat against her ribcage in an uneven *thump-thump*. "She's probably hungry." Her voice sounded high and breathless in her ears. "I need to fix her a bottle."

"I'll hold her while you do it. We don't want her waking everyone in the house."

Indeed, they didn't. Her father and mother slept down the hall. Only a few yards from where Iris had received that long-awaited gift of her first kiss. All those nights when she'd stood on the porch watching Aidan drive away, aching, disappointed, uncertain, agonizing over why that first kiss never came. God knew. God had a plan for her. For Aidan. For Mahon. At the doorway, Iris turned back to look at him. He held Lilly in his arms. He crinkled his nose, clucked, and then made *chirp-chirp* sounds. Lilly's cries subsided. Mahon eased into the rocking chair and looked up.

The words came easily. "You're worth waiting for too."

His smile widened. "It's *gut* you think so." His Adam's apple bobbed. "And you're right about not being able to hold a *bopli* and not get attached."

"You'll be a *gut daed*." Their gazes held. Lilly began to fuss again. "I better get the bottle."

"No rush. We'll be right here."

Her heart no longer felt so heavy. In fact, she felt so light she looked down to make sure her sneakers still touched the floor.

# CHAPTER 12

The weather had turned unexpectedly warm for Salome and Ethan's wedding. Nearly limp with exhaustion, Iris wiggled in the backseat of the buggy and tried to stay awake. A whirlwind two weeks of preparations and now it was over. She and Rachel had served as Salome's witnesses. Mahon and Joseph had been Ethan's. She couldn't help but glance at Mahon. He winked at her, his face crinkled in a smile. That wink. It was all she could think about through the rest of the ceremony and the festivities. No time to talk to him. They both had their duties, making sure his sister and her best friend had a beautiful, special day. Iris smiled at the thought. She couldn't wait to talk to Salome in the next few weeks to get her impressions of the daylong event. After the dust settled. She straightened, then tickled Abigail's neck. The girl was nodding off against Louella's shoulder.

"Stop." Abigail whined and shifted so she leaned against the other side. "Leave me alone."

Iris chuckled and leaned back, her arm around Lilly's basket. Lilly had been passed around and loved on by many of the guests. She should sleep well. Home would feel good for both of them tonight. Maybe tonight Mahon, who'd been busy helping with the preparations, would make another visit.

Another kiss.

Her cheeks and neck warmed. Thinking about kissing Mahon in a buggy full of family wasn't a good idea. She couldn't help it. Between mulling over Lilly's fate—so intertwined with her own—and thinking about the possibility of a future with Mahon, she couldn't think straight.

"We have company."

*Daed*'s gruff voice held surprise. In farmer time, it was late. Past their bedtime. Dusk had long come and gone.

*Mudder* sighed.

"Who is it?" Iris leaned forward and peered into the dark night. An unfamiliar green truck with Iowa plates sat parked at an odd angle—as if turned off in a rush—in front of the house.

Iris's happiness disappeared into a sudden knowing. She gripped the handle of Lilly's basket with both hands as if it might fly out of the buggy. The joy of seeing her best friend married slipped away, replaced by a sense of impeding anguish that must be faced and then accepted. His face twisted in a deep frown, *Daed* swiveled on the buggy's front seat to look back at her. "I knew it would come to this."

"We don't know what it's come to yet." *Mudder* patted *Daed*'s thigh with her gloved hand. "Let's just see who it is."

*Daed* pulled in next to the car. "I'll do the talking."

A gray-haired woman in baggy black pants and a short green coat eased from the car, using a cane to pull herself upright. She put one hand on her hip and stretched. "Hello there. I was getting worried you might not come home tonight. I've been sitting out here for hours."

Hours. For something important.

Iris hoisted herself from the buggy and turned to lower the basket.

"Is that her? Is that Jessica's baby?" The woman limped on rubber-soled rain boots toward Iris. An anxious smile bloomed on her face. She had dimpled cheeks and bright-blue eyes behind dark-rimmed glasses. Her hands fluttered. One came to rest on her ample bosom. "It's her, isn't it? The girl at the grocery store—Kathy Myer—said you have Jessica's baby."

His expression all deacon, *Daed* stepped between Iris and the woman. "Who are you?"

"I'm Jessica's grandma. Sherri Turner." The woman's voice trembled. She sniffed and wiped at her nose with a crumpled tissue. "That makes the baby in that basket my first great-grandchild. Could I see her? Please."

Iris stumbled back a step. "How do we know you are who you say you are?"

"Why would I lie?"

"We're sorry you had to wait so long. We've been at a wedding." *Mudder*'s smile encompassed them all. It landed on *Daed* last. "It's getting chilly. Let's go inside. I'll make some coffee. You can tell us your story."

"I'll come in and restart the fire before I tend to the horses." *Daed* tied the reins to the hitching post and nodded at the girls. "Abigail, Louella, go on upstairs and get ready for bed. We'll be up for prayers in a bit."

Eyes wide with interest, the girls went in first, taking their time, not wanting to be left out of whatever excitement was about to happen. *Mudder* shooed them through the door and held it for their guest.

A strange buzzing in her ears, Iris trudged up the steps and into the house where she set Lilly's basket on the front room table and removed her coat. She couldn't think. Sounds reverberated. Time stood still and sped up at the same time. As if that were possible. This was it. The baby who'd come into her life in the middle of a snowstorm would now leave just as abruptly.

Sherri edged toward the basket. "Could I see her?"

"Please sit down." *Mudder* pointed to the rocking chair situated by the fireplace where *Daed* was restarting the fire. "Have you come a long way?"

"From Des Moines. I drove straight through after I heard about the Facebook post."

"Facebook." Iris hung her coat on the hook by the door. Every muscle in her body wanted to grab the basket and run, run far, far away. But then she would be like Jessica and Quinn, who couldn't face what life offered them, and instead, dodged their responsibilities. "You heard about Lilly on Facebook?"

"It would be best if you start at the beginning." *Daed* stoked the fire with the poker, then stood. "The sheriff's office gave us temporary custody of the baby until something permanent could be worked out. We'll have to let them know if family has come for her."

"After Jessica and Quinn took off and I realized

they weren't coming back, I started looking for them.
I tried all their friends, everyone I could think of. I
didn't think they would go far." Her gaze still on the
basket, Sherri removed her glasses and blotted tears on
her wrinkled cheeks. "Weeks passed and nobody knew
anything. Then yesterday I got a call from my great-
niece Tanya. She's on social media night and day. She
said a friend of a friend had seen a post on Facebook
that had been shared so many times it got to a friend
of Tanya's. A girl named Kathy Myer from Jamesport
had posted a picture of two sketches. She said the kids
were wanted by the Daviess County Missouri Sheriff's
Office for questioning in a theft at the grocery store
where she works. Tanya said they looked just like
Jessica and Quinn. She printed it for me."

Sherri delved into her gargantuan, black patent
leather pocketbook and produced a ragged manila
envelope. It held dozens of photographs. Jessica in a
red cheerleading outfit. Jessica eating a slice of watermelon. Jessica blowing out candles on a birthday cake.
Jessica in short denim cut-offs with frayed hems and a
halter top leaning against the green truck now parked
in the Beachy's front yard. Behind the smaller snap-
shots was a larger one, an eight-by-ten. A photograph
of Mahon's sketches.

Iris forced herself to look from the sketch of Jessica
to her grandmother. The resemblance was slight. The
eyes. The shape of her face. It was hard to say with a
woman now in her late sixties and a sixteen-year-old
girl.

"Iris."

She started at the sound of her father's voice. She glanced at him. He nodded toward the basket. Swallowing a lump the size of a ten-pound sack of potatoes, Iris stood. She leaned over the basket and slid her hands under the quilt that kept Lilly warm. The baby's eyes opened. After a lazy yawn, she stretched and gave Iris a sleepy stare. With a heart this heavy, how would Iris manage to pick up this tiny baby and hand her over to a great-grandmother who hadn't wanted her?

"Iris."

This time her father's voice held a warning. She turned and moved toward Sherri. Every step seemed to cover too much territory, bringing her closer and closer to a precipice from which she would leap and there would be no return. She gritted her teeth, adjusted the quilt, and held Lilly out.

Tears rolled down Sherri's face. She accepted the bundled baby with no notice, no acknowledgment, of Iris or her pain. "My baby quilt."

Iris tried to follow her train of thought. "Your quilt?"

"I have chores to do," Daed interrupted. "I'll leave you two to talk."

His sharp tone told Iris what his expectations were. She nodded. His gaze softened and he smiled. "Be sure to give your guest something to eat. She's had a long drive."

Iris waited until the front door closed. She turned back to Sherri. "What were you saying about your quilt?"

"My mother gave it to me when Melissa was born." Sherri shook her head, her voice breaking. She used her free hand to shuffle through the photos. "Look. Jessica when she was a newborn."

A photo of a baby wrapped in the same nine-patch crib quilt with purple, pink, and lilac squares. "Your mother made it?"

"No. My grandmother. When she was pregnant with my mother. It's a family heirloom."

Like the one in *Mudder*'s chest down the hallway. A different pattern, but the same tradition of family and love and celebration of new birth. English or Plain. Family traditions created bonds between generations. Lilly belonged to that tradition, just as Iris belonged to hers. She swallowed her pain and cleared her throat. "I'm glad it didn't get lost in all the turmoil. Did you give it to Jessica?"

"I didn't intend for her to keep it. I wanted her to see that when the time was right, she would have a baby and we would do all this the right way. We had an argument. I told her after she finished school and got married and was ready to have a family, I would give it to her. It would be waiting for her." Sherri's voice quivered at the memory. "She looked at me like I was a monster. She snatched it up and ran out of the room before I could stop her."

Iris's shoes were cemented to the floor. She should back away, but she couldn't. If she did, she would never get Lilly back. "Jessica said you wanted to give her baby away. How could you?"

"I watched her get bigger and bigger. She looked more and more like her mother. It broke my heart to think of what the future held for her, for the baby, for me." Sherri tore her gaze from Lilly. "I've been through this before. With Jessica's mother."

"Where is she? Why doesn't she help?"

"She's dead."

"I'm sorry."

"Melissa was a wild thing. I was divorced. A single, working mom. I didn't have the time or the energy to corral her. In high school she went crazy. She got pregnant. I took care of Jessica so Melissa could finish school, make something of herself. Instead, she sank deeper into the life she'd chosen. Then she died of a drug overdose, leaving me with another little girl. Jessica. I raised her. I raised her the best I could."

She bowed her head and closed her eyes as if praying. Maybe she was praying—for forgiveness, for discernment, for her dead daughter and her missing granddaughter, for this new life in her arms. She opened her eyes and stared at Iris. "I didn't think I had the strength to do it again. I'm old and tired, and I have arthritis and bad back trouble. I told Jessica I couldn't do it. I'm too old. I wanted her to put the baby up for adoption. I'd already looked into it. That's why she ran away."

"Then she ended up giving the baby to me." Iris stifled the urge to shout. None of it made sense. Plain people didn't do these things. They grew up, they married, they had children, they raised them, they died. An orderly existence. "How is that different?"

"It was the one single selfless act Jessica has ever performed." Sherri smiled the saddest smile Iris had ever seen. "I've never been so proud. I'm not sure I'll be able to do the same, now that I've held this precious baby in my arms."

"How is it selfless to throw away a baby?"

"No one is throwing away a baby." Her voice grew fierce. "There's a couple in Des Moines who are desperate for a baby. They can't have one of their own. My granddaughter left her baby with you because she realized I was right. She's too immature to take care of a baby. Giving her to you was a selfless act of love. Giving this baby to that couple would also be an act of love."

Iris fought to control her own voice. She breathed. In and out. In and out. Shame assailed her. "You're right. Jessica wanted to do the right thing. So do you."

"Now there's a slight problem."

A slight problem. Hysterical laughter burbled up in Iris's throat. "Only now?"

"Now that I've held her, there's no way I can give her up. She's my flesh and blood. As long as I have breath in my body, I'll care for her. I need to tell Jessica this. I need for her to come home. Together, between the two of us, we can raise this baby."

"What about Quinn?"

"He's another child I'll have to raise, I imagine . . ."

Her voice trailed off. The pain on her face spoke to Iris. It told her a story of love, regret, pain, and uncertainty. While Iris took care of Lilly, this grandmother had suffered the agony of not knowing where her grandchild was. "They'll come home. In her note, Jessica said they would come back here. When they do, we'll send them home to you."

"You're a dear, sweet girl. I can see why Jessica took to you so quickly."

Lilly fussed. Iris gripped her hands behind her back to keep from reaching for her. Sherri laid her on her shoulder and patted her back. The cries grew in volume. *"Hush, hush, little baby, don't you cry,"* Sherri began to sing. *"Momma's gonna buy you a rocking horse . . ."*

The cries turned to screams. Iris's hands flew to her ears. Swallowing tears that couldn't be allowed to fall, she forced them down. Sherri shook her head and tutted. "She wants you."

"She's probably hungry. I'll fix her a bottle." Iris had to get out of the room. If she didn't, she would snatch Lilly back and never let her go. She inched backward. "She'll like you when she gets to know you. She's a friendly baby."

"You're the only mother she's ever known."

It seemed an awful thing to do to a baby. With God's grace, perhaps she wouldn't remember. Abandoned twice. "She'll adjust."

Iris turned and fled to the kitchen.

Her mother sat at the table, sipping her tea. "You and *Daed* abandoned me."

The irony of those words chilled Iris. She caught the sob in her throat before it escaped.

"You did a good thing, child."

Then why did her heart and her throat throb with pain and her eyes burn? She turned her back and picked up a bottle from the counter. She swallowed hard against the lump in her throat. "I feel heartbroken."

"You specialize in selfless acts of love."

Bottle still in her hand, she faced her mother. "You were listening."

"I know what you've done. You let Aidan go because you knew he belonged with someone else. It's what you're made of."

"You knew about that?"

"*Mudders* know everything."

"You took care of Lilly to give her mother time to grow up. You've fed and rocked and burped and diapered her for the first six weeks of her life. You've given her a fighting chance. It's time for Lilly to go home, and it's time for you to get on with your life."

Delivering other people's babies. Holding them when they come into the world and then handing them over to another woman to love? She stared at the bottle in her hand. What she did gave joy to others, which brought joy to her. Was it enough? Should it be enough? "What do you mean?"

"I mean don't keep Mahon waiting any longer. There's a crib quilt in that chest down the hall waiting for you."

Iris didn't bother to ask how *Mudder* knew. *Mudders* knew everything.

Her throat tight with unshed tears, Iris fixed the bottle and returned to the living room where Sherri cooed to her fussy great-grandchild. "It's late, and there are no hotels nearby. Do you want to spend the night? You can have my bed."

"The bed where this baby was born?"

"Yes."

"I couldn't do that to you."

"It's okay. I'm not tired."

She wouldn't sleep, not with her heart in pieces and Lilly no longer hers. It would be a long night.

# CHAPTER 13

The half-moon and thousands of stars lit up the inky April night sky. Iris welcomed their company. Feet bare, she eased into a rocking chair on the porch. Still, it squeaked, the noise loud in the stillness. She winced and sat unmoving for a few seconds. Nothing stirred. Everyone slept, oblivious to the frogs croaking, the crickets chirping, and the occasional questioning hoot of an owl. Lilly slept in her crib next to the bed Sherri had taken in Iris's bedroom. No cries emanated from the room. Surely the fact that Lilly was sleeping through the night meant the baby felt safe and secure next to her great-granny. Iris leaned her head back and closed her eyes. For the first time in weeks, she had no responsibilities heavy on her shoulders like a wool winter cloak. No bottles to fix. No diapers to change. No need to keep one ear awake while the rest of her slept. Her duties had ended with an abruptness that left a void where mothering had been.

Tears pricked her eyes. She swallowed the knot in her throat. *Gott* knew best. Always. *Thy will be done. Thy will be done. What would you have me do now?*

The *clip-clop* of horse hooves in the distance,

interspersed with the clatter of buggy wheels, brought her straight up from the chair. She sped to the railing and peered into the darkness. Headlights appeared in the distance. Her heart banged. Mahon. It had to be Mahon. He had known somehow that she couldn't sleep. Maybe he couldn't sleep for thinking of her. What a prideful thought. She pried it from her mind and tossed it in a heap with all those prideful thoughts of how she would be the best mother for Lilly.

The buggy drew closer. She couldn't see the driver behind the brilliant lights. She padded down the steps and let her feet sink into the cold grass. Finally, the buggy pulled into the yard. Mahon. It was Mahon. Her fingers entwined themselves in the strings of her *kapp*.

"Iris. Iris, I'm here. It's me, Jessica. I'm back."

Jessica's high voice trembled.

Iris froze.

Jessica had come back for her baby.

Mahon halted the buggy and hopped from the seat. "She came to the door and asked for me. She wanted to come directly here."

"Why did you go to Mahon?" Life began to move forward again. *Gott*'s plan pulled her along with it. With Him. She held out her hand. Jessica took it and jumped down from the buggy. Her T-shirt was stained and her jeans dirty. She smelled of stale cheeseburger and pickle juice. "How did you get to Mahon's?"

"Is that Nana's truck? It is. It's Nana's truck." Jessica wrapped Iris in a quick, fierce hug. "It's her truck. Is she here?"

"Yes, she's here. She was looking for you."

"I was in Dallas with Quinn, but I couldn't do it. I couldn't stand being away from my baby."

"Where's Quinn?" Iris looked over Jessica's shoulder at Mahon. He shrugged, then cocked his head toward the house. Iris nodded. "Let's go inside. You can tell me the whole story."

"Where's my baby?"

"Sleeping. With your grandmother. She got here a few hours ago."

"I had to get my baby back." Jessica's voice broke. "Quinn wouldn't bring me back so I hitchhiked."

The idea of a young girl accepting rides from strangers all the way from Texas to Missouri made Iris's stomach twist. She put her arm around Jessica and led her up the steps to the house. Mahon followed. "I'm so glad you made it safely."

"The truckers were mostly nice. One dropped me off on the highway right by the turnoff to Mahon's house. I walked the rest of the way. Mahon's was closer, and I knew since he's your boyfriend—"

"Let's go inside." Iris held the screen. "Are you hungry? I'll fix you something to eat."

"I just want to hold my baby and tell her how sorry I am. I want to tell Nana how sorry I am."

The tears came in buckets. Iris hugged her again. "You'll scare Lilly and your nana. Dry your tears first, okay?"

Jessica nodded. She hiccupped one more sob, then wiped her face with her sleeve.

"Don't mind me." Mahon sank into the nearest chair and heaved a sigh. "I'll wait here."

Together, Iris and Jessica walked down the hall to the bedroom. Iris held up the kerosene lamp and opened the door. Jessica tiptoed across the room to the cradle. "Baby, my baby," she murmured. "I've missed you, baby."

She scooped up Lilly and wrapped her in her arms, tight against her chest. Iris opened her mouth to protest. The baby had never slept this long uninterrupted. She closed her mouth. Her job had ended. Soon they would say good-bye and go about their business as if they'd never met. As if she'd never mothered this baby as if she were her own.

"You're so beautiful. I'm so sorry. I'm so sorry," Jessica crooned. "I'm here now, baby, I'm here. I'll never leave you again. I promise."

"Jessie, is that you?" Sherri sat up in bed. "Are you really here? Where have you been, girl?"

"Nana, I'm so sorry." Jessica didn't move. "I've missed you so much. Forgive me?"

"I'm just so glad you're safe. I was afraid you were dead." Relief mingled with tears filled Sherri's voice. "Get over here so I can hug your neck."

Sobbing, Jessica rushed to the bed where more crying ensued.

Lilly wailed.

"Oh, you poor thing, we woke you." Sherri patted the baby's cheek. "You're okay. Your mommy's here now."

Mommy's here now.

Lilly's wails turned to screams.

Both women looked at Iris. She tightened her grip

on the lantern and her emotions. "She's always cranky when she wakes up. She's probably hungry. I'll get her a bottle."

"No, you've done enough. I have to figure out how to do this." Jessica rocked Lilly back and forth, then lifted her to her shoulder and began to pat her back. The wails subsided to a low roar.

"Thank you so much for taking care of my baby." Jessica's voice wobbled. "It was so wrong of me to dump her on you like that. I'm not a bad person. I just got confused for a little bit. I promise I'll take good care of her from now on."

"I believe you." Iris took a deep breath and let it out. Her time with Lilly had ended. "You're her mother. You'll do fine."

"We'll go into the sheriff's office tomorrow." Sherri patted the spot next to her on the bed, and Jessica slid under the blankets next to her. "We'll face the music and make this right, whatever it takes. Me and Jessie together."

They had a long road ahead of them. The legal system was a mystery to Iris. "I'll pray for you, all of you."

She would pray for God's will and God's grace and for Lilly's safe journey through this world. And for Quinn. Babies needed both their moms and their dads.

"Thank you, Iris." Sherri nodded, her wrinkled face streaked with tears. "You're a good girl. You'll be a good mother to your babies."

In God's time.

"We'll send you pictures," Jessica added. "Lots of pictures. You'll be like an aunt. She can come visit and learn about farm animals. You can teach her to make baby quilts."

*Aenti* Iris.

"I would like that."

Iris backed out of the room and shut the door. She let her hands drop and stood there, in the middle of the hall, trying to identify the feelings that tumbled around in her brain.

Lilly had her mother. Her true mother. And her nana.

Every baby should have a nana to tuck her in for an afternoon nap, tell her stories, teach her songs, and hear her prayers.

The ache in Iris's throat was the preamble to acceptance and peace. A kind of contentment that all was as it should be. She whirled and trotted to the living room. Mahon rose from the chair. He held out his arms. She walked into them and leaned her head against his chest. His heart beat in a comforting *thump-thump*. His hands rubbed her back in a soothing circular pattern. "Who is Nana?"

"Jessica's *groossmammi*. She raised her. She is willing to help raise Lilly too."

"Then *Gott*'s will be done."

Iris snuggled closer. "That's what I keep telling myself, but sometimes it's impossible to know, isn't it?"

"Come outside with me." He stepped back, grabbed her hand, and tugged her toward the door. "I want to show you something."

Outside, she scurried to keep up as he tromped down the steps and strode across the yard. He stopped at the corral fence. "Have a seat." He patted the railing, then put both hands on her waist and lifted her so she sat on the fence. "Hang on."

Her mind still grappling with the feeling of his hands on her hips, she managed to do as she was told.

He settled next to her and inhaled a deep breath, then exhaled in a noisy sigh. "It's a beautiful night."

"It is."

"*Mudder* and *bopli* are together again."

"As they should be."

"Yet you have regrets."

"Not exactly regrets. It's been a strange time in my life, but a special time. An uncertain time." She struggled for words that could describe the bittersweet feelings that engulfed her. "I'm happy I had this time with Lilly. I'll always love her, but I know this is what's best for her."

"There is something you don't have to be uncertain about."

"What's that?"

His big hand covered hers on the fence railing. His fingers tightened. "Me."

She felt his smile as much as saw it in the moonlight. She felt it in the warmth of that single syllable. "You?"

"Do you ever look at the stars?"

"Sometimes, but mostly the moon."

"The light of the moon is only a reflection of the sun's light. It has no light of its own. I like the stars better. They make their own light. And there are so many. All made by *Gott*. I don't feel alone when I look at them."

She let her gaze follow his finger pointing at the sky. "They're beautiful."

His words penetrated. In his huge, overflowing family, he'd been lonely. She inched closer to him. "You don't have to sketch pictures of me anymore. I'm right here."

"It's still hard for me to believe. I waited a long time." His voice was low, barely a hoarse whisper. He took her hand and pointed her finger toward the sky. "Do you see the Little Dipper? At the tip of the handle is the North Star. Polaris. Some people think it is the brightest star, but it's not. Sirius is the brightest star."

"Why do the stars interest you so much?" She leaned against his shoulder and stared at the Milky Way, trying to see what he saw. "Your feet are on the ground, but your head is in the sky."

"*Gott* made the heavens and the earth. I'm awestruck by His power." Mahon's hand brushed against her cheek. He leaned in, and his warm breath touched her face. He smelled of peppermint. "He made man and then He made woman to keep man company."

The pounding of her heart increased. The cool night air turned warm as if spring had turned to summer. "I reckon He had a *gut* plan."

"I reckon He's happy you think so." Mahon chuckled, a husky, sweet sound. The air warmed even more. Summer in the midst of spring. "Like He needed our approval."

"*Nee*, I just meant life would be sad and empty if we didn't have that one person we were meant to share it with."

"You thought that person was Aidan."

"But I was wrong." She sought Mahon's hand and held it tight. "We hear over and over in sermons from the time we're old enough to understand that *Gott* has a plan. That we can't fathom it. We can only trust and obey. Everything that has happened to me over the last few years tells me the truth of the matter. *Gott* had a plan for me. Not the one I asked for. The one He has, the one that is best for me. And it is *gut*."

"This plan. It includes me?"

"Jah."

"*Gut.*" He slid from the fence and faced her. "I *lieb* you. I have always known that we were meant to be together. You haven't known as long, so I won't rush you, but I want you to know I plan to marry you some-day soon."

"That's *gut*." Iris hopped down and stepped into his space. "That's *gut* because someday I plan to marry you right back."

He laughed as he bent down. His lips sought hers. The kiss, long and sweet and sure, sealed the promise. She reveled in the taste and feel of his mouth, the way his huge, callused hands cupped her face with a gentle touch.

She reached up and tugged his glasses from his face. His eyelids fluttered open. He ducked his head. "Why'd you do that?"

"I like seeing your eyes. Without the glasses, I can see all the way to your heart."

He shrugged, his expression pensive. "They don't work well. I can't see a thing without the glasses."

She gently returned them to their place on his nose. "That's okay. I don't want other people to see what I see." She leaned into him, inhaling his scent of man, and smiled. "*Mudder* has a crib quilt her *mudder* gave to her. It's been passed down for generations. One day it'll be mine."

Mahon's arms tightened around Iris. His Adam's apple bobbed. He cleared his throat. "And one day you'll give it to our daughter."

Together, they turned and stared at the sky, endless in its beauty and possibilities. Together, they would forge a life that would fulfill her dream of being a wife and a mother. She would have babies of her own to love. Her dream and God's plan, bright as the evening stars, were one and the same.

# ACKNOWLEDGMENTS

I am thankful for so many blessings that it's hard to order my thoughts when it comes to acknowledgments. My thanks to God for richly rewarding me with these opportunities to write these stories. My thanks to HarperCollins Christian Publishing for allowing me to be a part of this novella collection. I'm so thankful for every HCCP staff member who had a hand in bringing this particular story to fruition, but especially editors Becky Monds and Jodi Hughes. Their attention to detail and love of a good story inspire me. I couldn't keep writing if it weren't for my husband Tim's support and love. He cooks, buys groceries, does laundry, takes out the trash, and cleans the cat box. That is true love. I'm thankful for readers who spend their hard-earned funds to buy books. I pray that this story blesses each one of you. I look forward to sharing many more stories with you in the future. God bless!

# Discussion Questions

1. Most Amish don't believe in having their photos taken. Their objection is based in scripture regarding "graven images." They also believe it's a form of idolatry that grows from vanity. This extends to Mahon's hand-drawn portraits of Iris. In the mainstream world, we've become handy with phone "selfies" and most people think nothing of regular posting of these photos on social media. Do you see any harm in this easy, instant access to photos and their online use? Why or why not? Does it have an impact on our sense of who we are and how "important" we are in the eyes of others? What impact do you think it has on children growing up in a "selfie" world?

2. Iris can't understand how Jessica can leave her newborn baby with a stranger. She says an Amish mother would never abandon or give up a baby, considered a gift from God under any circumstance. Jessica's grandma has found a couple who cannot have a baby who want to adopt her great-grandchild. They could provide a better home for the baby. Who do you think is right? Why? Is there room for both views in this complicated world we live in?

3. Cyrus is uncomfortable that Iris has brought a young unwed couple and their baby into his home. He's concerned for the example they set for his young children who live in the household. Do you believe children should be exposed to circumstances in which others have not lived up to God's commands or should they be taught these lessons in less obvious ways? Have you ever been influenced to do something you know is wrong because you spent time with friends who aren't Christians? What did you learn from that experience?

4. Iris spent three years courting with Aidan and waiting for him to propose to her. She prayed for God's plan to be revealed to her. In the meantime, Mahon was waiting for her to notice his feelings for her. Have you ever been certain you know God's plan for you, only to discover you were on the wrong path all along? How did you deal with it? What are some ways we can try to discern God's plan for us?

5. Do you think Jessica and her grandmother are making the right choice when they decide to keep Lilly?

# Enjoy these
# Amish Story Collections!

# AVAILABLE IN PRINT AND E-BOOK

# Enjoy these Amish Stories for every season!

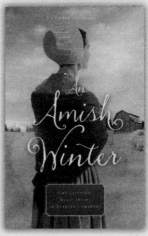

## AVAILABLE IN PRINT AND E-BOOK

978078521759 6-B